OATHBREAKER

Also available in the King Cnut series

The King's Hounds

The Word of a Villein (forthcoming)

MARTIN JENSEN

OATHBREAKER

Translated by Tara F. Chace

Published by
amazon crossing ⟨⟩

Text copyright © 2011 by Martin Jensen and Forlaget Klim

English translation copyright © 2014 by Tara F. Chace

Oathbreaker was first published in Danish in 2011. Translated from the Danish by Tara F. Chace. Published in English by AmazonCrossing in 2014.

Published by AmazonCrossing, Seattle

www.apub.com

ISBN-13: 9781477817360
ISBN-10: 1477817360

Cover design by Edward Bettison
Front cover crown illustration created by Edward Bettison
Floral pattern from *The Art of Illumination*, Dover Pictura, 2009, royalty-free

Back cover illustration inspired by public domain images found in the British Library Catalogue of Illuminated Manuscripts, http://www.bl.uk/catalogues /illuminatedmanuscripts/reuse.asp

Library of Congress Control Number: 2013915273

England, Anno Domini 1018

Prologue

Anno Domini 1016

htred shivered in the morning fog. He scratched his crotch, shifted his weight from his right foot to his left, and listened into the mist. He and his men had ridden a long way the day before in the drenching spring rain, which fell cold at this elevation. They had not reached the hay barn—where they had agreed to meet Uhtred's thanes—until well after nightfall.

"Did you say you heard hoofbeats?" Uhtred asked.

Ealdred was leaning forward attentively with his legs set wide apart. He nodded. Droplets hung from Ealdred's neatly tended dark-blond beard, and rainwater dripped from the worn ring-mail byrnie he had removed from a fallen enemy after a battle. That battle was so far in the past that Uhtred could no longer recall where it had happened or whom they had been fighting.

"Listen," Ealdred said urgently.

Was that a sound? Uhtred tried to see through the mist, but all he could make out was the grass under him—wiry, winter-gray grass, which had barely filled the bellies of the horses the night before. And their oat sacks were almost empty, too.

But hungry horses couldn't be avoided at the moment. The animals were still strong after weeks of eating grain during Uhtred's raids south into Mercia, but Uhtred had distributed all the spoils from the raids to his army, not keeping any for himself or his horses. To his mind, this conflict wasn't about plunder.

Though Leofwine, ealdorman of Mercia, had switched sides and sworn fealty to Cnut, the Viking king, Uhtred, ealdorman of Northumbria, had hoped to increase his own power by remaining loyal to the old Saxon king,

Ethelred. Why else would Uhtred have disowned his second wife to marry King Ethelred's daughter?

Uhtred had thus led his army southward, deep into Mercia, to strike at Leofwine. By ravaging his way through Mercia, Uhtred had shown the Viking king that England wasn't conquered yet, and that Ethelred still commanded battle-ready men.

Every burning farm, every granary consumed in flames meant fewer supplies for Cnut's army, and every warrior who fell to the spears of Uhtred's men and the swords of his thanes was one man fewer for the impenetrable shield walls of the Viking enemy.

And then, amid his hour of victory, Uhtred had received word from the south: King Ethelred was ill—so ill he might die. And Edmund, whom the men called Ironside—King Ethelred's son and Uhtred's brother-in-law—now reportedly waged a fruitless fight against Cnut, whose Viking force had won almost every skirmish the previous winter as it steadily swelled with reinforcements of Saxons and Danes switching to Cnut's side. Edmund could only clench his teeth in rage as he watched more and more of his sworn men change sides.

Uhtred had broken off his raids in Mercia after he was informed of the battle at Penn in Selwood, where despite the Saxons' greater numbers, the Saxon army had still not been able to break through the Danes' shield walls. When night fell over the stalemate, both armies had pulled back.

With King Ethelred on his deathbed, and his son unable to win battles even with a superior force, Uhtred had feared he would be trapped in enemy territory. Edmund had withdrawn to lick his wounds and raise new soldiers, and Uhtred knew his brother-in-law well enough to know that Edmund would avoid fighting for a while to rebuild his forces.

During this lull, the road north to Uhtred's lands would be open to both Cnut and Leofwine—and the latter was undoubtedly itching to march back north now that the war in the south was deadlocked. Once Leofwine had his army back in Mercia, he would be able to drum up more soldiers, while Uhtred would have only the men who had come south with him in the first place.

Indeed, Uhtred's scouts soon informed him that King Cnut was marching north. Since Leofwine was heading straight for Mercia, Uhtred withdrew to the northeast, afraid of being trapped between Cnut's and Leofwine's forces. Uhtred had dispatched his scouts forward, instructed skirmishers to cover his flanks, and made it back to his own Northumbrian borderlands without difficulties.

And that's where the surprise had been waiting.

As Uhtred's unit had approached a small hamlet, one of his forward scouts, Ulf, came riding back in such great haste that his horse's flanks were covered with foam. Before Uhtred had had a chance to raise his right arm in greeting, Ealdred had turned his horse away from Uhtred's and started barking orders to the men, who immediately dismounted and took shield-wall positions bisecting the trail, leaving a small gap they could close the second Uhtred and Ulf rode back through the line.

"There are soldiers in the hamlet," Ulf panted, his chest heaving.

Uhtred glanced up the trail. Everything looked so peaceful in the pale spring sunlight.

"Many?" Uhtred asked.

Ulf shook his head, saying, "They've set up a peace marker."

Uhtred nodded to Ealdred, who dug his heels into his horse's flanks and quickly rode ahead to confirm Ulf's report. He soon vanished behind a little grove of ash trees.

His hoofbeats grew fainter until they were completely gone. The trill of an early lark could be heard from the air above the shield wall. The men stood with their spear tips pointed at the sky, eyes alert and muscles poised to lower spears at the least sign of an approaching enemy.

Uhtred waited. His horse shifted beneath him, and he flexed his calves to tell the animal to stand still. A raven flew over him toward the ash grove.

Soon they heard hoofbeats approaching again. The men instinctively closed ranks, but kept their spears up and their shields resting at their feet. They peered calmly ahead.

"The mark of King Cnut!" Ealdred gasped, reining in his horse. There was no one behind him.

"Cnut?" Uhtred asked, eyeing him sharply.

"Just off the road in front of a farm, there's a spear stuck in the dirt, tip down, with Cnut's banner tied to the butt end," Ealdred replied.

The sign of peace.

"Did you see any men?" Uhtred asked.

"Four," Ealdred said. "They weren't carrying spears, and their swords were sheathed."

"Did you speak to them?"

"One of them held his hands up to his heart and then put his palms together."

Another indication of peace.

"Good," Uhtred said, tapping his horse with his heels and calmly riding forward. Behind him he heard his men remounting their steeds to follow him.

Ealdorman Uhtred of Northumbria rode into the hamlet with his thane Ealdred at his side. They passed three thatched farmhouses so low that their horses' heads reached the eaves. Then they passed a few dilapidated little outbuildings and a wattle sheepfold. No palisade protected the perimeter.

Sure enough, four Vikings stood in front of the largest farm. They weren't wearing helmets or ring mail, and their hands were far from their sword hilts. A spear stood in the ground behind them. Cnut's standard fluttered gently from the butt end of the spear in the mild breeze.

The horses' harnesses creaked as the men behind Uhtred dismounted. He didn't turn around as they reformed their shield wall.

One of the four Vikings stepped toward Uhtred. He was tall, as tall as Uhtred, with two thick red braids hanging down over his shoulders, water-blue eyes, and a fleshy nose over his thick lips.

"Ealdorman Uhtred?" the Viking asked.

Uhtred nodded.

"I am Erik, thane to Cnut, bearing a message from the king."

"Proceed," Uhtred said.

Erik closed his eyes for a brief moment to gather his thoughts. Then in a clear voice he intoned: "I, Cnut Sweynsson, bid you greeting, Uhtred of Northumbria, whom I offer my friendship. There is no cause for dispute between us. We are both lords in our own right, and I, Cnut, acknowledge your right, Uhtred, as you should acknowledge mine. Let peace and harmony prevail between us. Let us be true friends to each other. This is the oath I offer you."

Ealdred gasped at the offer of peace, but Uhtred remained calm.

"Was that the entire message?" Uhtred asked.

Erik looked surprised for a moment, then nodded. "And your response?"

Uhtred looked around and then said, "Cnut will have my response when it's ready."

For a day, Uhtred kept to himself, thinking. Then he summoned his thane Ealdred and apprised him of his plan, which Ealdred agreed with.

The wind was blowing Cnut's way. It was now common knowledge that King Ethelred was on his deathbed. No one knew where his son Edmund Ironside was; it was as though Ironside had sunk into the earth. Uhtred had no doubt it was to gather forces to oppose Cnut again, but it was widely agreed he didn't stand much chance. The soldiers crowding the roads and the thanes leading them were all moving in the same direction: Everyone was rallying around Cnut's standard. Everyone was pledging allegiance to Cnut.

Uhtred's greatest concern was Ironside's disappearance. How could he assess his brother-in-law's plans if he didn't know where to find him? How could he even know whether Ironside was still alive—and if he was, whether he had an army at his disposal?

It wouldn't have been hard for Ironside to find Uhtred. Cnut had, after all. And Ironside had ample scouts to predict which way Uhtred's men would move as they marched home from enemy territory.

But no Saxons had come looking for Uhtred. No messages reached him as he waited in the hamlet, and forced Erik to wait for his response.

After his talk with Ealdred, Uhtred waited another three days.

On the fourth day, Uhtred informed Erik that he would accept Cnut's offered friendship and would provide Cnut with hostages as a guarantee of his good faith. Seven of his thanes went with Erik the Viking and his thick braids, while Erik's three companions, mighty Viking chieftains whose names Uhtred knew all too well, stayed behind as assurance to Uhtred of Cnut's good faith.

Uhtred sent his wife word that he would no longer be her father's ealdorman. He was going to become King Cnut's jarl. That was the essence of Cnut's message—*I, Cnut, acknowledge your right, Uhtred*—which Erik had recited with his eyes half-closed.

Uhtred's family had ruled Northumbria for five generations. At times his ancestors had held only Bernicia—the northernmost portion of the current earldom. At other times, such as now, they also ruled Deira to the south and called themselves, as Uhtred did, ealdorman of Northumbria.

But their power had seen nothing but challenge, from Scots and Picts in the north, and, in the south, from the Danes who had settled in Northumbria a few generations back, displacing the Angles. The Danish settlers had taken over the Angles' farms or had cultivated new ground to live side by side with them—but always as the new masters, who worshipped the ancient gods and spoke a Danish tongue the Angles could understand only with great difficulty.

Uhtred had defeated the Scots himself back when his father was still alive. The Scottish king had thought an aging enemy would be easy prey, but they hadn't counted on Uhtred, who rallied the men from Bernicia and Yorkshire and pounded away at the Scottish army with such might that the Scottish king returned to Scotland only by the skin of his teeth, and with so few men in tow that the Scots had henceforth left the border unchallenged.

The victory had been great; the spoils, less so. However, the Scottish heads, which could still be seen on stakes here and there along the roads leading north, attested to Uhtred's fighting spirit and his willingness to take on anyone who would seek to avenge those heads, whose bodies rotted in the ground outside Durham.

But there were still Danes to the south who challenged Uhtred's power. And he had yet to directly engage with the most powerful of them, Thurbrand the Hold. Uhtred knew perfectly well that Thurbrand was merely biding his time.

Now that time would have to wait.

King Cnut had offered to make Uhtred the Angle his jarl, which meant that Uhtred—and not Thurbrand—had the king's favor.

About ten days after Erik had recited Cnut's message, Uhtred received word that Cnut was in Tadcaster but wanted to meet in three days in the village of Wiheal, about a half day's march from the old fort. The king would await him in the central hall in Wiheal before midday, accept his oath and those of the men swearing with him, and after that declare Uhtred his jarl in Northumbria.

Uhtred had immediately sent word for his own retainers and noblemen to meet him that morning so they could enter Wiheal together. Ulf the scout, who was from the area, had suggested a hay barn where they might meet. Uhtred and his retinue had arrived late the night before the meeting, getting a decent night's sleep in what was left of the hay after the winter.

Ealdred stood perfectly still at Uhtred's side outside the hay barn. The morning fog essentially blinded them. From behind, they heard the men's feet sliding through wet, winter-dead grass, followed by muffled orders. Uhtred's housecarls had assumed defensive positions around the hay barn. It was now half a moon since Erik had recited the king's offer, and today was the day Uhtred and King Cnut would finally seal their friendship.

Above the sound of approaching hoofbeats, they could also clearly hear saddles creaking and groaning under their riders' weight, the faint knocking of sword sheaths against leather-clad thighs, and a few coughs from fog-moistened throats.

As soon as the first heads became visible through the wisps of fog, it was clear the visitors were not there to fight. Uhtred recognized the helmet with the blond shock of hair topping its comb. It belonged to Hubert, Uhtred's own bannerman. The day after Uhtred had given Erik his response for Cnut, he had recalled Hubert from Mercia, ordering him to get word to the other noblemen of Northumbria that they should report immediately to swear their fealty to Cnut.

Now Uhtred stood wide-legged as the fog burned off, offering each nobleman in turn the same greeting: a clenched fist to the chest, the sign that as their master he acknowledged they had met their obligation to him. They would enter Wiheal together.

Thane rode beside thane, chieftain beside reeve. They were all from the finest families in the region, commanders of land and men. They had shown their mettle in battle and war and had fought with and for Uhtred—indeed, a few of them even for his father, just as their sons would one day fight for Uhtred's sons.

Uhtred had promised to bring forty men to swear with him—to pledge their fealty at his side as a promise that the jarl and all under him would live, fight, and die for King Cnut forever after.

Before setting out, the assembly ate a quick meal of bread and cheese, washing it down with the last of the ale from the kegs secured to their saddle pommels. The newly arrived men who were still in ring mail removed it, handing it over to their slaves and servants. The ealdorman, soon-to-be jarl, of Northumbria then mounted his horse to lead his retinue into Wiheal. The king had promised safe-conduct and that he himself would not be armed at their meeting, so Uhtred and his men did not ride as soldiers.

When Uhtred dismissed his housecarls, Ealdred's head drooped, realizing the order applied to him as well. But Uhtred was firm.

"Someone needs to lead my housecarls home," Uhtred said, "And make sure you go *straight* home and don't get caught up drinking and whoring."

"But—" Thane Ealdred began.

Uhtred shook his head and gestured with his chin toward the three Viking chieftains, whom Erik had left with them as surety.

"The lives of these Viking warriors is Cnut's guarantee that he will keep his word," Uhtred assured Ealdred.

They were finally ready. The men swung up into their saddles and followed their leader, Uhtred. He in turn followed Ulf, who would lead the way.

The three Vikings rode in a line behind Uhtred, each flanked by two of Uhtred's soldiers, spears pointed directly toward the Vikings' tunic-clad chests, so close that the spear tips would skewer the men before they could get up to any treachery.

Wiheal was larger than the hamlet where they had met Erik and his companions. From a distance they saw smoke rising from at least five farms, and once closer they could see that the palisade around the village was well maintained and strong.

Viking guards stood at the gate, which gave Ulf pause, but Uhtred ordered him to proceed with a soft hiss. Ulf breathed a sigh of relief when he saw the Vikings' swords hanging from the nearest tree trunk in the palisade's stakewall, so high up that none could pull them down without jumping.

An unarmed Erik waited in front of the village's central hall, which was just a farmhouse slightly larger than the others. Uhtred's seven thanes, who had served as hostages, surrounded Erik. The seven immediately stepped aside so the three Viking chieftains who had come with Uhtred could join them. Another Viking soldier then took up position behind the seven thanes, unsheathing his sword and holding it at the ready in his right hand.

Uhtred stayed in his saddle and nodded calmly at Ulf, who dismounted and took the same position behind the most powerful of the Viking chieftains, holding his own blade at the ready so he could swing it unimpeded through the Viking's neck.

Uhtred then dismounted—with difficulty; the weeks of military campaigning had taken a toll on his body—and his noblemen followed suit, passing their reins to the slaves who came scurrying over. Although the village square in front of the hall was quite large, it resounded with the commotion and noise of the weary horses. Quiet did not return until the slaves took the beasts to the stables outside the palisade.

Erik stepped toward Uhtred and waited as Uhtred unfastened his sword belt. The Viking then summoned a servant, who deferentially accepted the ealdorman's weapon before kneeling and vowing that he would guard the sword here until the ealdorman himself needed it back.

Other servants accepted the swords of the forty noblemen accompanying Uhtred, arranging them carefully in fastidious rows in the grass, and it wasn't until the swords were all arranged that Erik motioned with his hand for Uhtred to enter the hall.

It was dark inside.

Uhtred hadn't noticed if there were windows in the exterior walls, but if there were, they were closed now to keep out the spring chill. All he could see was dust dancing in the pale light that trickled in between the timbers. The coals of a fire glowed in the hearth in the middle of the hall, but with no flames that might have illuminated the room.

Uhtred squinted into the smoke, spotting a silhouette on the far side of the hearth—a silhouette that blurred as a draft suddenly rushed through the hall, flapping the tapestries covering the walls and flaring up the fire.

As the wind receded, Uhtred could make out the silhouette more clearly and was certain that the tall, broad-shouldered man with the prominent, hooked nose was King Cnut, even before he made out the narrow gold crown in the man's dark-blond hair.

Uhtred took a step closer and then waited for the king to pay him the courtesy of doing the same.

The king didn't move.

"My lord, I've come to pledge my oath to you," Uhtred said politely and in Danish.

"Your oath, Uhtred? What is your oath worth to me?" Cnut's voice was so quiet that at first Uhtred thought he had misheard. But then, from the astonished mumbling behind him, he realized that was not the case.

Instinctively Uhtred took a step closer, clenching his fists. He was about to ask the king what he had meant when he heard a sound behind him, like a tree trunk being pulled across the floor.

Surprised, Uhtred looked back to see that the enormous oaken door to the hall had just been closed. He directed his eyes back across the hearth.

The king's silhouette was gone.

Uhtred was looking around to see if Cnut had sat down when an enormous man on a stool by the wall suddenly stood. Uhtred hadn't noticed the man before, preoccupied as he had been with the king. Then suddenly the tapestries that lined the walls seemed to come to life as men armed with swords poured into the room from where they had hidden behind the wall hangings. It was then that Uhtred recognized the enormous man.

"This is the end of your road, Uhtred," Thurbrand the Hold announced.

"Treachery!" Uhtred's voice thundered through the hall.

Thurbrand's lips curled as he snarled, "Stupidity, Uhtred. Your stupidity led you here today."

Uhtred was the first to die, which spared him from seeing his forty noblemen sliced down, their reward for—like him—having taken the king at his word.

Chapter 1

Anno Domini 1018

fter a long, sunny summer, the harvest month had arrived. If I'd still held my father's estate, my mood would have been elevated by the thought of my serfs and tenants toiling away harvesting my crops for me.

Here in Oxford, on the other hand, the sun made the days unbearable. Heat waves quivered between the walls and woven fences. The only fresh air was down by the river and in the meadows. Everywhere else you inhaled the hot, dusty stink of town with each breath.

I've heard it said that when summer settles over London, the town is a reeking hell of stench. Though Oxford is scarcely a quarter the size of London, it could easily serve as the antechamber for the doomed.

King Cnut had left Oxford ages ago. The large joint meeting of the Danish Thing and the Angles' and Saxons' Witenagemot, along with the Danish chieftains from the Danelaw north of Watling Street, had formally agreed that Cnut would be king and rule England in accordance with the old laws. Cnut then spent a week divvying up the massive heregeld tax he had collected—more than eighty thousand pounds of silver. He distributed this among his jarls, thanes, and chieftains to thank them for their assistance in conquering the nation. After that he rode to Canterbury, where Archbishop Lyfing had been forewarned that the king had several matters to discuss with him.

The city of Oxford breathed a collective sigh of relief when all the visitors—not only Cnut and his retinue, but also the noblemen from the rest of the country and all who had crossed the sea to earn some silver by serving Cnut—left after the meetings. They left behind a city that, while it had known how to profit from their visit, rejoiced all the same at being able to once again walk the streets without fighting through crowds, enjoy an evening beer in the taverns with room to sit on the benches, and—not least of all—see the inflated prices at all the stands and stalls drop back to normal again.

Calm presided once again. In fact, it was *too* calm.

I had accepted a position working for Winston the Illuminator, a position I had expected to involve a fair amount of travel. When we first met, the good Winston had confided that he generally traveled from monastery to monastery and church to church at the behest of abbots and bishops, doing what he did better than anyone else in the entire land. Namely, he adorned psalters, prayer books, evangeliaries, and biographies with beautifully colored illuminations—which the religious men wanted to enrich their altars and libraries.

And so what was Winston doing now, that lazybones? Sitting on his behind in Oxford, satisfied to scratch on a little parchment here and a little slate there, while the alewife Alfilda looked after his body's every need—and I do mean all of them.

As my brother Harding used to say: If a man can eat his fill and have a willing bedmate in the same place every night, he quickly grows lazy.

After a few weeks of this idleness, I raised the issue with Winston. Not the part about his sleeping with Alfilda, of course, but his inclination to put down roots in this town by the river ford. His response was a coy look, and a brief smile flashed behind his curly blond beard.

"Are you dissatisfied in your work for me?" he asked.

By no means. The short time I'd been in his service we had already solved a murder for King Cnut, which had not only earned me the king's good graces but also a pound of silver, which I certainly knew how to use. Not that I said that. Instead I hinted that it was time for us to move on, to find a churchman who would pay handsomely for what Winston called work.

"There's no hurry," he mumbled, rubbing his chin.

"The king's silver won't last forever."

"Humph," Winston said. "Are you broke already?"

I certainly was not! A pound of silver was no small sum. I had bought myself a proper, nicely embellished sword befitting my lineage as son of a Saxon thane, and some new clothes to replace what I'd worn since those Viking brutes seized my inherited estate. The smith had accepted my old sword as part of my payment, and since I'd waited until all the crowds had left town before looking for cloth merchants and needlewomen, I had gotten both the cloth and the sewing for a price that I had all but named myself.

"My silver will last a while longer," I said. "But you're not paying me to sit around in Alfilda's tavern and drink, are you?"

Alfilda laughed openly and said, "Well, that's easy enough to fix. Maybe I should put you to work."

That was not my intention. I had no desire to leave Winston's employ. First of all, we got along well together. Second of all, my other prospects were not very tempting.

Men like me abounded, landless noblemen willing to serve whoever paid us the best. And thanks to the large number of soldiers looking for work these days, the going rate wasn't very good.

I had never felt a desire to be a common soldier. My lineage promised me something more. I was the son of a Saxon family, which had served our own kings well, and a Danish woman, whose family was no lower in rank than my father's. I was born to give orders. So if I was going to have to obey someone else, let it be a more important man than all the petty chieftains who sought to gather soldiers around themselves. Someone like the king, for example, which was where Winston came in. In his company I had served Cnut so well that—in addition to paying us—he had summoned us before he left for Canterbury and told us he trusted we would serve him again in the future.

"For a suitable price," I had said. King Cnut looked me in the eye when I said that, and I looked right back at him.

The reward I'd requested was an estate of my own. The king had scoffed and offered me silver instead. Very well. I'd understood his message. I would never ask him for an estate again. Though my side had lost, even the conquered have their pride.

Still, there must have been something in my expression, because the king narrowed his eyes at me.

"Is my silver not good enough, Halfdan the Half-Saxon?"

I returned the insult: "When Saxon silver flows through your fingers and ends up in mine, it is back in its proper place, King Cnut."

His face grew more serious, and a deep wrinkle appeared over his sharp nose.

I heard Winston's breath catch; then a laugh broke the silence. Thane Godskalk, the leader of Cnut's housecarls, laughed loudly.

Cnut turned to look at him and then looked back at me, a smile spreading over his thin lips.

"Then it's good for both of us, half-Dane half-Saxon, that the English have inexhaustible supplies of silver."

Winston reprimanded me later for baiting the king. Before I could retort, he snapped that as long as I was in his service, I would avoid provoking the person who had the power to separate our heads from our bodies.

"If Godskalk hadn't found it funny, it is likely that at least one of us would have stained the grass red," Winston scolded.

"My brother always said that you're only inferior to a man if you behave like you are."

"Your brother's body is rotting in Essex."

Well, if he thought that remark was going to silence me, he was right.

So I left it up to Winston to decide when we would leave Oxford. I left him and Alfilda in peace apart from mealtimes, when we ate together. Instead I spent my days in the company of other men like myself, and my nights with a willing Saxon wench with perky breasts and firm buttocks.

The idleness still perturbed me, however, so I welcomed it when a man approached me one hot afternoon when I'd sought refuge in the shady interior of Alfilda's tavern.

The man who leaned over my table wore a leather tunic, wool breeches tied below the knees, and felt shoes. A wide belt held his pants up, and a leather baldric lay over his shoulder. His face was broad beneath his graying hair. His mustache hung down on either side of his mouth, and strong, weather-beaten forearms stuck out of his tunic sleeves.

"I hear you're Winston the Saxon's man." His voice was rough, with a northern accent.

"You hear correctly," I said, then drank and wiped away the beer foam with the back of my left hand.

One of his eyes twitched, and then he smiled obligingly. "My master would like to speak to him."

I straightened up. A master who wanted Winston's services was as welcome to me as a Saxon victory would have been to King Ethelred. "And your master is . . . ?"

"Prior Edmund of Peterborough."

This was getting better and better: a churchman, just what I'd been hoping for.

"And where is the prior?" I asked, getting up.

"He's waiting outside."

So the monk was too good to set foot in Alfilda's tavern. I quickly finished my drink and adjusted my sword belt.

The alley outside was so narrow that the sun, which had now passed its zenith, cast a shadow over the entire lane. Four men stood in the middle of the street. Two of them were dressed like the man who had led me outside. One of those held two spears, and he handed one to my escort.

The other two were clergymen. One, presumably a subprior, wore a Benedictine cowl, held closed by a rope around his waist. The hood was off, hanging down his back, so I saw his chiseled face and his steely eyes watching me.

The second clergyman also wore a cowl, but his was edged in silk and held closed by a brocade band. His round, rosy face was also exposed. He had friendly gray eyes and a reddish-blond tonsure, which must have been freshly shaved that same morning.

"Prior Edmund," I said to him, bowing my head exactly as far as politeness dictated.

His friendly eyes looked me over.

"I am Halfdan, Master Winston's man."

"And your master?" Edmund's voice was gentle and accommodating.

"I will take you to him, if you will follow me."

Winston had gotten into the habit lately of sitting in the meadow north of town, where until recently so many noblemen were camped. He spent these hot days in the shade of the bushes lining a small creek, sketching with graphite on parchment or scratching with the tip of a stylus on his slate.

I led the prior and his retinue down the lanes and alleys, exited the town's northern gate unimpeded, the guards nodding at me lazily, and spotted Winston sitting in the distance with Alfilda at his side. After the dinner hour, the redheaded alewife would often leave the operation of her tavern to her buxom assistant, Emma, and join Winston. I had often found them together, she with her head in his lap admiring a drawing of a sheep, a man's head, a tree, a flower, or countless other things he had felt like sketching.

Today, too, she sat at his side. She looked up as we approached through the grass. She gave Winston a subtle elbow to the side, and he glanced up quickly but immediately returned his attention to the parchment in front of him.

I stopped a couple of feet in front of him.

"What do you think?" Winston asked.

The drawing was finished. It was Alfilda, as she lived and breathed.

"I've brought Prior Edmund from Peterborough," I announced. For goodness' sake, surely he could see that I wasn't alone.

Winston glanced up, squinting into the sun, which was behind my back. "Prior Edmund!"

The prior, his presence having been acknowledged, cleared his throat and began: "Winston the Illuminator, my abbot, Elsin, asked that I seek you out. He would like you to come to our monastery."

Winston filled in a shadow on his drawing. "Peterborough? No, I don't think that suits me."

I caught a flash of surprise in the prior's face and smiled slightly, despite my irritation at Winston. Here they were, setting a job in the palm of his hand, and he wasn't even considering what it would entail.

"We're otherwise engaged," Winston said.

It didn't seem to please the prior and his brother to be standing in the middle of a meadow talking to an illustrator, so it said something about Winston's reputation that the monk continued: "A nobleman left us a considerable fortune in his will to create a book about Seaxwulf, the founder of our monastery. It is a . . . significant . . . gift, which makes it possible for us to pay for the very finest work."

The lead fell from Winston's hand, which he then entwined in Alfilda's.

"There are other good illustrators," he said.

The gleam in the prior's eyes was no longer surprise, but growing rage. "We want you. That must suffice."

"Suffice?" Winston said, still holding Alfilda's hand. "Not for me. I'm not interested."

The other monk in Edmund's retinue took a step forward, but Prior Edmund's angry voice stopped him: "I am not in the habit of haggling with runaway monks. My abbot wants *you*."

Winston's upturned face was now every bit as angry as the prior's.

"Runaway monks, Edmund?" Winston said. "You're poorly informed. I did run away, yes, but I was never a monk. Walk away now, and I'm willing to forget about you."

This was too much for the monk accompanying Edmund, who stepped out in front of his prior, livid. The man paused briefly, apparently flustered at having stepped so close to Alfilda. Then he regained his composure and addressed Winston: "You're talking to your superior. Obey him, or I will make sure you never work for another monastery in England again."

Winston let go of Alfilda's hand and slowly got up.

"That, my unknown friend," Winston stated, "is beyond your abilities. As long as I can draw, which I can, the monasteries will want my work. But I never work for people who threaten me after I have said no to them."

I saw Prior Edmund blush all the way down his neck. The friar looked like he wanted to roll up the sleeve of his cowl and punch Winston. I warily loosened my sword in its sheath as I watched the three freemen, who apparently weren't planning to intervene.

Then the prior's body deflated a little. He nodded to his companion and, still looking angry, slowly turned away from Winston. To me he said, "We ride north in three days. For your and your master's sake it would be best if you changed your minds before then."

I shrugged, giving him a helpless look, and waited until they were out of earshot before I snarled at my artistic friend, "You just turned down a job that could have earned you a fortune."

"You're too thirsty for silver," Winston said, waving his hand flippantly. "I have something here that's better than money."

Only now did Alfilda speak: "Halfdan will never understand this, Winston."

Now I was angry. Did I not know the joys of a woman? I, who so rarely lacked a bosom to sleep against? But I refused to be drawn into a war of words with a tavern worker.

"It may not be wise to antagonize your superiors, Winston."

"Superiors?" Winston's voice was mocking. "Surely you don't believe that? From what I hear, you're only inferior to a man if you behave like you are."

Winston had a way of twisting a man's words.

Chapter 2

stormed off, steering clear of the tavern. I didn't want to sit there and glare at Winston, who would no doubt be making eyes at Alfilda the whole time. Instead I roamed through town and sat for a bit in an ale tent. I had a slice of bread with blood sausage that smelled of thyme, along with a tankard of sweet ale. Then I went to the house where my wild Saxon servant girl, Engelise, worked. But when I tried to enter the kitchen, her mistress brusquely dismissed me.

Instead I returned to the ale tent, which was full now that the sun was kissing the trees in the woods on the far side of the river. I found a seat across from two Viking soldiers, who gave me blasé looks and didn't bother to lower their voices as they continued their heated argument about which of them should sit on the outside, closest to the oar, in the longboat that would transport them and their spoils back to Scandinavia.

I gulped my ale while cursing Winston, who had apparently decided to keep sitting on his ass.

In absolute honesty, Alfilda's inviting body was likely not the only thing holding Winston back. In the time we'd been together, I'd learned a fair amount about him—including the fact that he preferred to be his own lord and master and spend his time drawing what *he* cared about. I had never figured out why he didn't like working for churches or monasteries. He did the jobs they hired him for, of course, but he just never seemed at ease in such places—though he certainly enjoyed the considerable income from the work. Which meant that Winston was not a poor man; he could afford to say no to Edmund and bide his time in Oxford with Alfilda and his art supplies precisely because he was so well paid.

I knew that Winston's aversion to churches and monasteries had something to do with his past. He'd been a novice at a monastery when he was younger, although I'd never found out where. The only time I'd asked him why he left, he gave me a vague answer I hadn't understood about faith being hard to explain.

Faith is not something we soldiers concern ourselves with. We have priests and monks for that. All men like me need to know is that when death strikes, if we've lived the way the clergymen tell us we're supposed to, we will open our eyes in Paradise.

Prior Edmund had dug his own grave when he accused Winston of being a runaway monk. I could have told the good Benedictine that was the stupidest thing he could say, as was abundantly clear from Winston's reaction.

It didn't seem to bother Winston that *I* found ambling around with nothing to do maddening. I worked for him, so I went where he went. That's how it was, unless I wanted to quit, and I've already explained why that did not seem to be the wisest choice.

I had another tankard of ale and then returned to the kitchen door, where to my joy I found Engelise waiting for me. Her mistress had forbidden her from receiving me in the room she shared with two other girls, but that didn't stop us from seeing each other. It had finally grown dark out, the night was warm, the meadow grasses were soft and inviting, and Engelise's embrace was just as welcoming under a starry sky as on her bed's straw mattress.

About a week later I spent an afternoon playing dice on the alehouse table in the pleasant company of some Saxon freemen. It had not been a bad day for me.

When I made my way that evening toward the house where Engelise worked, I saw a burly soldier riding across the square in front of the large hall where King Cnut had stayed.

The man sat very upright on his well-nourished horse. There was no spear at his side, but a gold-bedecked sword hung at his left hip. The sword bumped against his saddle as he rode. His helmet was edged in silver, and his belt was richly embroidered with both silver and gold thread. Such a splendidly equipped soldier was undoubtedly the housecarl of an important man. Indeed, when he briefly turned to look back, I recognized Godskalk, thane to King Cnut and captain of his personal housecarls.

Our eyes met from across the square. I greeted him with a subtle bow and was surprised when he raised his right hand and called me over.

There weren't many people about. The workday was over, and the market stalls were all closed. Most people were probably having their evening porridge, so I had no difficulty crossing the square. Godskalk dismounted and handed his reins to a servant, who had apparently been waiting by the door to the stables behind the hall.

Godskalk turned to me, and casually gave each leg a shake to loosen his thigh muscles after the ride. He let me walk all the way over to him before he greeted me.

"Halfdan," he said, "Just the man I'm looking for."

"*I'm* the man you're looking for?" I said, looking at him in surprise.

"You're one of them," he said, flashing a quick smile. "Is your master in the tavern?"

"Presumably." I didn't bother to elaborate, despite the puzzled look on his face. Godskalk served the king. I served Winston. He probably had as little idea where Cnut was right now as I did about Winston.

"Do you have a message for him?" I asked.

His nod kindled a little hope in me. Cnut had not dispatched the leader of his housecarls merely to inquire how Winston was doing.

"You can lead the way," Godskalk said, gesturing that I should go first.

As expected, Winston was in the tavern. He sat in his usual spot, at the table closest to the counter. He always sat with his back to the door, facing the counter. That way he and Alfilda could carry on a conversation while she took orders and made sure that Emma was serving the food and drinks to the right tables.

I noted a touch of worry in Alfilda's expression when she realized who was behind me. Then she nodded a welcome to Godskalk, who strode through the establishment, greeted her politely, and then sat down directly across from Winston, who looked at me in silence. I smiled at him.

"Jarl Godskalk has a message for us, Winston."

"Have you ridden far?" Winston asked.

Godskalk nodded and looked over at Alfilda behind the counter. "A round of drinks would be welcome."

Alfilda set a tankard of ale before each of us, and Winston and I drank to our guest.

"Well?" Winston asked. My master was not in the mood for small talk and wanted to know why the king had sent his most trusted man to Oxford.

"The king sends his greetings. He has a job for you."

Winston grunted that that much was clear while I watched Godskalk in curiosity. He took off his helmet and ran his fingers though his sweaty hair.

"You'll have to go north, to Mercia," Godskalk said. He gave Emma a look of gratitude as she set a dish of peas and fried pork shank in front of him. "To Peterborough," he continued.

A small gasp escaped my lips, and Godskalk looked at me in surprise.

Winston leaned forward calmly and said, "So Prior Edmund . . . ?"

"Was asking around in Canterbury for a good manuscript illuminator, and the king remembered you fondly to him."

It was clear from Winston's face that he didn't believe this any more than I did. I wondered if maybe things hadn't happened the other way around. Perhaps Cnut had been the one asking around, for a monastery in Mercia that might be enticed to hire a certain illuminator. Not that it mattered, it occurred to me, since the outcome was the same: either way, Winston would be getting off his ass now. Finally.

Chapter 3

inston tugged on his nose and glanced at Alfilda before looking back to Godskalk.

"We *have* to go to Mercia?" Winston asked incredulously.

Godskalk nodded.

"And arrangements have been made for us to accompany Prior Edmund?" Winston sounded insulted.

Godskalk shrugged. I guess a thane who led Cnut's housecarls was used to having things decided for him. Godskalk was plainly puzzled why this bothered Winston.

"And the job?" I asked.

"You are to be the king's eyes and ears," Godskalk said mysteriously.

As Winston and I exchanged glances, I tried to ascertain whether he knew something I did not.

"And who are we supposed to watch and listen to?" Winston asked, confirming that he didn't.

Godskalk looked around the tavern. People still sat at a few of the tables, most of them just finishing their tankards after having eaten. The evening rush of men looking for a place to pass the time together had not yet started. The tables nearest us were empty, but Godskalk remained silent, eyeing Alfilda warily.

"You can speak freely in the presence of the tavern mistress," Winston said with a bite to his voice.

Godskalk's shoulders rose slightly, and then he invited Alfilda to join us at the table so he didn't have to speak so loudly.

"The king wants to know what people are talking about in Mercia."

I couldn't suppress a snort. "Fall is coming," I said. "They're talking about how hard times are and the good old days."

Godskalk grunted before raising his tankard. He set it back down and leaned in over the table.

"You know who Cnut placed in charge of Mercia," he said.

"Leofwine is Cnut's ealdorman there," I said, taking a drink.

"The king doesn't trust his own man in Mercia?" Winston asked, cocking his head at Godskalk.

I saw a glint in Godskalk's eyes, which I took to mean that the king didn't trust anyone, but Godskalk wisely bit his tongue.

"Wait a minute," I said, pausing to think. "Leofwine doesn't control *all* of Mercia."

"Quite right," Godskalk said, nodding in approval. "Mercia is divided. Leofwine rules the larger part, in the northeast. Other men control the south and the east."

"Viking jarls," I observed. Now I saw what this was about. "Leofwine is the only Saxon ealdorman up there."

"And a man who has reason to harbor ill will toward the king," Winston said, nodding to himself.

"Like thousands of other Saxons—" I started, then realized what Winston had meant. "Oh, because of Leofwine's *son*."

When the joint session of the Witenagemot and Thing had concluded, with the ealdormen and jarls unanimously declaring Cnut the sole and true king of England, Cnut had promised to rule the land by the old laws and not impose new ones.

Some compromise had been required to reach that decision. Saxon thanes, Viking chieftains, Danish noblemen, and Angle freemen had all had to bend toward each other, an exercise that did not come easily to such men.

The king had paved the way for this compromise the previous year by assassinating those noblemen who opposed him and those whom he didn't trust to submit to his rule—suspecting that they would continue to undermine him.

One of the most powerful Saxon ealdormen, for instance, had fallen victim to the ax of none other than Erik of Norway—carrying out the king's order: "Give the ealdorman what we owe him."

Jarl Erik had had no doubt what Cnut meant by that order, nor had he hesitated. To the contrary, he'd separated Eadric the Grasper's head from his body with a single swing, thereby eliminating one of the most contemptible of contemptible creatures from the earth.

If I hated any man, it was Eadric, that grasping scum pot, who had always put himself first. The traitor had switched allegiance faster than the swallows change direction. Eadric's greatest treachery had occurred at the Battle of Assandun, when he abandoned Ironside's army midbattle, taking all his men with him to fight with Cnut. My father and brother died in that battle. Of course there were many casualties, but at least the fallen died true to their word, shoulder to shoulder with the finest soldiers in England, killed by a man who saved his own skin by betraying those who trusted him.

That single slice of the ax that severed Eadric's head was why I was willing to follow Cnut now. And if I should ever meet Jarl Erik of Norway, I would extend my hand to him in gratitude.

But another man cut down at Cnut's bidding was Leofwine's son, Norman. One rumor was that Norman had somehow been involved in Eadric's schemes. Another was that he had tried to lure Jarl Thorkell the Tall into leaving Cnut. But whatever the reason, everyone knew that King Cnut had had Norman killed.

"But," I began, "I thought Leofwine reconciled with King Cnut."

Godskalk apparently hadn't expected me to be so dimwitted, and the corner of his mouth twitched.

"Ealdorman Leofwine, honest man that he is, gave Cnut his word," Godskalk said, not quite hiding his sarcasm.

"Even an honest man must avenge his fallen heir," Alfilda said.

Godskalk looked at her in surprise. She smiled quickly.

"But Leofwine has other sons," Winston said.

"So Cnut thinks Mercia might rise against him?" I asked, stretching my legs out beneath the table.

"What Cnut would like to know," Godskalk said, slowly shaking his head, "is whether there is anything to *suggest* Mercia might pose a threat."

"But—" I began and then paused. Winston gave me a look of encouragement, so I proceeded. "All right, we know that Viking jarls rule southern Mercia. Jarl Erik of Norway now rules northern Northumbria. East Anglia belongs to Thorkell the Tall."

"Halfdan's right," Winston said, adjusting his position and leaning toward Godskalk. "Leofwine holds his station because Cnut permits him to do so. North, south, east, and west—Leofwine is surrounded by Viking and Danish jarls every way he looks. Is Leofwine somehow a threat to Cnut?"

Godskalk laughed grimly, which made us nervous enough that I whistled softly and Winston tugged on his nose. But Alfilda was the one who actually spoke.

"Cnut doesn't trust his own jarls?" she asked.

I wanted to point out that Erik was technically Norwegian, but realized it didn't matter—maybe Cnut had good reason to be suspicious. Instead, I asked if there were any indications that Thorkell was going to go back on his oath to Cnut again.

"Next to Cnut, Thorkell is the most powerful man in England," Godskalk said, shaking his head. "He's drunk on power, yes, but he's not stupid."

Now I understood! "It's Leofwine's family you fear."

"It's his family that the king wants to be sure of," Godskalk said, pushing his empty tankard across the table to Alfilda, who got up and refilled it. He waited until she was seated again before continuing. "As you pointed out, Winston, Norman has brothers. Apparently they accepted their father's reconciliation with Cnut, but they're young and hot-blooded. Leofwine put the eldest, Leofric, in control of the fyrd, the local militia. And this puzzles Cnut. The king appoints *jarls* to lead the fyrd's soldiers. So now why would Cnut's appointed jarl hand this power over to Leofric, who is merely one of the king's many thanes?"

The answer was obvious. "His son has some hold on him," I said.

"His *family* might have some hold on him," Winston corrected me. "Leofwine's relatives accepted his reconciliation with Cnut, but they want assurance that Mercia's fyrd is controlled by a man loyal to his own and not bound by any promise to a conquering king."

"Exactly," Godskalk said, nodding. "Leofwine gave the king his word, but is his family or his son Leofric also bound by that? The king would like you to head north into Mercia with your eyes and ears open. Listen to what people are saying. Look for signs about what the local soldiers are up to."

"But," Winston began, "wouldn't it be easier to simply get rid of Leofwine and his sons and name someone else jarl?"

"So soon after promising to keep the old laws and govern England by the joint resolution of the Witenagemot and Thing?" I asked. I couldn't help but smile. "There is only one Saxon ealdorman left in this entire land, and a living Leofwine is the proof the Saxons need that Cnut means what he says. If an ax struck Leofwine down, or even if he suddenly fell out of the king's favor, the joint resolution adopted here in Oxford wouldn't be worth anything in the eyes of the Saxons."

"And *that* is why you're going north," Godskalk said, leaning back.

"And *that* is why the king arranged for a job at the monastery in Peterborough to land in my lap," Winston said, resting his hand atop Alfilda's.

"Prior Edmund happened to be in Canterbury and was willing to listen to Cnut's proposal," Godskalk said with a shrug.

"But . . . ," I said, struck by a thought, "the prior arrived in Oxford last week, and you got here today. You can't expect me to believe a flock of monks rode here faster than the head of the king's housecarls."

Godskalk's response was a sly grin.

"The king simply suggested that the prior make use of Master Winston's talents," he said. "Prior Edmund isn't aware of Cnut's true motives. We had hoped the matter would be settled before I arrived, and that you would already have signed a contract."

I wondered if Edmund had sent a messenger to inform the king that Winston had refused to accept the job.

"The prior was furious after his conversation with you," Godskalk continued. "So much so, in fact, that one of my housecarls who was overnighting here on his way east overheard the prior ranting. I had previously arranged to meet that housecarl in Taceham, a day's ride to the south. And when I got there, he told me of the prior's anger." Godskalk smiled again. "So I thought I'd better ride up here and set things right."

"So if Winston had said yes to that fart of a monk, we would have set out north without knowing what the king wanted us to do?" I said, not following.

Godskalk gave me an almost pitying look.

"My travels are taking me north from Taceham," he explained. "I would have 'happened' to run into you, and we would have had a nice time over a few tankards of ale as old acquaintances from Oxford."

"The brethren left four days ago," I said. "Even though they're not riding the best mounts, they have quite a head start. All we have at our disposal is Winston's worm-ridden old mule, and there's no way we can catch up with them on foot."

"So," Godskalk said, standing up, "let's get you outfitted from the king's stables next to the hall as soon as possible."

Chapter 4

t took us a full day to ready ourselves for the trip. Winston pointed out to Godskalk—who was impatient to see us on our way so he could return to the king—that he could not start an illumination job without his tools and materials.

And so we spent most of a morning carefully packing away his pens; paintbrushes; sticks of lead; envelopes of gold leaf; jars of red lead; rolls of parchment; small pouches of lapis lazuli; bottles and pots of yellow, green, and black paint; rulers; and countless other items that Winston needed for his work. The afternoon sun gradually passed over the town while he painstakingly stowed his packages away into bags or rolled them up into cornets, which he stored in big leather satchels meticulously tied closed with multiple cords. By the time evening came, "our" room—as we still called it, although I was the only one who still slept there—resembled a merchant's stall with all the little parcels covering the bed.

After bidding a proper farewell to Engelise in the meadow grasses, I retrieved Atheling, Winston's slightly lame and extremely obstreperous mule, from his stall. Then Winston and I secured the bags to the mule's bony back. I was very careful to keep out of reach of his rotten teeth, which I knew all too well could still bite very effectively despite their apparent frailty.

Once Winston was convinced everything was properly stowed, I pulled Atheling behind us through the streets to the king's stables, where the two horses we'd chosen awaited us. Winston had selected a gray mare with a blocky head and a sweet-tempered look in her brown eyes, while I'd chosen a red gelding with good, strong pasterns and eyes that seemed to say he would stand his ground should we encounter any trouble.

I tied Atheling to the post in front of the stable. After I'd saddled the horses, Winston came to join me, having said his farewell to Alfilda. She had decided to stay at her inn and not see us off.

We bid Godskalk farewell as well and rode out the northern gate with my gelding and me in front and Winston and his mare leading the mule by the reins. I wore soft wool breeches and an open linen tunic, and had secured my baldric to my pommel. The hilt of my sword lay within reach of my right hand. I'd secured my small bundle of clothing behind me.

The day was bright and warm, with a gentle breeze that cooled my face and ruffled my hair. I was incredibly happy to get out of town. I kneed my mount and couldn't stifle my laugh of delight as he instantly obeyed, breaking into a canter. The sun, the wind, and the powerful horse moving beneath me returned me to a time when my father and brother, Harding, were still alive. When, as King Ethelred's men, we still had our estate.

I rode as far as five arrowshots ahead, testing the horse's responsiveness to the bit and to my knees. Satisfied, I stopped beneath a great oak that offered a pleasant shady spot while I watched Winston catch up calmly along the trail.

That night we slept under the open sky. The horses and the mule grazed peacefully side by side. Apparently Atheling realized that both the mare and the gelding were stronger than he was, because he didn't try anything with either of them. Winston snored next to me, and when I finally fell asleep, I dreamt King Cnut had made me a thane and granted me an estate that I could pass down to my heirs.

Given how eager Prior Edmund had recently been for Winston to illuminate his book, you would think he'd have been happy when we caught up to him. But he seemed almost annoyed when we walked into the hall where he was staying.

In the late afternoon of our third day of riding, we reached a small village named Brackley, where the road from Oxford crossed another road running from the southeast toward the west. Despite Brackley's size, it had a large hall, the home of the thane responsible for the crossroads. As we entered, four spearmen who were vigilantly keeping an eye on passersby hailed us.

I explained that we were riding to Peterborough at the request of the prior there, and after checking that we weren't hiding a flock of bandits in our mule's saddlebags, they informed us that we were in luck: the prior happened to be in the village hall right now as a guest of the thane.

We rode up to the hall and were again greeted by spearmen. They inquired within, and after demanding my sword, they let us enter.

A stocky Viking thane with red braids hanging down over his ring mail–clad chest sat in the high seat. His face was coarse, and he had a bright-red scar running from the corner of his left eye down across his cheek, where it disappeared under the beard that covered his strong chin.

His eyes followed us as we walked across the floor, but he didn't greet us with a slight nod of his head until we stopped and gave him our names. He told us he was Leif, the king's thane.

"And you're here on Prior Edmund's business," he continued, glancing at the monk by his side.

"You turned down my offer," Prior Edmund stated, eyeing us resentfully.

"I've changed my mind," Winston said, bowing politely and giving me a look to bow, too.

"Why?" Edmund demanded.

"My lady friend sent me packing," Winston explained.

I had to admire Winston's graceful lying skills.

"So you come running after me, crying for forgiveness," Edmund said, his mocking tone sounding almost pouty. "I seem to recall you informing Subprior Simon that no one could make you change your mind."

That wasn't completely true. What Winston had said was that Simon couldn't stop other monasteries from hiring him for his artistic abilities. But since Winston didn't correct the prior, I decided I wouldn't either.

"Fine, fine," Edmund said, leaning back. "Name your demands."

Winston dug a foot into the dust on the floor, and then he glanced up at the smoke-blackened ceiling.

"You would like a book done, as far as I recall," Winston said. "So at least eight full-page illuminations, I presume?"

The prior nodded.

"Initials?"

"Our own scribes will do those."

"Smaller illustrations?"

"Maybe. Let's say eight of them."

"Are your scribes skilled?"

"Our master scribe is," Prior Edmund said. "And he's a man who knows how to get the best work from his assistants."

"But are they skillful enough to draw *initials*?"

"The master scribe will handle those."

"Hmm," Winston said, scratching the back of one hand. "I get to approve the parchments."

"That's not going to go over very well," Edmund said, seriously but not harshly. Negotiating the details of the deal seemed to have dissipated his anger. His ruddy face seemed just as friendly as the first time I'd seen it.

"You mean with the master scribe?" Winston said. "Yes, I realize that, but that point is nonnegotiable."

"*All* the parchments?" the prior asked. A furrow now appeared between his eyes.

"Any that I'm going to draw or paint on, yes," Winston said with a sigh.

"Fine," Edmund said. Although Edmund was apparently unaccustomed to hearing the word no, he also didn't seem to be one to quibble over details now that Winston had accepted the assignment. "And your price?"

Winston closed his eyes. I saw his lips moving, as if he were talking to himself. Eventually he looked up. "One and a half pounds of silver."

"That's outrageous!" Edmund exclaimed, shaking his head.

"Outrageous?" Winston said. "By no means. Eight fully illuminated pages and an equal number of half-page illustrations for me to color and complete. You've heard my price."

"Which is much too high." There was no trace of merriment left on the prior's face now, nor in his voice.

"Well then." Winston turned to Thane Leif, who had been listening to the haggling in silence. "My lord, would you permit my man and me to spend the night in your village?"

"You can sleep here in the hall," Leif said, nodding. "I'm sure your man will find himself a spot."

"Would you permit me to carry my sword?" I asked, glaring at Leif.

Sadly, this hint that I was a man of noble lineage left Leif unswayed concerning my *current* social rank.

"If you give me your word you won't unsheathe your sword unless you're attacked, then I grant your request," Leif said. "But you'll have to find your own shelter for the night."

I turned away and heard Winston's footsteps behind me as I strode toward the door.

"You cover the cost of food and drink for you and your man," Prior Edmund called out before we left the hall.

Winston turned around and said, "A pound and a half of silver, a place to stay, and *my* food. I will cover Halfdan's necessities myself."

Edmund bit his lip and then nodded.

"Shall I draw up a contract?" Winston asked.

"No," the prior said, shaking his head. "We'll have the sacristan do it once we reach the monastery."

Winston bowed.

Once outside, we led the horses and mule to the meadow a spearman pointed out to us. I watched with some satisfaction as Atheling demonstrated who he thought was in charge of the paddock, sinking his teeth into the shoulder of a well-fed mule mare. I hoped it was the prior's mount.

Chapter 5

he square outside the hall bustled with a ragtag group of wayfarers. The vulnerable travelers were availing themselves of the military retainers protecting Edmund and Simon.

Of course such retainers often provided a false sense of security, because the thane or other nobleman who'd hired them determined the speed of travel. Typically the people clinging to the group for safety couldn't keep pace. They would fall behind and risk falling victim to outlaws who wisely waited for the armed group to pass before attacking the stragglers.

But apparently the monks moved along at quite a leisurely pace, befitting the ruminative religious men, wobbling along on the broad backs of their mules with their spearmen following them, always close enough to defend the monks should an enemy be sighted.

Perhaps Prior Edmund still took the responsibility to care for the poor to heart enough that he intentionally kept his pace slow, so that even the poorest, most hunchbacked wayfarer could keep up. Wandering around in the grassy square, I realized that must be the case. I watched some people settling in around a cooking fire and erecting a makeshift shelter. Although the eldest and most infirm among them certainly looked tired from the day's travel, none of them seemed completely exhausted or run ragged.

Peddlers sat in groups, sizing up one another's bundles, their minds busily comparing the quality of the others' wares to their own. These were men equipped for life on the road, passing around full casks and jugs as they blabbered on. They told the kinds of stories that peddlers like to pass the time with—stories that are pretty much all about a huge sale almost made, before the unfortunate peddler either loses the goods or finds the item to be so readily available that no one is willing to pay the outrageous price named.

For as many peddlers as I've met who claim they've almost made a fortune, it's amusing how jealously they all guard their purses and coffers from prying eyes, leaving it all too clear that they've never *actually* made those fortunes. I've always wondered how they pay for their good shoes, their durable breeches and soft shirts; how it is that they always carry full bags of food and frothy kegs to put to their lips; and how the heavily laden horses, asses, or mules they pull along behind them are always well fed and glossy coated.

Other groups settling in for the night were families, quite obviously Saxons who had lost their farms and land under the new king and now hoped there was land to be had up north. It was more than likely that the Danes up north would stubbornly insist the arable land was theirs. The luckiest of these Saxons would get a chance to become tenant farmers, peasants working some Danish farmer's land. And the unluckiest would end up selling off their children, then their wives, and finally themselves, all into serfdom to those same Danish farmers, just so they would have a chance of not going to bed hungry at night.

The other people I saw on the village green—the ones who couldn't afford any wood for a cooking fire, let alone food to cook—consisted of myriad small bands of riffraff. They eagerly watched for someone to toss aside an already-chewed bone, a crust of bread, or maybe a chunk of meat full of cartilage.

When that happened, they would pounce, frothing at the mouth, biting and hitting each other to make it to the tidbit first. And the man who succeeded would scarf the morsel down while holding his less fortunate fellow sufferers at bay with his free hand.

The ones who succeeded most often were men who had already paid the price for escaping a battle alive: one-armed or handless men; men with stumps of limbs dangling between crutches and men supporting themselves on a wooden leg; one-eyed men, no longer useful in a spear wall since they can't see to the side and are therefore a risk to those standing next to them; young men with arms hanging limp after a sword blow to the shoulder or a spear through the armpit; men whose fingers had been chopped off and could no longer hold a spear shaft. These were all men who had served fallen masters and had never earned their hoped-for pay. In the end it hadn't mattered if they'd marched ahead in the dust, waited fearfully within the shield wall, or hacked away at the enemy's shields, limbs, and necks while foaming at the mouth with a drive to fight. They had all wound up traveling the back roads, hoping somewhere or other there would be a patch of ground where they, too, might settle down, where a handless man could become a shepherd, a one-eyed man could drive a ploughshare, and a legless man could carve spoons or wooden shoes.

Prior Edmund's housecarls also occupied the square: a dozen spearmen seated around a wooden table under a tree. One of them was the housecarl who had approached me in Alfilda's tavern. He happened to look up just then, and our eyes met. I nodded in greeting, which he returned uncertainly. Then he finally recognized me, stood halfway up, and gestured for me to join them.

I didn't have any better offers, so why not socialize with the soldiers? Which is just what I did. I walked across the grass, stopped a couple of steps from the table, and gave them my name.

My acquaintance responded by giving me his name. His friends nodded at me but apparently found no need to be any more polite than that to the son of a Saxon nobleman, since I had so obviously been cast out of the finer company in the hall.

The spearman's name was Wulfgar, and he willingly made space for me next to him and pushed a tankard of ale my way. I don't know if he noticed his colleagues' rudeness, but he smiled at a couple of them, who looked up in surprise when I asked how they could all be off duty at the same time. I had asked the question in the Danish I had learned from my mother. Her accent was hardly as grating as the Danish they speak in the north, and even Saxons can understand it, although some claim they have to concentrate so hard it gives them a headache.

"So you're a Dane, even though you're dressed like a Saxon and travel in the company of Saxons?" Wulfgar asked, taking a pork shank from the platter in the middle of the table and passing it to me.

"Saxon, Dane," I said. "I am who I am."

Wulfgar gave me a quick glance and then apparently decided it was my own business who I chose to be.

"And, yes, we can all stuff ourselves tonight since Leif's housecarls are on duty," Wulfgar added.

I bit into the shank, which was fatty and smelled of rosemary.

"Of course the thane's men are responsible for security here, but isn't it customary for a visiting nobleman to offer to have his soldiers serve a shift?" I asked.

"Yes, that's true," Wulfgar said. "And Prior Edmund made just such an offer, but Leif turned him down. Apparently Leif would like the king to hear word that Leif does his duty and doesn't need help from others."

"Noblemen are like that," I said, spitting a bit of bone onto the grass.

"If you say so," Wulfgar said with a shrug.

I didn't detect any sarcasm in his voice, and I decided to change the subject.

"What kind of man is this Prior Edmund?" I asked.

"Like most high-ranking monks," Wulfgar said. "He was a nobleman by birth, and I guess you can't set aside your upbringing just because you swap your cloak for a cowl."

I cocked my head and studied Wulfgar's face, but it was calm, and there was no derision in his voice.

"For example, he doesn't tolerate being disobeyed," Wulfgar said, now with levity in his voice. "Oh, how he raged after your master turned him down."

"Yes," I said, swallowing a chunk of fat. "It's never pleasant to be put in your place."

Wulfgar chuckled. He was obviously enjoying the memory of the prior being on the losing end. Then he leaned over to me.

"And yet," he said, "after all that, you're here anyway?"

"Your master isn't the only one with strange ways," I said. "Mine is always changing his mind depending on his mood. The prior struck the wrong note in that meadow, but when Winston had a chance to think it over, he realized he could use the money."

I didn't care if the soldier believed my explanation, but he did seem to have given some thought to the issue.

"I heard that your master was a prosperous man," he said.

I looked at him with one eyebrow raised.

"So perhaps it's not the profit that motivates him," Wulfgar said, taking the ale jug and pouring more for both of us.

"That's what he told me, anyway," I said shrugging. Neither of us said anything, so I decided to turn the conversation back to Prior Edmund. "But noble-born, you said this Edmund is?"

"Aren't they all?" Wulfgar replied. "Abbots, bishops, priors. A farmer's son like me can become a monk if he wants to, but to *lead* monks or clergymen, you have to come from a noble family."

"Maybe I know his family?" I said. It was always good to know as much as possible about people, especially the ones who thought they were your superiors.

"I don't know if you'd know them. North of Watling Street they're not unknown. Edmund's father was Edgar, son of Edwin, and the family has owned land up by the border with the Scots for many generations."

"So Edmund's family is Saxon," I said. "And they still have some power up there?"

"Noblemen are noblemen first and foremost," Wulfgar said, giving me a look that was hard to interpret. "Only after that are they Saxons or Danes. And the answer is yes. Edmund's brother is Jarl Erik's trusted man."

We drank for a bit in silence; then I decided I might as well take advantage of his talkativeness.

"And what about the subprior?" I asked. "Is he also of noble birth?"

"Simon?" Wulfgar chuckled. "Or should I say Harold—as he was called before he crawled into his cowl. He's the son of a Saxon priest whose church is in western Mercia. Simon is the conscience of the monastery."

I gave him a quizzical look.

"Prior Edmund and Abbot Elsin both think that the Peterborough monastery needs to become large and powerful to prove the greatness of God," Wulfgar said. "They've gone about acquiring amazing altar cloths, tapestries woven with gold thread, and, well, lavishly illuminated books—all of those things are supposed to show the glory of God. That's how noblemen think, you know? Simon, on the other hand, believes God doesn't want to be honored with gold or silver. He would prefer for the monastery to use its wealth 'feeding the hungry, curing the sick, and soothing the suffering,' as he says."

Wulfgar paused when he noticed me shaking my head.

"You don't believe me?" he asked.

"Sure, of course, but that doesn't add up. Simon was the one who threatened Winston back in that Oxford meadow."

"Oh yes," Wulfgar said, laughing loudly. "It actually adds up quite nicely. These are all monastery men, and to them any monastery—but, let me add, especially their own monastery—is the noblest entity in the world. So whether they believe God is best glorified by gold and gems or by helping the needy, no one had better cross them. The abbot and the prior believe they speak for God. By opposing Prior Edmund, your illuminator defied Our Lord himself. And Simon doesn't let that kind of thing go unpunished."

"But that's just what Winston did," I said, puzzled. After all, Winston *hadn't* been punished.

Wulfgar gave me a vaguely pitying look.

"Didn't you just tell me that he changed his mind?" Wulfgar said. "If you ask Simon, he'll say your Winston did not change his own position. God changed it for him. And you can be sure that Simon also expects that Winston has learned a thing or two about humility, having been schooled by the Good Lord himself."

I smiled. I was rather looking forward to seeing what would happen when those two should come up against each other again.

Chapter 6

I slept well. Better, I'm confident, than if I'd been lying in that hall with all *those* folk. People always come and go in a nobleman's hall, all night long. Snoring and snorting erupt from the sleeping benches, men have to piss in the middle of the night, and guards clatter their weapons when starting a new shift.

After I bade Wulfgar good night, I pissed good and long until I was sure I'd emptied out the ale he had generously offered me. Then I retrieved my cape from my saddlebag next to the horse paddock.

A full harvest moon hung golden over the treetops on the far side of the road to the west, and the usual muffled ruckus came from inside the hall, from men who'd eaten their fill of the thane's meat and drunk his ale until their thirst was quenched. Apart from that, a peaceful stillness had settled over the village.

A hay cart sat outside a freshly thatched house, so I crawled under it, wrapped myself in my cloak, and fell asleep with the sound of the grasshoppers in my ears.

When I awoke, the sun was between the trees to the east, and a sleepy-looking maiden was walking across the small fenced-in croft that belonged to the thatched house. My eyes followed her until she reached a sheepfold, where she squatted down with her back to me and pulled up her skirt. What I saw of her white backside made me wish I could see more of her body, which was sensibly encased in the gray clothes that told me she was some type of serf.

On her way back, she spotted me and my lustful eyes and gave me a teasing wink. Then she walked back inside with a playful little swivel of her hips.

I walked over to the sheepfold for my own morning piss and then continued through the square's dewy grass to the stream, which ran just outside the palisade surrounding the village. I pulled off my shirt and waded out into the water, where I dunked my whole torso. Shivering from the cold, I climbed back onto the bank and started rubbing my arms.

I was warm and dry by the time I returned to my hay-cart lair. I dressed and strapped on my sword belt before heading to the hall.

The guard willingly opened the door for me, and after my eyes adjusted to the darkness and my nose to the stuffiness of a shut-in room full of sleeping men, I spotted Winston sitting at a long table, gobbling porridge. He grunted good morning and made some space next to him. A girl promptly placed an earthenware bowl in front of me. The sweet aroma of honey wafted up. The bowl was followed by a tankard of ale, and soon my belly was full of oatmeal and my mouth was satisfyingly malted.

Winston reported that he'd slept extremely well, but he needed to get some fresh air after being shut in for the night with "so many deep breathers." So we headed out into the morning, which was no longer as quiet as it had been when I entered the hall.

We heard voices from the paddock designated for the visitors' mounts, where Wulfgar and his colleagues were saddling up the monks' mules. The many wayfarers were also noisy as they broke camp. They knew how important it was to be ready the instant the prior swung himself up into his saddle, and they didn't want to be left behind.

Winston put his hands on the small of his back, stretched and took a deep breath, exhaled, stuck his arms out straight sideways, inhaled again, and then suddenly smiled at me.

"There, now the day can begin," he said.

"Speak for yourself," I retorted. "For some of us it began in the stream a couple of hours ago." I was already heading toward our horses.

Winston shivered.

"Leif is a generous man," he said. "He has his girls bring guests warm water to wash with."

I left it up to Winston to load his paraphernalia onto Atheling, who eyed me peevishly. I saddled the gray mare and my own mount and then led them out of the paddock and tied them to a fence pole to wait. I sat down to wait for the monks to say farewell to Thane Leif.

It wasn't long before the thane and Prior Edmund appeared in the doorway. Edmund stopped as soon as he was out on the grass, held out his hand, and apparently politely thanked the thane for the night's shelter before striding decisively over to Wulfgar with Simon in tow, the latter's face hidden under the hood of his cowl.

The emergence of the monks was the sign the wayfarers had been waiting for. They quickly flocked onto the lawn in a particular order: first the mounted merchants, then the peddlers in their sturdy shoes, then the landless families on their way to what they hoped would be a brighter future, and finally the slovenly poor and other riffraff, including the one-eyed and handless.

Among these, I happened to notice a broad-shouldered man with a beard. He held his head down like someone ashamed of his condition. He wore the leather tunic and buckskin breeches of a soldier and carried a long package on his back that I decided contained a sword, presumably the last relic of his former life, which I expected he would cling to as long as possible. A nobleman who has fallen as far as a person can fall will let hunger ravage his gut for many days before he parts with his sword.

Wulfgar led the prior's mule forward, helped the two monks into their saddles, and handed them their reins before nodding at three of his men to lead the way north. We fell in behind: first Wulfgar, the only spearman traveling on horseback, followed by the two monks, riding side by side. Then came Winston, who led Atheling while I rode at his side, and then the rest of the monks' spearmen, followed by the motley crowd. All told, there were close to sixty people stretching out into a procession a good arrowshot in length, with those at the very back eager to keep up and stay as close as possible to the spearmen.

It was a clear day with blue skies and a sun that quickly warmed the dry ground, so I was glad to be on horseback and not walking in the swirling dust kicked up by all the hooves and feet. Prior Edmund had his mule maintain a good, steady pace, but he looked back at regular intervals to make sure that everyone was keeping up. So I was correct that he took his duty to care for the poor quite seriously.

Winston rode in silence while I enjoyed the day's warmth and light. I noted Wulfgar's vigilance and was satisfied with his expertise. He continually scanned the countryside ahead of us and to the sides, and he looked back at regular intervals as well.

Our trail cut through the woods, and occasionally we spotted smoke from one of the small, adjacent villages. At one point we heard someone working with an ax, and occasionally we would pass scattered, already harvested fields, where a swineherd would let his drove root around in the stubble. The swineherds eyed us with curiosity, but the sight of the monks always seemed to reassure them. None of them ever decided to run away and leave the pigs to fend for themselves.

Just as the sun reached its zenith, we arrived at a small village called Syresham. The farmers kindly let us rest on their green for a while and brought ale to the two monks. They permitted the rest of us to buy ourselves a couple of tankards if we wished.

We stayed long enough that even the rabble looked rested. Then we climbed back into our saddles and rode on through the shady woods, the sun no longer directly overhead.

Wulfgar returned from a short ride ahead and told Edmund that we were approaching Watling Street's crossing over the River Tove. Suddenly we heard yelling and shouting from behind us. I turned my head and saw a band of armed men, weapons out, charging at the peddlers, who were screaming at the top of their lungs to get Wulfgar's attention.

Wulfgar bellowed an order, and his spearmen lowered their weapons and rushed back to fight off the attackers. I grabbed the hilt of my sword next to my pommel, unsheathed it, and dug my heels into the horse's sides, yanking on the reins to turn the animal around. Then I rushed back down the trail.

I had to ride in an arc around the spearmen and noticed to my joy that my mount willingly followed the pressure commands from my knees. The horse didn't show the least sign of fear as we hurtled toward the armed men.

Ahead I saw a redheaded outlaw fleeing after he had managed to rip a leather sack away from one of the peddlers. I brought my horse up to his left, swung my sword down with a whoosh, and passed the man's body before his head had even struck the ground.

Behind me to the left I saw the spearmen catching up with the bandits, who—like the man I'd just dispatched to eternity—were running away after grabbing what they could hold from their victims. A spear whistled through the air—apparently the monks' soldiers were strong—and another bandit fell to the ground. I got my horse up to speed again and rode forward in front of the fleeing thieves. I saw Wulfgar come thundering in from the other side with his spear lowered. A press of my knee sent my horse to the right. Wulfgar skewered a screaming bandit as I slammed my sword down into the shoulder of one scoundrel, who bellowed loudly. The blade bit in and stuck, so I had to let go. I turned my horse with a frustrated growl and leaped out of my saddle. I gripped my sword and twisted it free of the man I'd struck down, who lay screaming before me. Then I slit his throat in one slice.

The robbers who were still alive around me yelled as the spearmen closed in on them.

"Wulfgar!" I bellowed. From his horse he turned to me with a smile on his face and a spear in his hand. "Take one of them alive!"

He nodded and then I realized to my delight that my gelding was standing calmly only a few paces ahead of me. I reached out and grabbed the reins and got back into the saddle again.

The spearmen were looking for the last of the outlaws, who were trying to escape into the woods. I saw only one of the thieves still nearby, swinging an ax at a swordsman. The swordsman was the bearded soldier I'd noticed that morning.

From the way the soldier avoided the swinging ax and maneuvered his opponent around, I could tell he wasn't a bad swordsman. Then I heard Wulfgar yell to him that he should make sure just to wound the outlaw. The bearded soldier feinted at the outlaw's chest. The outlaw fell for the trick and whacked his ax down, trying to parry the sword away, but then suddenly the sword wasn't there anymore. Instead the soldier swung it in from the left in a formidable backhand swing, slicing into the bandit's unprotected neck.

Suddenly it was quiet around us. No screaming, no yelling for mercy, just the agitated voices of the peddlers, hurriedly inventorying their wares to find out what they were missing.

Wulfgar rode up to me and dismounted.

"Do we have any of them alive?" I asked him.

He shook his head and looked despondently from the dead man in front of him to the soldier who'd slain him.

"I asked you to spare his life," Wulfgar chastised the soldier.

The bearded man shrugged and then bent down to wipe his blade on the dead man's clothes. I noted that he had a beautiful old sword—the kind our Saxon forefathers had forged back in the day—with a silver ring on the hilt.

Wulfgar shook his head.

"It might have been nice to know if they were just a pack of roadside brigands or if there was something more organized afoot," Wulfgar explained to the soldier, who just stared back at him.

"Do you understand me?" Wulfgar asked. He clearly wasn't sure why the soldier had disobeyed his order.

The bearded man nodded.

"You could at least do me the courtesy of responding, then," Wulfgar said sternly.

I put my hand on the man's arm to take the edge off Wulfgar's scolding.

The man pulled his arm free, brought his hand up before his mouth, and shook his head.

"You're mute?" I asked.

He nodded.

"But you can hear?"

Another nod. Then his lips slid apart and he showed me his tongueless mouth.

Chapter 7

ulfgar and I turned away from the mute man.

"Just let him be," I urged quietly.

Wulfgar glanced over his shoulder at the man and then nodded. "Let's see how badly we were hit."

I surveyed the group. Silence prevailed among all the wayfarers following us. The riffraff stood in a joyful huddle, glad to be alive, but shaken. Prior Edmund stood in his stirrups and looked back down the line at us.

Two bodies lay in the grass. A pool of blood spread beneath one of them, a merchant, and it didn't take much looking to determine that the man was dead.

The other body sat up, cursing, just as we reached him. He clutched his bloody arm and spat angrily in the grass, looking up at us. He was one of the peddlers.

"Some protection you're providing!" the man complained.

Wulfgar gave him a testy look and countered, "Did you by chance enter into some sort of agreement for protection from my master, the prior?"

The peddler bit his tongue.

"Come on, the prior's waiting," Wulfgar commanded me.

It didn't even occur to me to retort that I was Winston's man, not the prior's. I just followed Wulfgar, satisfied I had proved that I was his natural equal.

"Well?" Edmund asked, looking down at us from his mule.

"One merchant killed," Wulfgar said, handing his sword to one of his men, who started wiping the blood from the tip with a cloth.

"You didn't see them coming?" a disgruntled voice asked.

I turned to see Subprior Simon scowling at me from his horse, but didn't feel like clarifying that that wasn't my job; *I* wasn't one of his hired spearmen.

"They struck after we passed," Wulfgar said, as though explaining the obvious to an idiot.

"These men were counting on our protection," Simon said indignantly.

"If you wanted me to protect them instead of you," Wulfgar stated calmly, "you should have ordered my men to march alongside them and not in a closed formation around you."

"Quite right," Prior Edmund chimed in. "What about the outlaws?"

"We got them all," Wulfgar said, running his hand through his hair. "Would you like us to bury the dead merchant here?"

Edmund nodded. "Bury him, but hang the outlaws up."

Wulfgar raised his hand to summon one of his men, whom he instructed to oversee the digging of a grave. Then Wulfgar asked me to come with him.

"I'll be right there," I said. Winston had dismounted and had subtly caught my attention as he pulled his two animals to the side of the road.

I stepped over to him, taking care to make sure the mare stood between Atheling and me, and Winston gave me a questioning look.

"I don't know," I replied, "but I'm on my way to find out if this was anything other than a band of outlaws on the lookout for loot."

"Who could have known why we're here?" Winston mumbled.

"No one, I assume," I responded with a shrug. "I doubt Godskalk would have let anyone else in on the king's secret request."

"I hope you're right."

"There is one thing that suggests I am," I said.

Winston bit his lip.

"True," he said nodding. "The attackers did go right for the peddlers."

I nodded in agreement and rushed to catch up with Wulfgar. He had assigned a group of spearmen to gather the dead outlaws. By the time I reached him, a pile of six shabbily dressed bodies lay in front of him, and two more were quickly tossed onto the heap of their dead companions

I walked around the pile, studying the bodies. They were dirty, with uncut hair and tattered, threadbare clothes. Only one of them wore shoes. Two of them didn't even have shirts and had made do with sacks with holes cut out for their head and arms.

Wulfgar watched me as I reluctantly leaned over and passed my hands over each of the bodies.

"I'm looking for clues about who they were," I explained.

He stood there waiting until I finished and wiped my hands in the grass.

"Nothing," I announced.

"Humph. What did you expect?"

I couldn't very well say I was afraid I would find evidence that they'd been sent by Jarl Leofwine.

"Maybe a coin—"

Wulfgar laughed aloud.

"If any of these asses had had a coin, the others would have killed him to get their fingers on it."

He was right. These were not the housecarls of some powerful jarl, hunting down their master's enemies; this was a flock of desperate outlaws, the type the whole land was crawling with. They were Viking soldiers whose masters had no further need for them now that Cnut was on the throne, or they were Saxon soldiers whose thanes had fallen in battle—or been assassinated on the king's orders. Now they all roamed the countryside without a bread-giver, living off what they could rob from the weak and powerless.

Even their weapons indicated this. A lone rusty sword lay next to the pile of bodies along with three axes, whose edges hadn't been sharpened in a long time, and four spears, only one of which still had its shaft intact.

They had been desperate, daring to attack a group protected—even if only indirectly—by a dozen spearmen.

The prior and subprior were already at the freshly dug grave when Wulfgar and I reached it. Winston and a couple of peddlers were standing with them. Two spearmen lowered the dead merchant's body in, and Prior

Edmund said a prayer. Then some farmers in threadbare clothes filled in the grave, and we all turned away.

"What about the dead man's possessions?" Simon asked.

"We have divided them among ourselves," grunted one of the peddlers, a fat man with a red nose and a thin wreath of hair plastered to his pate.

"One-third must be given to the poor," Simon said, his voice not welcoming any opposition. The other peddlers nodded, although I had my doubts that even a quarter penny would find its way to the riffraff sitting on the grass behind us.

They didn't get to sit for very long, because the spearmen rounded up the men and boys and forced them to grab hold of the robbers' bodies, tie nooses around their torsos under their arms, and hang the bodies from the tallest trees lining the road, to scare and serve as a warning to anyone else similarly inclined.

By the time they were done, the sun was getting low in the west, and Prior Edmund ordered everyone—even the weakest of the rabble—to keep a swift pace since he wanted to reach the fortification guarding the crossing over the River Tove by sundown. Faced with the choice of a quick march or spending the night in the dark forest alone, everyone was happy to comply.

The order of the procession hadn't changed. The spearmen fell in again behind Winston and me; maybe the monks felt safe from any further attacks. They probably thought it unlikely that *two* bands of outlaws would be roving within the same small area.

Winston nodded his acknowledgment of my report that common roadway robbers had committed the attack. He rode along in silence by my side, preoccupied with the obstinate Atheling. The mule apparently thought that if you stopped twice in one day, the second time was it. As a result, Atheling was extremely unwilling to move on. He staggered along the track in a half-sideways trudge and impeded the progress of the spearmen and everyone else behind us.

Eventually it got to be too much for the spearman at Atheling's tail, a bony young man with big ears. He lowered his spear, positioned the tip against the beast's rump, and poked.

Atheling brayed bitterly and flashed the whites of his eyes but started moving forward close to his normal speed, in a bumpy walking gait.

I thought about the mute man.

That morning I had wondered if he had a sword on his back, assuming he was one of so many soldiers who had lost their employers or their able-bodiedness and had been forced to live off handouts.

But now I knew not only that he *had* been carrying a sword, but that he knew how to wield it. He was a true swordsman, thus of a certain rank and presumably also noble-born. And if he'd been living on handouts, they had been generous; the strength in his arm proved that. His final feint—fooling the scum-pot thief he was fighting into striking downward with his ax and thus leaving his neck exposed—was not the move of an inexperienced swordfighter.

Now I had also beheaded the first outlaw I attacked. But I was on horseback, and the animal's forward thrust combined with my downward swing from above had added strength to my blow, so my sword sliced hard enough to sever the head from the body.

By contrast, the tongueless man had been fighting on foot. And yet he still had the strength to cut so deeply into the thief's neck that his sword plowed through the vertebrae, beheading the thief as he toppled over.

What had cost the man his tongue? What crime had he committed? I knew of only two for which a man would forfeit his tongue: spreading malicious gossip about the king or those closest to him, and blaspheming either the Lord or His Holiness the Pope.

But I had never heard of Cnut actually having a man's tongue cut out—not that the king refrained from abusing those who, in his opinion, deserved it, but Cnut mostly stuck to having noses cut off and eyes gouged out.

And these days, what with the country inundated with newly arrived heathen Vikings, you'd be hard-pressed to find a clergyman who would dare insist on having someone's tongue ripped out for blasphemy, for fear of retribution.

The fortification came into view just as I concluded that every man was entitled to his secrets. Nonetheless, I decided to keep a vigilant eye on the mute man. And in the meantime, I would rejoice that our procession included an experienced swordsman who had not hesitated to throw himself into the fray in our defense.

Chapter 8

owcester was a stone-walled, fortified burgh, which sat on a small hillock just far enough from the river that it wouldn't flood during the spring thaw. From that elevation, there was an extensive view up and down Watling Street, the dividing line between Wessex to the south and the Danelaw to the north. Inside the town walls was a crooked stone hall, the west side of which had settled somewhat. It was surrounded by three post-and-plank buildings that housed the garrison.

A few farmers had built homes outside the town walls, although none of the homes were actually big enough to merit being called farms. I could tell from the inhabitants' clothing, and their posture as we rode by, that not long ago they had been in the same lot as the wayfarers in our procession.

The jarl had put a one-eyed man in charge of defending the river ford. He had a gray beard, but sturdy shoulders and a booming voice. The guards on duty at the gate must have woken him up, judging from the way he yawned and busily scratched the gray chest hair jutting out of the neck band of his leather tunic as we approached. But he still managed to bid us a resounding welcome as we rode past him through the gate and came to a stop. He jogged—or rather, given his stature and heft—jiggled over to Prior Edmund's mule and steadied the stirrup so the prior could dismount.

Three guards rushed over and took Edmund's and Simon's mules, Winston's horse, and Atheling. They then led the animals, with Wulfgar and me leading ours in tow, back outside the gate and to a pen down by the river.

By the time we returned, the gray-bearded man had already led his guests into the hall. Wulfgar, who hadn't taken his sword belt off since the attack, made sure his men understood that they were allowed to accept the tankards offered to them so long as they also understood they would be on watch duty that night along with the local guards. Then he and I ducked through the low door and joined the others in the murky hall.

It was dark and stuffy, the smell of moldering straw mixing with the sour smoke wafting up from the hearth in the middle of the room.

A couple of stooped slaves scurried over and handed each of us a tankard of ale. I drank thirstily and found the ale quite good—to my amazement. Wulfgar evidently shared my opinion, since I heard him smack his lips in satisfaction.

A long bench ran along the far wall opposite the door. Edmund, Simon, and Winston were seated on it, while the man with the gray beard sat in a chair reminiscent of a throne, although its lack of armrests suggested it was the chair of a lowborn man.

"Yes, we've had our hands full dealing with those outlaws," the old man was saying. He didn't seem to notice Wulfgar's and my arrival, preoccupied as he was with his finer guests. "It's all heath and forest from here to Brackley, so there are plenty of hiding holes for those kinds of wrongdoers. As recently as last week, we rode out to give them their just deserts, but they managed to ambush *us* yet again."

Edmund's expression made clear that he didn't think tricking this aging soldier would be that hard, but he didn't say anything.

"You should be glad that the road south is safe now," Simon said instead.

"Definitely, definitely," the old man assured him, only now noticing Wulfgar and me standing in the middle of the room. "Welcome to you, soldiers," he said. "I am Humbert, the jarl's man here."

Wulfgar and I introduced ourselves.

"If you'd like to share the long bench tonight with the holy men, you are most welcome," the old man said, nodding graciously to us and gesturing for the slaves to fetch us more ale.

Wulfgar accepted the drink, but declined the offer of shelter for the night, saying that he slept best with his men. I thought this would be a good opportunity to spend some time alone with Wulfgar and try to find out if he knew what the king had sent us north to learn, so I wasted no time explaining I preferred to sleep with my peers as well. Winston gave me an odd look and then made a face, revealing something I had never seen in him the whole time I'd known him: jealousy. No doubt he, too, would have preferred not to spend the night in the stuffy hall.

I grinned at him, handed my empty tankard to a slave, and made my way out by myself to the fortification's close, where I gratefully inhaled the evening air for a bit. Then I set off after Wulfgar, who was heading straight for his men.

It didn't take him long to assign them shifts for the night, but it took him slightly longer to impress upon them that their job was to assist the local guards, and that if any of them were found drunk, he would face Wulfgar's wrath. I could tell that this information was not new to them, nor apparently was it an empty threat.

Wulfgar then turned to me.

"I could easily eat half a hog. Would you like the other half?" he asked me.

"As far as I can see, there aren't any cooking fires burning," I said, although my hunger pangs had been troubling me for a long time.

"Damn," Wulfgar said, looking around. "You're right. Hey," he said to one of the local guardsmen, "don't you guys here by the river ever eat?"

"Of course," the guard replied, laughing. But he said Humbert, who lacked a woman of his own, had forbidden his men from having any women around to cook. So instead the fortification had an arrangement with the farmers outside the wall, who kept them in food and drink. It was an arrangement that the farmers, Humbert, and his men were all happy with.

I pondered how you could get away with requiring men who lived the boring lives of guardsmen in an outpost like this to forgo female companionship. Wulfgar and I walked back outside the gate and down toward the nearest farmhouse, where, sure enough, we found a farmer who assured us his wife would have our meal ready shortly. Unfortunately he couldn't provide a whole pig, he explained, chuckling at Wulfgar's request, but our bellies would be filled if we came back an hour later.

While we waited, we strolled through the fields lining the river and made sure the rest of the wayfarers from our procession had gotten their camps set up. We knew they would sound the alarm at the slightest provocation, since none of us believed we'd gotten rid of all the outlaws in the woods earlier.

Wulfgar sternly ordered two peddlers who had built their fire too close to one of the haystacks dotting the fields along the river to douse it. We listened to a family heatedly argue with two poor beggars afflicted with favus or some similar skin disease. The father claimed the men had stolen a loaf of bread intended for his children. The beggars ran off when Wulfgar decided to intervene, and we laughed when one of them tripped over a pair of legs sticking out from beneath a wagon and fell face first.

The owner of the legs grunted unintelligibly, and when I bent over I saw why. It was the tongueless man. He'd found himself a place to sleep where he'd be sheltered from the dew that would cover the fields by morning.

I bid him good night and followed Wulfgar, who walked with more purpose now, back toward our promised meal.

The farmer had not lied. A linen cloth was spread on the grass, set with bread, boiled pork shank, smoked ham, a roasted chicken, and a round cask of ale. We sat down and dug in. The food was delicious. These farmers may not have been living out here around the fortification for very long, but their women were not novice cooks—and I enjoyed the best meal I'd had since Alfilda's tavern.

Wulfgar and I didn't say much as we chewed our meat and bread. Only after we had both comfortably stretched out our legs and freshly filled our tankards did I belch and give Wulfgar a satisfied smile.

"Now that was a meal fit for a nobleman," I said.

"Close to it," he said, putting his hand on his stomach.

"And tomorrow," I said, pointing north, "we'll be in the Danelaw."

Wulfgar glanced up and down Watling Street. It was deserted, since the travelers who could afford to were enjoying an evening ale somewhere, and those who couldn't knew better than to be out on a well-traveled road-way as darkness settled in.

"Yes," Wulfgar said, belching into the back of his hand. "Although now that the Danes rule the entire land, I suppose it matters less, in the northerners' eyes, whether we're Saxons, Danes, or Angles."

I looked at him. His light-brown hair was braided down his back, and he wore a mustache that hung down on either side of his mouth in the Saxon fashion.

"You're Saxon," I said.

"My grandmother was Danish," he responded with a nod.

Ah, that explained his unusual dialect.

"And your father?"

"Saxon, farmer, soldier," he said with a shrug.

"You're from the north?" I asked.

He nodded, gesturing vaguely with his chin over the river.

"And you would rather serve as a prior's housecarl than be a farmer like your father?"

He frowned at me, and I raised my shoulders in an apologetic gesture.

"Not that it's any of my business," I added.

"Humph. Curiosity is the mother of knowledge," he said. Then he smiled and held out his hand to me. "Was this made to hold the handle of a plow?"

His hand was fairly narrow, strong, and sinewy. He was right. It was more suited to a spear shaft or a sword hilt than a plow.

"I suppose I would have become a farmer if I had been the elder brother," Wulfgar said. "But as it was, my brother got the farm, and I became a spearman—most recently for the monks."

"I thought everyone inherited equal parts up north," I said. That's what I'd always heard, at least. Where I came from in the south, the eldest son inherited everything but had to buy himself free of the younger brothers. I had thought that in the Danelaw all the land was divided equally between the sons.

"We do," he said. "Unless one of the sons would rather swing a sword than shear sheep."

Ah. I understood. He let his brother buy him out of his inheritance because he *wanted* to be a soldier.

"And you?" Wulfgar asked me.

I told him briefly about my estate back home, about my father and my brother, Harding, who had both fallen at the Battle of Assandun, and about how I had subsequently lost my estate to a pack of Viking assholes.

"Hmm," Wulfgar said, scratching under his chin. "So you're familiar with the fate of the vanquished."

"I used to be a jarl's man," I said with a shrug. "Now I'm my own."

"Isn't that illuminator your master?"

"We have an agreement, yes."

"How long have you been working for him?"

"Six months," I said. "And you?"

He looked confused, so I explained: "How long have you been working for the monks?"

"Oh. A couple of years now," he said.

Now I was getting to the part that interested me.

"Mercia's control extends a ways into the Danelaw now, doesn't it?" I said, fishing.

"King Cnut reigns over the entire land today, and he decides the extent of each jarl's territory."

"And who will be jarl," I pointed out.

"Yes, that, too," he said, giving me a dirty look. "That's how it is with kings."

Culturally, he was definitely all Saxon, one who had obviously not forgotten the time when we were masters of our own houses.

"They say," I started hesitantly, "that Jarl Leofwine has a hard time . . . forgetting."

He shot me another pointed look. "Forgetting what?"

"The death of his son Norman."

"Jarls have as much trouble as anyone else forgetting when they have been wronged," Wulfgar snapped.

"So you believe Norman was innocent of the accusations?"

"I believe . . ." he began, but suddenly he stood up, fidgeting like someone who needs to move. "I believe that I don't give a damn about Jarl Leofwine. I serve the monastery in Peterborough, and I couldn't care less what the nobility is up to. Let's you and me just let the jarls and kings do their thing, while we worry about the folk who are paying us."

I stood up, smiling. "As long as they pay us well."

"Exactly."

The sun had set during our meal and subsequent conversation. Now that he was up, Wulfgar looked around.

"I'd better go check on the guards. You want to come?"

But I had spotted a familiar silhouette in the gateway.

"No," I said. "The man who pays me appears to need me for something."

When I reached the gate, Winston started walking down the street away from the fortification without a word. I followed until we were an arrowshot from both the wall and the surrounding buildings. Winston stopped by a large mulberry bush.

"Well, did you get anything out of him?"

I grinned. "You guessed that was my goal?"

"Of course. You're not hard to read," Winston said.

"Well, Wulfgar is a farmer-turned-soldier who works for the monks and couldn't care less about kings and jarls and their games."

"Hmm, as expected," Winston said. "But still good to know."

"And what about the monks?" I asked. "They're probably more interested than a simple soldier in what the various noblemen get up to."

"One is more stuck-up than the other," Winston said with a snort. "They hired me, so in both men's eyes I'm their inferior. If I ask them a question that's not about food or travel, they just glare and go back to talking between themselves."

"It may not be so easy for us to gather the information Cnut's looking for," I said. "Well," and I smiled, "unless I start hanging out with some noblemen, and you put those monastic asses in their place."

"Perhaps," Winston said, eying me grumpily. "The former will no doubt be easier to achieve than the latter."

Chapter 9

e'd been riding for a while the next morning when it occurred to me that something was wrong. The sun, which in this harvest month should have been coming from our right, was warming our backs and casting our shadows straight out ahead of us.

I squeezed my knees and brought my horse up even with Wulfgar, who was riding alertly with his hand close to the hilt of his sword and his eyes continually scanning the countryside.

He looked at me when he heard the hoofbeats.

"Shouldn't we have taken the track to the northeast?"

Wulfgar's eyes twinkled. "You have a good eye, Halfdan," he said.

"Which is why I'm still alive. Why are we riding north?"

I expected him to say he'd sent out scouts, who had reported that outlaws lurked on the main road to Peterborough.

But no.

"The prior wants to spend the night in Brixworth."

I'd heard of the place. Apart from cathedral towns, Brixworth was home to the largest church in the country. They say the monastery there had suffered greatly back when Cnut's father, Sweyn, and the Norwegian Olav Tryggvason ravaged the land, but I didn't understand why Edmund would postpone his return home to Peterborough to visit Brixworth.

Wulfgar smiled when I shared my thoughts with him.

"Wait and see," he said.

I'm sure he knew that would pique my curiosity, but when he refused to answer any of my subsequent questions and returned to scanning our surroundings instead, I fell back and took up my place at Winston's side again.

We rested in Northampton, which many generations before had been the capital of the Mercian kings. It could no longer boast many reminders of its heyday. But the town's thane had ale, bread, and cold meat brought out to the square for Wulfgar and his men and placed a freshly cooked pike in front of the monks, who ate by themselves. The monks sat on a blanket one of the spearmen spread on the grass at a good distance from the ragtag band.

The spearmen politely invited me and Winston to share their meal. The ale was strongly malted and the roast pork loin tender. Once I'd eaten my fill, I offered to take over a watch shift from one of the four spearmen Wulfgar had instructed to ensure our safety while we ate, an offer that was gladly accepted. So I took up my position at the edge of the grassy area.

It was an easy shift. Northampton was the home of King Cnut's consort, Ælfgifu, and so was already being guarded by a large troop of soldiers. Not that I had seen any sign of Ælfgifu or had any idea if she was currently staying in the enormous hall—the thane didn't think he owed the monks or anyone else any information about the lady's business. It felt a little superfluous to be on guard here inside the fortifications, but Wulfgar was obviously a man who didn't take any chances.

Prior Edmund gave the last of the rabble accompanying us time to rest properly before he announced that we were setting off again. Although it was only about five miles from Northampton to Brixworth, the sun was already in the west by the time we rode up the hill to Brixworth's church. The building towered like a vigilant dog, the glowing rays of the autumn sun warming its brown stone.

The village of Brixworth sat at the bottom of the hill and looked well maintained and prosperous. About four wattle-fenced farms surrounded a wide, green central square. Brixworth also boasted an inn, easy to recognize by the green branch hanging over the front door. Another three farms were set back somewhat from the square. Five cottages with newly reed-thatched roofs lined the street leading up to the church, three on one side and two on the other. A lone stooped slave stared wide-eyed from the doorway of one of the cottages. Children played in the square, and we could hear hammer blows from a smithy sitting off on its own, about an arrowshot from the farms.

And then I noticed a long, solid building set apart a bit from the other buildings. It didn't look like a barn or a farmhouse. It definitely did not look like a church, although men dressed in cowls stood outside it. But before I could figure out what it was, we reached the church.

The church building was surrounded by a solid palisade, a reminder that the church and the monastery within had learned from the looting raids of the past and now wished to make it as hard as possible for a pillaging enemy to access whatever riches Sweyn's and Olav's Vikings might have missed.

Prior Edmund bowed his head, signaling that Wulfgar should ride ahead to the palisade gate. Soon the sound of Wulfgar's spear knocking on the solid wooden gate boomed through the early evening air.

We waited. An impatient cough from the subprior caused Wulfgar to make another resounding blow on the plank gate door.

A little more time passed, and then we heard a grating sound as someone raised the crossbar out of its iron supports and then the door slid open a little. A stocky man in a peasant coat stepped out toward us.

"Prior Edmund from your motherhouse wishes to enter," Simon said.

The man raised his sunburned face toward Simon, looked at him for a brief moment, then looked at Wulfgar, and then finally settled on Prior Edmund.

"Abbot Turold bids you greetings. All guests are welcome at Saint Winfrith's monastery, even those who unjustly claim rights that are not theirs."

I saw Edmund's lips tighten, but before he opened his mouth, the door slid open and the man gestured an invitation to enter. Edmund and Simon exchanged glances; then Simon shrugged and Edmund, who obviously interpreted the shrug as a signal, rode forward toward the gate, following the three spearmen who led our procession.

To my and everyone else's surprise, the man in the peasant coat stepped in front of the spearmen, stopping them with his right hand raised imperiously.

"Our father expressly forbids any weapon from entering onto this holy ground."

Edmund's eyes held a spark of rage.

"I am Prior Edmund," he said, obviously affronted. "And I wish the protection of these armed guards."

The door guard didn't waver. "Abbot Turold is in charge here."

Winston, who had sat in silence up to this point, whistled softly to himself. Over Winston's shoulder, Wulfgar winked at me. So this was what I'd been waiting to see.

Edmund's face reddened with barely contained rage. Then he apparently realized that if he did not do as told, he'd have to sleep outside the palisade on the bare ground. He gave a curt order for his spearmen to obey.

Simon turned angrily toward Edmund but then lowered his head meekly after Edmund quietly told him—and any of the rest of us within earshot—that it would be time to put things in their proper places soon enough.

After the men's spears were leaned up beside the gate, the man in the peasant coat finally stepped aside and let the monks and their guards ride in but raised his hand again to stop Wulfgar. "Your sword, sir."

I was half-expecting either Wulfgar or the monks to point out that Wulfgar was not a thane, but when that didn't happen, I rode up next to him and said, "I, too, am carrying a sword."

The gate guard gave me a look and said, "I see that."

I bit my lip in annoyance. "It's worth significantly more than a spear," I said. "And I do not wish to risk having it stolen by some random down-on-his-luck farmer, who wishes to enrich himself at my expense."

"The abbot is familiar with this objection," the gate guard said, his lip twitching, "and permits men of rank, if they swear to uphold the peace while here, to place their swords at the Lord's altar."

I could tell that he did not believe I really counted as a "man of rank," but before I could give him a piece of my mind, I heard Winston's voice behind me: "Oh, for heaven's sake, Halfdan, just do what he says so we can get our rear ends off of these saddles."

With a nod to the gate guard, I dismounted, tossed my reins to the spearman who held Wulfgar's horse firmly by the halter, and followed Wulfgar across the grass toward the church entrance, which was on the western end.

As we approached from the south, the enormous Brixworth church loomed before us, extending to our right as far as a seasoned soldier can hurl a spear. The chancel and apse were off to our right. Along the base of the nave in front of us there were six little straw-roofed side chapels, each with a window looking out over the churchyard. It was quite simply the biggest building I had ever seen.

We headed toward the entrance at the west end. The inside of the church was dark. Candles glowed in some of the side chambers, which I guessed contained the saints' altars. A steady murmur of voices from within confirmed this.

Through the great chancel arch ahead of me I saw the altar, made of rough stone and decorated with a single candle sitting between a silver container—the ciborium—and a silver chalice. I undid my sword belt and followed Wulfgar, my weapon in my right hand. I knelt down beside him and placed my unsheathed blade before the altar.

I heard heavy footsteps in the nave behind me and instinctively slid to my left, turning to see who was coming. Then I suppressed a curse as it occurred to me, too late, that I should have just stuck my hand out and grabbed my sword. Wulfgar grinned at me in the dim light. He had already figured out that the footsteps belonged to the tongueless man, who was obeying the abbot's orders by bringing his sword to the altar.

The tongueless former soldier held his unsheathed weapon in his right hand. As we just had, he kneeled, respectfully kissed the blade, and laid his sword between our two. Then he stood back up and walked away, back down the entire length of the nave without so much as a glance at us.

Wulfgar and I walked back through the church and out the door together, shoulder to shoulder. I had just shared with him my hope that the monks had something other than fish and porridge for us to buy when I heard horses tramping through the gate.

The gate guard had stepped aside for a group of riders led by a skinny, black-haired thane on an equally black stallion, which danced across the churchyard grass toward us. We watched in silence as the new arrival handed his sword to a weaponless spearman in his group and ordered him with a hand gesture to bring it into the church. Then the thane turned his horse without a word and rode off toward the monastery buildings that stood before us, lit from behind by the light from the setting sun.

Whereas the church was made of brown stone, the monastery was built of cob, a reminder that the original buildings had burned during the North Sea robbers' raids.

The main monastic building consisted of a hall surrounded by low rooms. Behind that lay a guesthouse with four sleeping chambers, which each slept eight men, and next to that, the monks' sleeping hall, an unfinished room with a reed-and-fern-covered floor. Although I didn't learn this until later that night—when I saw the room Winston and I were going to share with three spearmen—the monks apparently slept right on the floorboards.

Behind the guesthouse lay another row of outbuildings up by the stable, where we determined that someone had taken good care of our horses and Atheling as well as the monks' mules. On our way out, we made room at the doorway to the stable so the newly arrived riders could lead their animals in.

Wulfgar and I reached the hall just as the thane stepped in and greeted the monastery's abbot, a small, wizened old man with vigilant eyes. Abbot Turold was apparently in the middle of some dispute with Prior Edmund, an exchange that was interrupted when the thane, Wulfgar, and I entered.

"I am Ælfgar," the thane said in a deep voice, the kind you might expect from someone who needs to be heard above the din of battle.

A sudden movement next to Prior Edmund made me stifle a smile. Simon had crossed himself vigorously over his chest with his right hand, and I thought I knew why. Simon had changed the Saxon name that he was given at birth, Harold, to Simon, the name of the Lord's loyal right-hand man. In his eyes, it was probably not fitting for a monk to bear a soldier's name: Harold meant Leader of the Army. Simon must be shitting himself to meet a Saxon thane who wore his old pagan name with such pride. *Ælfgar*, after all, meant Elf Spear.

When Simon crossed himself, Abbot Turold looked at him sternly. However, the abbot was immediately calm again, welcoming Thane Ælfgar in a voice that was surprisingly steady given his age.

"Thank you, Father," Ælfgar said, standing confidently in the middle of the hall and not deigning to even glance at anyone else. "On behalf of my master, I demand a night's lodging for myself and my men."

That got my attention. That master could only be the Mercian jarl, Leofwine; no one else would be entitled to demand lodging. Was it a coincidence that Leofwine's man had arrived at the monastery the same day we had? One glance at Winston told me he'd had the same thought.

The abbot bowed his head a fraction to Ælfgar and said, "The jarl demands only what is his due. Our monastery grants this with pleasure."

Prior Edmund straightened, cleared his throat, and chimed in: "Although it is polite to word a just demand as a request, we concur with our brother, the abbot."

Ælfgar looked from Edmund to Turold in astonishment.

"Enough!" Turold said tersely. "As I told you just before Thane Ælfgar arrived, Edmund, you and your subprior and your men are welcome to partake of our monastery's hospitality, but as our gift. You can drop your nonsense about our monastery here in Brixworth being somehow subordinate to yours in Peterborough."

"Abbot Turold," Simon said, stepping forward, his eyes radiating rage. "It is common knowledge that Brixworth was founded by brothers from Peterborough, back when our monastery was still known as Medeshamstede. The document proving this is kept in our monastery from olden times, and we have come here today to summon you, Turold, to accompany us back to the motherhouse so that we can once and for all resolve the fact that your and your brethren's obstinate denial of our right to give you orders is wrong and in defiance of church law."

A deep, rumbling voice sliced through the room: "So what you're suggesting is that we here at Saint Winfrith's are so stupid that we can't recognize a forged document when we see one?"

I stiffened in surprise, as did Wulfgar. We turned to see who'd spoken and saw a broad-shouldered, relaxed-looking monk standing in the doorway to one of the chambers along the side of the hall.

"Brother!" Edmund hissed nervously, and then he pursed his lips. "I command you to be silent when your superiors are speaking."

"Look, Edmund," the broad-shouldered monk said, still sounding relaxed. I couldn't have been the only one who noticed that Edmund was offended not to have been addressed as *Prior* Edmund. "As Abbot Turold just told you, you're not my superior. Father Turold, do you wish me to be silent?"

"No, Brother Godfrid. You may speak. In our monastery, everyone is equal," Abbot Turold said. "I'm merely the one who implements whatever mutual decisions we reach."

Murmurs arose around us, and suddenly it occurred to me that monks were sitting along both of the long sides of the hall, and I hadn't noticed.

"You take our venerable Father Benedict's rules too lightly in your monastery," Edmund said, his voice trembling with indignant rage.

"In our monastery, we keep all three of our vows," Godfrid intoned, and then despite Simon's attempt to silence him with a hand gesture, he continued: "We remain inside the palisade wall, we live in chastity, and we obey the communal decisions."

"You say you keep your promises," Simon said, both scandalized and outraged, "but you don't care about the sacred founders of our order."

Godfrid leaned forward. He was a large man with a red tonsure that jutted out like a halo around his broad head. He made Simon, who stood across from him, look almost little by comparison.

"That's because we don't belong to your order," Godfrid said condescendingly. "Listen up, you gnome, we are growing weary of repeating this message: Our monastery dates back to a letter from King Oswig himself, a letter that is every bit as old as the one that founded your monastery. We have no interest in whatever forgeries you've fabricated. Here in our monastery we live by age-old rules, as I'm sure you do in yours. Just go off and follow Saint Benedict, and let us live as we wish."

Simon was practically hopping up and down with rage and indignation, but before he could open his mouth, Abbot Turold's voice cut through the hall: "Silence, both of you! Our two monasteries have discussed this matter long enough. Now we must set it aside. To that end, Prior Edmund, I want to make this clear for the last time. My message for you to take back to Abbot Elsin is that we have never obeyed and never will obey any other monastery. And that is the final word on that matter. You may stay here as our guests, but do not try to come as our superiors."

Prior Edmund, whose ruddy complexion was by now copper-colored with rage, opened his mouth but couldn't manage to get a word out, he was so livid. Instead, Simon said, "Those might be your final words, Turold, but we know the Holy Father in Rome will see this matter differently."

Godfrid could no longer restrain himself. He stepped forward, tossed his head in disgust, and hissed to Simon: "Complain to the pope, you little shit, and it'll be the last thing you do."

Chapter 10

he monastery's hall was like a henhouse with a marten loose in it following Godfrid's outburst. Simon seethed with indignation, and all he could do was make a spluttering sound. Prior Edmund, on the other hand, kept full possession of his faculties of speech and screamed at the top of his lungs that Godfrid was an impudent monk who would pay dearly for his blatant disdain of his superiors. Abbot Turold merely shook his head at this.

I could scarcely conceal my amusement at the whole scene. When my eyes met Winston's, he rolled his and smiled scornfully, as he always did when conversation fell to monasteries or church leaders.

The monks seated along the walls stood up and started shouting menacing obscenities at the two visiting monks from Peterborough, while Thane Ælfgar looked from one monastic brother to the next, shaking his head.

I sensed movement at my side and glanced at Wulfgar, who looked like he couldn't decide whether or not to get involved in someone else's conflict. Then apparently he made his decision, and he took a step forward, his right hand clenched, toward the impudent Godfrid, who had maligned his superior. But he froze when Turold, now standing, demanded silence in a voice that was firm and resounding despite his advanced age.

No one but Wulfgar seemed to listen to him. Abbot Turold's own monks continued to scream at the visitors. Simon spluttered like meat over a fire. Edmund continued chastising Godfrid, who listened with a sneer on his lips.

Winston exchanged looks with the thane; then they both shook their heads as if they had reached a joint decision that none of this had anything to do with them.

Wulfgar finally reached the same conclusion and remained casually at my side, apparently relaxed, although he was watching Godfrid. If Godfrid made the slightest sign that he was going to resort to physical violence against Simon, Wulfgar would be ready to hurl himself into the fray and separate the two.

I glanced up at Abbot Turold, who stood completely motionless, silent now that he'd realized no one was listening to him. Even so, he radiated authority. He seemed bigger and younger than he had when seated. His posture was straight, and he held his head high as he surveyed everyone.

His own monks were the first to settle down, their tongues quieting as his eyes lit on them, one by one.

Prior Edmund, still lobbing threats of churchly penalties at the insolent Godfrid, apparently realized that his voice was now the only one responsible for the noise. He stopped abruptly and glared at the abbot. The abbot gazed calmly at the indignant Simon, whose sputtering had dwindled to labored wheezing.

Only when the hall was totally quiet did Turold sit down and indicate with a nod of invitation that Ælfgar was welcome to sit next to him. But Edmund managed to pull himself together before Ælfgar reached the chair that one of the monks pushed into place for him.

"I summon Brother Godfrid to Peterborough for sentencing in accordance with the monastic disciplinary rules," Edmund commanded.

The words triggered a rumbling, scornful snarl in Godfrid's throat, but this was drowned out by Turold.

"Silence, Prior Edmund," Turold demanded, no longer seeming like an old man at all. "I have once and for all put an end to your and your monastery's silly claim of superiority over us. We are our own monastery. We make our own decisions, and if you try to claim otherwise one more time, you will lose the right to enjoy our hospitality."

"This is a matter that must be determined between us," Edmund countered, his head scarlet.

"Silence!" Turold ordered. He took a labored breath, then exhaled and turned toward Ælfgar. "Well, we seem to have gotten off topic. I believe I was bidding you welcome."

If Turold thought he'd subdued Edmund, he was wrong.

"I demand that Brother Godfrid be punished," Edmund said.

Turold's lips tightened as he was yet again forced to turn his attention to Edmund.

"You're right on that count," Turold said. "It's not appropriate to use that kind of language when speaking to a fellow monk."

Turold looked across the hall at Godfrid, who hadn't moved an inch. "You have displayed anger and spoken improperly to a fellow brother, though he does not belong to our order. Go to the church, where you will spend the night kneeling before the altar contemplating how a brother of the Lord should properly behave."

Godfrid's jaw tensed as he stared at Turold in disbelief. Turold calmly looked back at him.

"Go, Brother Godfrid. As your abbot, I request this," Turold said. His voice was quiet, but had a bite to it that I couldn't put my finger on.

Winston was also watching Godfrid attentively. I'm sure he, too, expected Godfrid to defy Turold to prove how deeply he despised the two visiting monks. But to my surprise and—I admit—relief, Godfrid suddenly bowed his head and turned on his heel. He walked to the doorway, where he appeared to change his mind: he stopped and turned to face Simon, who still hadn't recovered his powers of speech. Then Godfrid raised his right hand and slowly traced an exaggerated cross in the air in front of Simon before calmly turning and proceeding on his way.

Once he'd exited, Turold turned his attention back to Ælfgar and asked, "And can I serve you or the jarl in any other way?"

By dinnertime, people's tempers had more or less settled, but it had certainly taken awhile. A few monks still shot irritated glances at the two visiting brothers even after the bell summoned us and we all made our way back into the hall, which had now been transformed into what the monks called their refectory.

Whereas the center of the room had been bare before—aside from the abbot's chair and one for the thane—it was now occupied by six dining tables made of planks and supported on trestles. There were benches along one side of each table.

At the head of the room, where Turold's chair had been earlier in the day, there sat a wide table covered with a cloth. The two visiting monks were seated there, one on either side of the abbot, thus demonstrating that the abbot did not harbor any grudge over their previous disagreements. Next to Edmund sat Ælfgar, followed by another local Brixworth brother. On the abbot's other side were Simon, then Winston, followed by yet another of the local brothers. Maybe Ælfgar and Winston were there because Turold didn't trust his brothers to keep the peace during the meal. In any case, Winston grimaced at me when he realized he would have to make polite conversation with the haughty Simon for the entire meal. I smiled widely in return.

Spearmen and monks sat at the other tables. I sat with two of the thane's men and four monks. The monk next to me, who introduced himself as Brother Edgar, was older and gray-bearded, with cheerful eyes and an unkempt tonsure.

A well-dressed spearman sat on my other side. He wore arm rings, which showed that he must be one of the highest-ranking soldiers, an assumption he confirmed when I asked. He was Alwyn, the thane's second-in-command.

The food was plentiful, the ale strong. Leg of mutton, chine of pork, and a stew of what I thought must be hare were carried out along with large loaves of bread made of a blend of rye and wheat flour. Young brothers walked from table to table offering everyone butter and salt, but the ale was set out in big pitchers from which we could each help ourselves.

To begin with, I talked mostly with Alwyn, in hopes of learning information that the king could use, but either he was not as deeply in the thane's confidence as he said, or he was as skillful at avoiding answers as I was at asking questions.

I learned limited information: the thane was riding on his jarl's business, and they were on their way north yet again. That made me prick up my ears, but when I asked where exactly they were headed, he made a sweeping gesture with his arm and responded—while chewing his pork, possibly to obscure his response—that they had business at one of the jarl's properties in the Danelaw.

After long enough that I felt compelled by politeness, I turned toward Brother Edgar, who had been digging into his food in silence, apparently uninterested in our conversation.

"You eat well here in the monastery," I remarked.

"Better than the Benedictines," he responded with a coy smile.

He was looking up toward the main table, where Edmund and Simon appeared not to have been served the same food as everyone else. Edmund poked at an eel stew while Simon bit into a piece of what looked like undercooked stockfish. They did not seem to be enjoying their meal.

"We really weren't expecting visitors," Edgar said, by way of a fake apology. "You know how dry preserved stockfish is. The fish had plenty of time to soak, but maybe not quite long enough to cook."

Only then did it hit me that Edgar and all the rest of the local monks were not very ascetic about their meal. They had plenty of pork and hare stew and seemed to relish eating it. Were monks allowed to eat meat?

"So was Edmund right when he said you don't follow Saint Benedict's rules?" I asked.

"Well, give or take," Edgar said, spitting a little gristle into his hand and setting it on the table in front of him. "We're not Benedictines, and God willing, we never will be, either."

"You won't?" Even I was starting to find this interesting.

Edgar shook his head. "Our monastery—it used to be rich before the Vikings pillaged it—remains loyal to our founders, who wanted to start a place where men and women could live a life of work and prayer to the glory of God. And part of that entails enjoying his gifts, which are the riches of the fields and forests as well as the surpluses of the rivers and seas. Unlike the Benedictines, we enjoy the flesh of four-footed animals."

"Did you say *women*?" I looked around out of curiosity. "Are there women here?"

"Not anymore," Edgar said. "On that point we had to bend to a papal brief. In return we received the Holy Father's word that on all other points we could live as our founders wished."

"And Edmund doesn't know this?"

Edgar snorted. "Of course he does. He just claims our papal brief is a forgery."

I laughed. "And you claim that his is."

"The difference is that we're right," Edgar said with a shrug.

I had learned enough from Winston to know that forging a document is very easy, but since I wasn't here to take sides or decide which monastery possessed the authentic brief, I bit my tongue and instead asked: "Saint Winfrith? I've never heard of him."

Edgar exhaled dismissively in response, implying that he doubted I was familiar with very many saints.

"But perhaps you've heard of Saint Boniface?" he asked.

I shook my head, conceding his assessment of my ignorance.

"Saint Winfrith was a Saxon from southwestern Wessex," Edgar explained. "After his nomination, he became a missionary in Frisia and Germania. He suffered a martyr's death and was buried abroad under his new name, Boniface. Since this is a Saxon monastery, we call him by his true name. They," he nodded disdainfully toward the main table, "who've adopted Benedict's rules and laws call him by his Latin name and have threatened that as soon as they force us to accept their dominance over us, our monastery will have to change its name. I hope that day will never come." Edgar spat on the floor.

"Do you mean to say," I asked in astonishment, "that all that fuss earlier was a disagreement over a saint's name?"

Edgar's response was tolerant. "Of course not. And yet . . . well, it wasn't about whether we follow the old rules either. It was about something else entirely."

I waited for him to continue, and then the answer dawned on me.

"Money," I said.

"Exactly." He nodded approvingly. "We are a rich monastery."

"You don't look like one."

He laughed. "We don't spend our money on towering buildings, opulent furnishings, or lavishly appointed chambers for our superiors. Unlike certain other monks we know." He winked. "No, here we all share the beds of poverty on the floor and make our decisions as a community—which is a thorn in the side of the Benedictines—and aside from staying true to our founder's wishes and enjoying God's gifts, our wealth goes to alleviate need and suffering.

"I," Edgar said, sitting up straighter, "am trained in the medical arts. I have the best herbs and remedies anyone could wish for at my disposal. If you like, I'll show you my apothecary stall tomorrow. Brother Hubert over there," he pointed to a strong, blotchy-faced monk, "is the best nurse you can imagine. We are a house of healing, a monastery that uses its means to reduce the suffering in the world."

Now I understood. "So that large building out there?"

"That's our hospital, where we tend the sick."

Strange to think that Simon's views were really more aligned with these monks than with his own order.

Because we were sharing our room with several spearmen, Winston and I didn't get to talk much before we went to sleep. From the few whispered words we exchanged, I learned that he hadn't had any more success at coaxing information out of Thane Ælfgar than I had from his second-in-command, Alwyn.

Luckily the monks didn't require their guests to sleep on the floor. We lay on fresh-smelling hay mattresses, and I slept the sleep of the just.

For as long as it lasted.

Chapter 11

was sound asleep until my bladder woke me. I went outside and made sure to walk all the way over to the palisade. I pissed and then stood there for a moment, yawning and shivering in the cold night, staring up at the starry sky. There were no clouds, and the Tears of Saint Lawrence showered down where the light of the waning moon did not illuminate.

I noticed something move over by the gate. Two guards checked to see what had attracted my attention, but when I raised a hand to put them at ease, they waved back.

Back in the bedchamber, I crawled under my blanket, wrapped it snugly around my shoulders, and fell back asleep, not as deeply as before, but into the comfortable dozing state you sometimes fall into after having been awake, where you glide back and forth between dreams and oblivion.

It was still dark when he stepped in. I had heard the door open and assumed one of the other men in the room must have left to pee, but when I realized I hadn't heard anyone pushing their blanket aside or putting their feet on the floor, I was suddenly alert.

With my eyelids half-raised, I watched the dark figure approach my bed, hesitate, and look around. I silently cursed my weaponless state and carefully rolled over onto my left side, laying my right hand on the mattress, ready to push off and jump the intruder, when the person startled me by whispering my name.

Did I recognize that voice?

Until I was sure, I remained quiet, still ready to pounce. Then the whispered voice grew firmer: "Halfdan!"

"Alwyn?" I got up.

"My master requests that you two come to the church," Alwyn said, stepping all the way over to my bed.

I heard my bunkmates muttering and saw Winston get up from his bed. "You *two*?" I asked.

"You and Winston the Illuminator, yes."

Obviously Thane Ælfgar wouldn't have us brought to the church in the middle of the night like this so we could participate in communal prayers. Winston must have surmised the same thing, because he was already at the door, watching us through the darkness.

"Shall we go?" Winston prompted.

The moon was no longer visible, but a pink glow came from the east. I shivered in the early morning cold, as I was wearing only the breeches I'd slept in. Alwyn was fully dressed. With some annoyance I saw that Winston had had the presence of mind to bring his shirt out with him.

"To the church, you said?" Winston asked, pulling his shirt over his head, muffling his voice.

"Thane Ælfgar awaits you there," Alwyn confirmed, leading the way across the dewy grass.

We both knew better than to start asking questions. Winston raised his right eyebrow at me, as if to ask why, and I responded by shrugging my shoulders. Then we set off after Alwyn in silence, toward the west end of the church.

The entrance was blocked by two men with their spears lowered. They raised them at the sight of Alwyn, who led us in through the entrance porch into the dark nave. Three arches at the far end of the nave led into the chancel, and when we got there, we saw some figures lit by torchlight in the apse through the great arch. As far as I could make out—it was hard to see clearly since the men cast long shadows up the walls—two torchbearers stood on either side of a group of four people, who were bent over by the altar.

We quickly walked the length of the church to the great arch, and in the flickering torchlight I saw a man wearing the monastery's grayish brown cowl lying on the floor in front of the altar. One look at his red tonsure told me who he was: Brother Godfrid.

But it wasn't the tonsure that held my attention, it was the pool of blood at his right side, covering a section of floor as wide as the entire altar. The sea of blood continued into the darkness, beyond the light from the torches, toward the wall on the north side.

We stopped just as the four men became aware of us. Without saying hello, Winston walked right past them, leaned down over the man on the floor, and carefully looked him over. I noted the surprise in Ælfgar's eyes then I followed my master's lead and nodded to one of the torchbearers, signaling that he should come a step closer so that we could see better.

As Winston had taught me, I strove to memorize as many details as possible. Once you have enough details, you can imagine the bigger picture. That's what he always said.

Godfrid lay on his back with his arms outspread. His dull, unseeing eyes stared up at the ceiling, his mouth distorted as if in painful mockery. His cowl was held together at his waist by a leather belt, too narrow to be a sword belt, but too expensive-looking to be part of his monastic outfit.

I thought back. Had he been wearing that belt yesterday?

We could find the answer to that later. Right now we needed to take note of as many details as possible.

A splendidly ornate sword leaned against the altar. The hilt and sheath were inlaid with silver, and I knew that if I drew the weapon, the blade would be handsomely chased. Apparently the thane's man had felt that his master's weapon should stand upright and not lie down like the other swords.

The candle on the altar burned brightly. The ciborium and chalice remained where they'd been yesterday afternoon.

Wulfgar's and my swords were lying where we'd placed them. The mute man's sword was between them. Had he put it there? Yet another question that could be answered later.

I looked back at the body. Godfrid was lying in the shape of a cross, which was odd. A man who was bleeding to death would not lie quietly and let it happen.

And he *had* bled to death. His severed right hand was lying on his chest, over his heart. The pool of blood began as a narrow stream at the end of his severed arm.

Someone cleared his throat loudly, which made me look up. It wasn't Winston. He was still studying the body, but he looked over at me. *Whatever it is, Halfdan,* his eyes said, *you take care of it.*

"Yes?" I asked, looking into Edmund's angry face.

"Well, don't you have anything to say?" Edmund growled, his forehead furrowed like a freshly plowed field.

Abbot Turold stood behind Edmund and looked at me with concern. I smiled reassuringly back at the abbot and then turned to ask Wulfgar: "Is the gate secure?"

"The gate?" Wulfgar said.

I nodded. "There were guards on duty out there when I got up to take a piss," I said. "Are they still there?"

Wulfgar glanced uncertainly at Turold, who nodded.

"We have our own guards at the gate every night from sundown to dawn," Turold said. "They're unarmed, of course, but they're there."

"Good," I replied. "Wulfgar, go ask them if they saw anything."

"Me?" Wulfgar asked.

I glared at him.

"Yes, you. You're not doing anything useful here as far as I can see. Then go to my sleeping chamber and bring me my shirt."

Wulfgar turned on his heel and walked back down the length of the church and out.

"I asked you a question," Edmund growled, still infuriated.

"And I heard you," I replied. Then I looked at Ælfgar. "You had us summoned?"

Ælfgar cleared his throat. "Yes."

"Why?"

Ælfgar stared at me, astonished. "Why?" he repeated.

"Yes," I said. "We're guests at the monastery. There are many guests staying here. Why did you summon us?"

"Oh," Ælfgar replied as his face lit up with understanding. "I was in Oxford for the Witenagemot."

Ah, when Winston and I had solved a murder for King Cnut. That answered my question.

"Who found him?" I asked.

"I did," Prior Edmund began. "But I—"

I interrupted him. "What were you doing in the church?"

"Doing?" Edmund's voice was shrill. "I would like to ask—"

"We're asking the questions here," I retorted. The key was to pretend we were in charge. And I intended to keep it up as long as Ælfgar would allow, or at least until Winston was ready to take over. "What were you doing in the church in the middle of the night?"

"Praying," Edmund spluttered, his ruddy face glowing with outrage. "I'm a prior. And although this monastery hardly cares about the sacred Benedict and treats *ora* like dirt, some of us are faithful to our founding tenets."

"And yet apparently you've forgotten about *labora*," Turold said in a voice that creaked angrily, so unlike the powerful voice he'd used the previous day.

"Enough about that," I said, waving my hands. "So, you came in here to pray. When?"

"When it was time for Prime," Edmund replied, referring to the canonical prayers said during the first hour of daylight. So not that long ago. It being the harvest month, the rays of the sun shone through the small windows now.

"By yourself?" I asked.

"Huh?" he said uncertainly.

Good, I made him unsure, which suited me just fine. If he was lying, he would be more likely to trip up now.

"When you came to pray, were you by yourself?"

"Yes," Edmund replied, striving to make his voice sound authoritative.

"What about Simon?" I continued.

"He had prayed Matins. We figured," Edmund went on, now with definite traces of uncertainty in his voice, "that since the brothers here don't say the liturgies at the canonical hours, no one would mind if only one of us were in the church."

Winston stood up and gave me an urgent look, as if I couldn't think for myself.

"So Simon was here for Matins last night? By himself?"

Edmund nodded.

"With Godfrid?" I asked.

"Of course not," Edmund said.

Now it was my turn to be surprised.

"Of course not?" I asked.

Edmund explained patiently: "Simon left our chamber and came over here. Godfrid was already here before that."

"So they didn't pray together?" I queried.

Edmund's face became uncertain. "I don't know."

"You don't?"

"I haven't talked to Simon," he snapped.

"And where is Simon now?" I could see in the dim light that Winston still stood, with his eyes trained on Edmund.

"I don't know," Edmund said. "Why?"

Was the man an imbecile?

"Yesterday Godfrid threatened Simon. Then last night someone killed Godfrid. Think about it."

"That's . . . that's . . ." Edmund's voice choked with indignation. "That's unheard of."

"One man killing another?" I imbued my voice with scorn. "Definitely not."

"Blaming a man of God for such a gruesome act committed in the house of the Lord," Edmund said, wiping his brow with the sleeve of his cowl.

"Someone did it," I said.

Edmund sighed. "Yes, and that's terrible, whoever the culprit is. But to suggest that Simon . . . no, it's unthinkable."

From complete conviction to doubt. I let it sit for a moment, then asked, "Well, where is he then?"

"He was sleeping when I left," Edmund said with another sigh.

I looked at Winston. He shook his head; I didn't need to go to their guesthouse to check. Instead Winston stepped forward and said, "Abbot Turold?"

The old abbot nodded, his eyes moist.

"Who informed you of what happened?"

"The prior sent someone to my chambers."

So Edmund had recognized after all that Turold must be informed as soon as possible. Or maybe it suited him to let the old man take responsibility for this crime.

"And?" Winston prompted.

"When I s . . . saw this," Turold's mouth trembled, "I sent a brother to fetch the thane."

"Did anyone look in on Godfrid last night?" Winston asked.

"I thought about it, but then . . ." Turold hesitated.

Winston gave him a look of encouragement.

"I was mad at him," Turold admitted. "Not for what he'd said. For the way he said it. It is outrageous to threaten another person that way."

I suspected Edmund would say that the outrageous part was that the threatened person was a monk, but I remained silent.

"So you didn't come over here?" Winston asked gently.

Turold shook his head. "I thought it would do Godfrid some good to learn humility in private."

"Because he was not a humble person?" Winston said.

Turold nodded in silence.

To my surprise, Winston left it at that and turned to Ælfgar. "And may I ask what brought you here?"

Ælfgar looked up in surprise.

"I ride at my jarl's behest," he said.

Winston surprised me again when, after a moment, he nodded.

"But you want me to investigate the murder?" Winston asked.

"That is my wish," Ælfgar said, looking at the body. "Until . . ."

"Until?" Winston's voice sounded surprised.

"I need to send a message to the jarl's reeve. In my opinion, until he decides to take over the case, you're the best person to take charge."

"Let's hope it's resolved soon, then," Winston said.

I stifled a smile. Winston felt he wasn't just the best person until the reeve took over, but the best person for the job overall. I was inclined to agree with him.

We heard footsteps approaching through the church.

"The gate is closed," Wulfgar announced. "And no one came through it all night." Wulfgar handed me my shirt, gasping for breath. He had apparently hurried.

Everyone realized what that news meant. The murderer must be one of the men who'd been present in the hall yesterday afternoon.

Chapter 12

ulfgar and Alwyn!" Winston said. "Could I ask you to go to the door and make sure that no one enters or exits until I give the word?"

They went, but not until Ælfgar had nodded his tacit approval, giving Alwyn permission to obey Winston.

"And I . . . ," Edmund began. He paused to glare at the hand Winston held up to silence him. Then Edmund continued anyway: "I would like—"

"To get this murder cleared up, of course," Winston said. "And to that end, I will need a little peace and quiet so I can work. Would you all be so kind as to leave the torches here but give us the room?"

Abbot Turold looked gloomily from the dead man to Winston, then shrugged with apparent acceptance, and turned away. He pulled his hood up over his head, possibly to keep the evils of the world out.

Edmund, on the other hand, stood his ground.

"I—" he began to protest.

"Now, Prior!" Winston ordered. Winston gestured with his head, sending me over to Edmund. I put my hand on his arm. He glared at me, tore his arm free, and stiffly followed Abbot Turold, who had reached the great arch. The torchbearers followed them, but stopped at the door.

Winston's eyes now fell to Ælfgar, who had stood by calmly, watching the clergymen go.

"You, too, Ælfgar," Winston said quietly.

"Me?" the nobleman said, looking at Winston in surprise. "You're ordering me out?"

Winston nodded.

"Does that mean that you . . . ?" Ælfgar paused. He had realized the obvious: until the murderer was found, everyone—including him—was a suspect.

I furtively studied Ælfgar from the side. He clenched and unclenched his jaw muscles. He pursed his lips, and the muscles in his right forearm flexed as he clenched his fist.

It is difficult for the eagle when the sparrows oppose it, as my brother once said.

Ælfgar bit his lip, then shook his head and strode down the length of the church. I followed him and took the torches from the two men at the door. Then I stuck my head out and asked the two guards on duty outside to make sure no one entered the church. They peered uncertainly at Ælfgar, who nodded briefly.

Then I returned, handed one of the torches to Winston, and pulled my shirt on over my head. "Are we looking for rope?"

He gave me a look of approval.

"No," Winston said. "I agree that he didn't voluntarily lie still while someone chopped off his hand, any more than he remained still while he bled to death. But I don't think he was tied up. Look here."

Winston held the torch over the dead man's face, and in the glowing torchlight I saw a bluish lump on the corpse's forehead.

"My guess is that we'll find a similar swelling on the back of his head," Winston said.

Winston waited while I moved the severed hand from the dead man's chest and set it on the floor. Then we turned him together and saw a two-inch-wide mark from a blow across the back of his head.

"So he was praying. On his knees?" I guessed.

"Yes," Winston said and looked around. "Either he didn't hear the person approaching through the church, or he thought it was someone coming to join him in prayer."

"So it was easy for whoever it was to whack him on the back of the head. Then while he was unconscious, someone chopped off his hand and let him bleed to death." I looked around. "What was he struck with?"

Winston raised an eyebrow. "How should I know? A stick? A cane? Whatever."

"Maybe a spear shaft? Well, no," I said, thinking aloud. "Everyone had to hand in their weapons." My eyes met Winston's as we both came to the same realization. "The guards outside the door have spears," I said.

He nodded, but said, "They're not going anywhere." We could question them after we were finished in here.

"But," I said after a brief pause, "why kill him that way? Why not just run him through with a sword?"

Winston gestured past the dead man to where he might have been praying.

"I don't know how deep in prayer he was," Winston said, "but maybe he would have noticed if his attacker had come in past him and picked up one of the weapons from the altar?"

"The murderer could have smuggled in a sword."

"Not likely, but possible." Winston gestured for me to follow him to the altar. "Unsheathe the swords."

I started with Ælfgar's. His blade was every bit as finely adorned as I'd expected but showed no trace of having been used. Then I drew my own sword. We saw the steely gray gleam of the blade in the torchlight. The mute man's sword was next. Even as I grasped the hilt, I knew I held the murder weapon. The hilt stuck to my hand. I pulled the weapon from the sheath. The blade was covered with a greasy red film. I held out the weapon, toward the light of Winston's torch. The blood formed a herringbone pattern that extended down the blade. The murderer either hadn't cared about cleaning the blade or hadn't had time to wipe it off.

In response to Winston's nod, I pulled Wulfgar's sword as well, just to be sure. Not a drop of blood.

"The man was struck down and then had his hand chopped off." Winston stared at the severed hand, which lay pale on the stone floor. "That raises a number of questions."

"And one in particular," I said, nodding.

Winston looked at me questioningly.

"Why take the middle sword?" I asked. "Wouldn't you expect the one on the right to have been used?"

"If the man was right-handed, that would have been closest, yes."

I nodded.

"And a left-handed man would have taken the one on the left," I said. "But no one would reach for the one in the middle, would they? Unless," I paused to contemplate, and then continued, "unless he wanted to throw suspicion on the mute man. I suppose he would have a hard time defending himself since he can't speak."

Winston didn't say anything. A few moments later, he nodded toward the church door.

"Have the guards fetch the tongueless man," he instructed.

One of the spearmen obeyed me immediately, handing his weapon to his colleague—so much for respecting the rules of the monastery—and striding off toward the guesthouse. I decided to make use of the time until he returned.

"You're defying the abbot's rule that no one bear arms inside the palisade," I pointed out to the guard.

"My master ordered us to fetch our spears," the spearman said, eyeing me apathetically.

"When?"

"When he told us to stand here," he said, looking smug now.

Of course he was calm—he had no idea there had been a murder in the church. He was simply obeying an order, as he had so many times before.

"And the gate guards let you do that?"

"Yes," he said, with a cavalier shrug of his shoulders that told me the guards had protested, but lost. But it also confirmed that there hadn't been any spears present before the murder occurred. As far as I knew.

I waited with my back to the church door. It was light out now, and men were coming and going between the various monastery buildings. My eyes fell on the gate. It was closed, as Winston had ordered. I raised my hand in greeting to Wulfgar and Alwyn, who were standing on either side of the gate, each of them positioned next to a local guard.

I surveyed the palisade and realized something I hadn't noticed or taken an interest in before: the palisade was a true defensive enclosure. Built of tree trunks, sharpened on top, the palisade stakewall ran from the gate around behind the monastery buildings, around the cemetery, behind the church, and then curved all the way back around to the gate. It enclosed quite a large space, a good four arrowshots across. It was as large as a palisade you might find around a village, but the palisade around a village would have guards stationed along it at intervals. The monastery's enclosure was completely unmanned apart from the gate guards.

In other words, anyone could have just climbed over the palisade during the night. Or maybe there was an opening where one could crawl under it. As soon as I could, I would come back and check if the wooden stakewall had been breached.

I saw the mute man's stocky form emerge from the guesthouse along with the spearman who'd been sent to fetch him. The mute man walked straight over to me and stopped when he was a couple of paces away.

"We need your help, my friend," I told him.

He nodded and followed me into the church.

Winston stood where I'd left him, next to Godfrid's body, his face turned toward the swords before the altar. When we reached him, he snapped out of his deep thoughts, nodded affably to the tongueless man, and asked if he'd heard what had happened.

The man came to a stop next to the body—having glanced at it indifferently the way a person who's seen a lot of dead bodies is wont to do—and nodded.

"Who informed you?" Winston asked.

The mute man brought his hand up to his hair and made a circular motion. I stifled a smile. Well, necessity teaches the naked woman to spin, and so it must teach the tongueless man to speak with his hands.

"Turold?" I didn't think that was who he'd meant, and sure enough, he shook his head no.

"So, Edmund," Winston surmised before continuing: "Would you be so kind as to place your sword where you put it yesterday?"

The mute man looked at Winston in surprise, then reached his hand out for the sword, which Winston handed to him, hilt first. Winston had a firm hold on the sheath.

"There's blood on the hilt," Winston said.

The man shrugged in a gesture that indicated this wouldn't be the first time. He took his sword without reacting to the blood, which must still have been sticky, and placed it between the other two swords on the floor.

Winston and I both looked from the sword to each other.

"And this was the way you positioned it?" Winston asked.

The mute man looked at the sword; then he reached out and pulled it toward himself a bit so that it was no longer even with the other two.

Winston and I exchanged looks again. Now we knew why the murderer had chosen that sword. The hilt was sticking out, by the width of a hand, compared to the other two. That had obviously made it easy to grab.

I cleared my throat and held out my hand. The mute man gave me a look, then understood what I meant. He picked his sword back up and handed it to me.

I unsheathed it and shone the torch over the beautiful old blade. In the flickering light, I saw runes running down the blade just below the hilt. I pointed them out and Winston leaned forward.

The runes were easy to read, even for me, a man not very skilled in letters. Winston, who knew both his Latin letters and the runic alphabet, read the inscription aloud: EADWULF.

"Is that your name?" Winston asked.

I wasn't surprised when the mute man shook his head. The inscription seemed old. I glanced at Winston, who clearly had no more idea who Eadwulf was than I did. The name was not that unusual, even in our time, and I smiled at the thought that Simon would have to put up with another man with a heathen name, though one which meant something as simple as Rich Wolf.

"But it is your sword?" I asked. The mute man hesitated before he nodded.

"Are you sure?"

The man set down the sword and then mimicked slicing through the air, like a man chopping with an ax. Then he pretended to fall, and then grabbed for the sword again.

"You took it from a fallen man?"

He nodded. That's how soldiers get their weapons: they loot them from fallen enemies. I'd seen this man fight and knew he could defeat even the best.

An exclamation from Winston interrupted my thoughts. Winston held out the sword to show us another inscription on the other side of the blade. Below a cross, runes ran down the left side of the blade from the hilt: ULF REVENGE.

"Are you Ulf?" I asked.

He nodded.

"And you got your revenge when you took this sword from this Eadwulf?"

He hesitated and then shook his head.

"It doesn't have anything to do with revenge?" I guessed.

Ulf's nod indicated that it *did*.

Now Winston stepped in. "But it wasn't Eadwulf you killed?"

The man nodded.

Of course the runes indicated the name of the man who'd originally had the sword made. But it could have had many owners since the original owner had been gathered to his fathers. And what did that mean for us? This soldier had taken the sword from a man he had killed as an act of revenge, a man who in turn had probably kept it as a trophy after having killed its previous owner.

At least now we knew two things about this soldier. His name was Ulf, and he was a proud man, so proud that he inscribed on his sword that he had taken his revenge.

"You took revenge for your tongue being cut out," I said, after it suddenly dawned on me.

The soldier's eyes glistened with tears.

I understood. It must hurt to think about the day it happened.

It made sense that he wanted to flaunt that he'd taken his revenge.

Chapter 13

bench sat to the right of the altar, probably so that Turold and other elderly or infirm brothers could rest a little during the sometimes lengthy masses.

Winston took a seat on it, following Ulf with his eyes. After a quick bow to us, Ulf gracefully sauntered away through the church. A soldier who's had his place in the ranks dictated for years, advancing through sun, rain, and rough weather, doesn't waste any unnecessary energy on movement.

The church door shut behind him, sending a draft through the length of the nave and causing the torches to flicker. Then silence settled once again in the cold building.

"Shall we get to work?" Winston asked.

My response was a sigh.

"The signs point undeniably toward Ulf," I said.

Winston didn't respond.

"Godfrid's right hand was chopped off," I continued. "He wasn't just killed. A murderer who just wanted to be rid of him would have used his knife, strangled him, crushed his windpipe, or hit him so hard with whatever he used on the back of his head that Godfrid would have died from that alone."

Silence.

"We both saw what Godfrid did," I said.

"When he made the sign of the cross, yes," Winston said, finally opening his mouth. "And like everyone else present, we knew it wasn't a gesture of blessing."

"He was mocking the subprior," I said with a snort.

"Simon?" Winston eyed me sharply.

"Of course. He's the one Godfrid crossed himself to."

"But was he the one being mocked?" Winston asked.

Now I didn't follow. "Godfrid and Simon snapped at each other. Godfrid was punished and sent away because of Simon."

Winston nodded. "But who sent him away?"

"Turold," I said, replaying the scene in my mind. I knew that Winston wouldn't dwell on this topic if he didn't have his reasons, reasons it often took me a long time to clue in on. "You mean he was mocking the abbot?"

"Abbot Turold agreed with me just a few minutes ago that humility did not come naturally to Godfrid," Winston pointed out.

I concentrated, but still didn't see where Winston was going.

"Godfrid stood up to the brothers from Peterborough," Winston said. "He wasn't speaking like a monk who has promised to obey—which I'm assuming the monks here would do, even though they're not Benedictines. Maybe his sign of the cross was meant to show Turold that he would obey, but also that he could have chosen not to."

He was right. Edmund and Simon had behaved like what they were, nobleman monks. I remembered what Wulfgar had told me about them: Edmund had a powerful family from somewhere north of Watling Street. Simon was the son of a priest, and a force to be reckoned with if someone opposed his monastery. And Godfrid had argued with them as if he were their equal, even though he was just a common monastic brother.

"Let's undress him," I suggested.

Winston looked surprised but then nodded.

Beneath Godfrid's cowl, which we removed with some difficulty, he wore a linen shirt that I eventually wiggled up to his neck. Winston moved the torch over the body and nodded to me at the sight of the scars, which covered his torso like bird footprints.

I knelt down and studied them more closely. I saw point-shaped scars, where arrows had slammed into a ring-mail shirt hard enough to nick his skin; a star-shaped scar, where a spear had had enough force behind it to split the iron rings and penetrate a few finger widths into his shoulder; and several scratches from sword blades, a few so deep that the edges of the scars were raised. I noted that his left collarbone curled upward and ran my finger from his neck to his shoulder. At some point a war hammer or the butt of an ax had broken the bone.

We put the dead man's clothes back on, and then Winston sat down on the bench again.

"How long was he a monk?" Winston wondered.

I shrugged. The answer wouldn't be hard to get.

"But," I said, "that certainly opens up several other possibilities."

Winston nodded. "At least one."

It was Winston's idea for us to begin with Thane Ælfgar.

"We have a job to do," Winston said. "We mustn't forget that. Maybe if we question Ælfgar about the murder, we can get him to speak a little more openly about what the king is interested in."

I had to agree with him. It made sense to interview Ælfgar first, because we could be sure Simon wasn't going anywhere. As long as we acted in the place of the shire reeve, we had a certain authority even over the monastic brothers. And if we believed it served the investigation to keep them nearby, they couldn't demand they be allowed to travel on.

Ælfgar was another matter. He had bestowed our authority on us, and, if I knew anything about noblemen, he could surely take it away again in a heartbeat.

And yet as we walked toward the monastic buildings after ordering the spearmen not to let anyone into the church, Winston changed his mind. Instead of heading straight for the guesthouse, he stopped abruptly and then turned toward the chapter house.

I followed him, annoyed that he gave no explanation for his change in direction. It wasn't until we had Turold in private that I had to concede Winston was right. We would be best prepared for our conversations with both Ælfgar and the monks if we knew more about who Godfrid had actually been.

Getting Turold to ourselves, however, proved rather difficult.

He sat in his chair, looking gray and harried. Whether that was because his monk had been murdered or because Edmund and Simon were letting him have it, I couldn't speculate.

Edgar, the gray-bearded monk I'd sat next to at dinner, stood behind Turold. He glanced at us and then turned all his attention back to his abbot.

When we stepped into the room, the Benedictines went quiet, albeit just for a brief moment. They both turned to look at us, but it was Edmund who asked, "What news?"

Winston ignored Edmund and said, "A word, Turold?"

My eyes focused on Simon, who looked angry, but not worried. Well, I'd seen murderers be as cold as the bottom of a root cellar, so I did not take that as a sign of his innocence.

"I asked, *what news*?" Edmund said indignantly.

"And I heard you," Winston replied, sounding quite calm. "But my business is with Abbot Turold."

"Your business?" spluttered Edmund, gesturing in annoyance for Simon to shut his mouth. Simon had been about to say something but refrained. "Don't forget you work for me!" Edmund said menacingly.

Winston can have quite an edge when it suits him, which it did now.

"Work for you, Prior Edmund?" Winston said. "There you are mistaken. I have been hired to perform a task, which no one else can do for you. I have agreed to do it, and once it is complete, you will pay me and I will move on. I am not your or anyone else's employee, and it would be best if you understood that now."

Edmund's eyes bulged, and although his lips moved, only a dry croak came out of his mouth. Simon stepped forward indignantly to come to his superior's rescue, but before he could make a sound, Winston's voice thundered through the room: "Silence!"

Simon blinked his eyes in surprise, and Winston continued: "I am acting on behalf of the shire reeve, at the bidding of Ælfgar, the jarl's man. You heard him yourselves not long ago, as we stood beside the deceased."

Edmund and Simon looked at each other uncertainly, and Winston made use of this pause: "I am reluctant to give orders in the abbot's hall, so . . ." Winston turned to Turold. "Abbot Turold, I would like to speak to you. Could you ask these men to leave us?"

Winston could be slick like that. He had silenced the two monks by reminding them of his authority, and then he had reminded everyone that here in this monastery, Turold was truly in charge.

I watched Turold tensely. Would he know to seize the opportunity Winston had created for him?

"Edgar," Turold said firmly. "Would you be so kind as to escort our brothers-in-spirit back to the guesthouse and then return?"

The gray-bearded Edgar bowed and then stepped over to the Benedictines. With a sweep of his hand, he indicated the door. Edmund and Simon both stood, stiff as pillars. Then Edmund turned on his heel and walked toward the door, followed by a fuming Simon.

They had made it only a few steps when Winston's voice stopped them: "I would like to speak to you as soon as I'm done here, Simon."

Simon stiffened and then kept walking without so much as turning to look back. His shoulders didn't relax, even once he reached the door.

Edgar, however, turned his head and winked at me from the doorway.

Turold exhaled a long sigh. "These monks who don't believe we can think for ourselves! Edmund has been lecturing me—ever since we returned—about how the ghastly act that took place desecrated the church. As if I hadn't realized that on my own. And that's not all. He wanted to send a messenger to the bishop to have him come as soon as possible to reconsecrate our church. *Our* church," Turold sputtered. "He called it *our* church. I don't care what forged documents they can present."

"So you're implying that the good prior is concerned about something other than the church's well-being?" Winston asked slyly.

"Don't pretend to be dumber than you are, Illuminator," Turold scolded.

"In my experience," Winston said with his head bowed, "a person generally stands to benefit more from appearing dumber than he is rather than smarter."

"Not when you're among smart people," Turold countered.

Winston didn't respond. My brother Harding used to say: Some people are so smart that they're dumb about the most important things.

We stood in silence until Edgar returned with the news that the Benedictines were deep in prayer for the soul of the dead man.

"In the church?" Winston asked tersely.

But the Benedictines had realized that they wouldn't be let in there, so they were praying in their guestroom.

Turold sighed. "You wanted to speak to me?"

"Perhaps it would be possible to have a little breakfast while we speak?" Winston asked.

That hadn't occurred to me, preoccupied as I had been, but now I noticed the hunger chafing away in my gut.

"How could I forget . . ." The abbot flung his hand up to his mouth in horror. "You must be hungry."

He leaned forward and gave a quiet order to Edgar, who left us again. Turold stood up and invited us with a gesture of his hand to a door I hadn't noticed before, behind his chair.

A small room with a table and eight chairs lay behind the door. We sat down on one side while Turold took a seat on the other. Edgar came in a moment later carrying a pitcher and two leather mugs, accompanied by a young brother who carried a wooden tray with bread, ham, and a pot of honey. Edgar sat down next to Turold, and the young brother left us again with a bow.

"Have you eaten?" Winston asked Turold, breaking the bread and passing me a hunk. I sliced some ham for both of us.

"It would not be appropriate for us to eat until our brother has been laid on his bier," Turold said, sounding apologetic. He remained firmly resolved on observing the fast.

Thankful he didn't extend it to include us, I ate greedily. The bread was mouthwatering, freshly baked from dark bolted flour, the ham not too salty, and when I got to the honey, it tasted like meadow flowers.

We ate in silence. Then Winston pushed the tray to the middle of the table, and I wiped my mouth with the back of my hand and poured us each another mug of strong ale while I waited for Winston to begin.

He chose an indirect approach: "How many brothers do you have here at the monastery, Abbot Turold?"

If this beginning surprised the monk, he didn't show it.

"Twenty-two," Turold replied.

"And are any other monasteries in your order?"

"Not anymore," Turold said with a frown. "If we ever really had an order. We were founded by King Oswig, and as I'm sure you know, Peterborough was originally founded by King Peada."

Winston nodded.

"Who was Oswig's son-in-law," Winston said.

Sometimes he surprised me. How did he come by his knowledge of the northern royal houses?

"Yes, so I'm sure you see that when Edmund and his abbot claim we should be subordinate to them and their monastery, it's a bunch of hogwash," Turold said, flushed with emotion.

"Because Oswig was Christian, whereas Peada didn't convert until he married Oswig's daughter," Winston stated. He must have illustrated a book about these long-dead kings.

"Yes, yes," Turold nodded.

"And you've never belonged to an order?" Winston asked, bringing the abbot back on topic.

"There weren't any orders back then. A monastery was a community of men—and women—who wanted to live a life of prayer and work."

"But now you're just men."

Turold nodded.

"Who pray and work?"

"We run a hospital."

"And own the village out there?"

"That village and another four," Turold said. "We're a rich monastery."

"That isn't readily apparent," Winston said, smiling to take the sting out of his words, which he needn't have done.

Turold's response was self-confident. "Our wealth does not go to splendid adornment or magnificent buildings."

"It goes to the sick?"

Turold nodded.

"I don't understand," I interrupted. "Why is the hospital outside the palisade, where the sick will be in danger?"

"The palisade isn't there to defend against external enemies," Turold said, distractedly scratching at the gray stubble inside his tonsure. "It's a reminder to all who come here that the monastery and church must be separate from the world, a place of peace. That's also why we demand that everyone lay down their weapons." There was my answer to my musings on the usefulness of the palisade as a defensive structure.

"And if the brothers from Peterborough succeed in convincing whoever decides these matters that you should be subordinate to them, will that have any consequence for the hospital?" Winston asked, and then drained his mug.

"To begin with, no," Turold said, and then made a face. "People will say that the hospital should remain. But eventually more and more of our profits will be siphoned off to the northeast and wind up in their coffers."

Just as Edgar had told me the previous night at dinner, it was all about money.

"And Brother Godfrid?" Winston asked, getting to the point.

The corner of Turold's eye quivered very faintly.

"Yes, Brother Godfrid."

"Had he been doing hospital work for long?"

"Are you asking me questions you already know the answers to?" Turold asked, suddenly angry.

"I'm asking questions we think we might be able to guess the answers to," Winston admitted. "So, he hasn't been with you long."

"A little more than a year," Turold said and then exchanged glances with Edgar, who still hadn't said anything.

"Perhaps," Winston said with a sigh, "perhaps it would be easiest if you told me about that."

Turold glanced at Edgar again, then pushed himself forward in his chair and began: "He came just before the harvest month. He stayed in the guesthouse for a few days at first; then he started lending a hand with various tasks, and after a few weeks he asked if the monastery would admit him."

"Which you allowed?" Winston asked, watching Turold.

Edgar was the one who responded: "In a monastery like ours, decisions are made communally. Father Turold is our abbot, chosen to lead us in the sense that he makes sure our communal decisions are carried out. He is not an abbot like in a Benedictine monastery, a king whose word is law."

"Right," Winston said. "So you *all* allowed him to enter the monastery. Just like that?"

"Of course not," Edgar said.

"But," Winston said, furrowing his brow, "you said he'd been with you a year. That's not enough time for him to have completed his prescribed novitiate period. Was he already a monk when he arrived?"

Edgar shook his head and said, "Any adult man who declares that his true intention is to enter our monastery can take the monastic vows if he has no unfulfilled obligations and is willing to accept the rules we live by."

"So you allowed a man you knew nothing about to enter as your brother?" Winston asked, his forehead wrinkled in skepticism.

"Oh, we certainly knew the most important thing," Edgar said, his voice like honey.

I sat up straighter and noticed Winston also preparing himself to finally learn something tangible.

"We knew that he wanted to become a monk," Edgar said.

We scowled at him. I stood up halfway but stopped when Turold leaned over the table and quietly said, "And we knew he was running from his past."

"What past would that be?" Winston asked in a voice as sharp as a freshly sharpened scythe.

"That was and will remain his secret," Turold replied, shrugging his shoulders apologetically.

"You mean," I asked dejectedly, "that none of you ever asked him about it?"

"Of course we didn't," Turold said, sounding offended. "If a man wants to start over again in life, we must respect that. Here we live for God, who judges each of us. We face His judgment alone, and none of us can bear another's burdens."

"And yet Saint Paul says we must."

All three of us looked at Winston in astonishment. He merely looked placidly back at us.

"True enough," Turold replied after a pause. "And perhaps . . . perhaps it is conceivable that I could have helped him bear his yoke if he'd shared it with me."

"But I'm sure you guessed," Winston said.

Turold looked down at the table.

"It was obvious, for example, that he was a nobleman," Winston continued.

"He tried to hide his aristocratic behaviors," Turold said, rubbing his forehead.

"Well, they were certainly on display yesterday," Winston said relentlessly.

"Whenever he encountered arrogance, well, yes . . . then he would forget he was a monk and revert to being a nobleman."

Winston leaned forward. "But you had no doubt that he bore some burden?"

Turold and Edgar both nodded their heads in affirmation.

"Hmm," Winston said. He looked at me, and I nodded in response to his unspoken question.

If we learned what that burden was, it would point us to his murderer.

Chapter 14

inston stood up. He raised his shoulders for a moment, as if he were about to say something, then relaxed them again and turned toward the door. But I had more questions, so I cleared my throat, which made him hesitate.

"You said several times, Father, that you are all equals here in the monastery," I began.

"It's been like that from olden times," Turold said. "We are a community of brothers who worship God by tending the sick. We discuss everything here in the chapter house and reach our decisions together. Each brother is entitled to speak and has an equal say when a decision needs to be made. After that it is my duty to see that we comply."

"And," I pointed out, "as Edgar just said, your word isn't law as it would be with the brothers in Peterborough."

"It is as he said," Turold acknowledged.

I saw a twinkle in Turold's eye—he suspected where I was going with this.

"Godfrid obeyed you yesterday when you sent him to the church," I said. "So you have some authority, even though you deny it."

"I have never denied that I have authority," Turold said. "But that authority arises from the community."

I remembered the previous day, when Turold had told Godfrid to go pray. There had been an inscrutable snap in the abbot's voice. Was the dearly departed Godfrid a man who would bend to the community's representative?

Perhaps the answer was self-evident: yes, once a man like him accepted someone else's superior rank, he would fall in line. Noblemen bind themselves by oath to their superiors. Godfrid was a nobleman and he had taken his monastic vows. In his eyes, that bound him to obey just as much as if he'd placed his hands between a king's hands and sworn allegiance to him.

All the same, I continued: "But the community did not say that Godfrid had committed an offense."

"Because that wasn't necessary," Edgar said, sounding a little sanctimonious. "Of course we cannot allow the harassment of guests—no matter how impolite their own behavior may be. Some things are so obvious that even a soldier like yourself ought to realize them."

I flashed Edgar a grin. Apparently the arrogant Benedictines weren't the only ones who could get on the nerves of these charitable brothers.

"My thought was simply that a nobleman like Godfrid wasn't used to being sent away like any other oaf," I said.

Winston shot me a look. I was getting closer to something he had forgotten, and he nodded for me to proceed.

"So the sign of the cross was not a challenge to your authority, Father?"

Turold bit his lip. I saw the corners of his eyes glistening but held my ground, awaiting a response.

"I've been giving that a lot of thought," Turold said, and although his voice quavered, it also took on a sharp edge. "I'm not dumb, my young friend, and I do realize the significance of the severed hand."

Edgar was mad. He scowled at me and said, "Are you accusing the abbot of having killed and mutilated a brother as punishment for abusing the Lord's benediction?"

I didn't respond. My eyes were locked on Turold, who sighed and said, "I suppose the truth is that if the gesture wasn't meant for me, then the murderer is obvious."

"Did you do it?" I asked quietly, but urgently.

"Of course not," Turold said, shaking his head sadly.

I believed him and could tell from Winston's face that he did, too.

"Would Simon commit murder as revenge for an affront?" Winston asked calmly.

"Simon?" Edgar's lower jaw dropped in surprise. I smiled in sympathy. Not everyone can figure out what's important in cases like these. "Do you think he did it?" Edgar asked, dismayed.

No one answered.

Winston and I watched Turold, who sat for a moment in silence, and then sighed and said, "I shouldn't like to think so."

"But you can't rule it out?" Winston's voice was still calm.

"I don't know him that well," Turold conceded, and to my amazement, Winston didn't push any harder. Instead he asked me if I had anything else. I nodded.

"He'd been here a little more than a year, you said. Where did he come from?"

"I asked him," Turold said, "but he never told me."

If only Turold had even a fraction of the kind of authority Prior Edmund wielded. I was certain the good Benedictines wouldn't have accepted a brother's refusal to provide information about his past.

"And you didn't pressure him to respond?"

Was that a slight hesitation? Winston cocked his head—he'd noticed it as well.

"We believe men must be allowed to put their pasts behind them," Edgar said. Why did Edgar keep jumping in instead of allowing Turold to respond?

"I was so preoccupied with everything that was going on yesterday, I can't say that I really paid attention to Godfrid," I continued. "So I don't remember how he spoke. But you must have had plenty of opportunities to hear him speak. Did he have an accent? What kind? Where was he from?"

"Mercian," Turold said, but he was contradicted by Edgar, who responded with equal certainty that Godfrid was from the north.

Then the two of them looked at each other.

"He was a Viking," Edgar said.

"A Viking?" I protested. "But he spoke English yesterday."

"He spoke English flawlessly when it suited him," Turold said. "With a West Anglian accent. But Edgar is right now that I think about it. That first day, he spoke Danish like a Viking."

Winston cleared his throat, and I knew what he was wondering. Was the abbot hiding some deeper knowledge about the murdered monk by conceding so quickly that Edgar was right? Or was he just an honest old man, whose memory occasionally failed him?

"We'd like to thank you for your time," Winston said, walking to the door. I followed, wondering why Winston suddenly seemed to be in such a hurry. As soon as we were alone on the grass outside the hall, I asked what the sudden rush was about.

"Are you convinced Turold told us everything he knows?" Winston asked in response.

"Definitely not." I shook my head.

Winston watched a flight of geese cross the sky high over our heads. The harvest was drawing to a close.

"Me neither. I think he knows more about Godfrid than he wants to tell us. And his lips are shut with a seal we cannot break."

"The confessional."

"Yes," Winston replied. "We might have been able to entice a regular monk or priest into revealing secrets confided to him, but the good father abbot's faith and will are too strong for that."

"And did he try to mislead us by suddenly agreeing with Edgar about Godfrid's accent?"

"Possibly," Winston mused, tugging at his nose. "Or maybe they were both telling the truth. Maybe Godfrid was a Viking who learned to speak English with a Mercian dialect. Whatever the facts may be, we have just learned an important piece of information about him."

Before I had a chance to ask what he meant, we heard hoofbeats coming from the stable. Winston scowled at me, as if I somehow had any control over the fact that Ælfgar had had his horse saddled and now rode toward the gate followed by two mounted spearmen.

I grinned innocently back at Winston and followed him when he stepped in front of the thane.

"I'd hoped to have a word with you, Ælfgar," Winston said. He raised his hand to grab the beast's reins but dropped it again when he saw the dismissive look on Ælfgar's face.

"You can have your word," Ælfgar said politely, "when I return."

"So your errand is urgent?" Winston asked, fishing for information.

The nobleman's horse stamped impatiently, blowing and tossing his head. He was obviously eager to get moving after having spent the night and most of the morning in the stable. The sun glistened off the horse's sleek black coat as Ælfgar forced him to remain still.

"You asked me to let you work, Winston the Illuminator. And I have been waiting patiently since then, as politeness dictated. Now you must permit me to exercise my horse." He forced the stallion forward with his heels.

Winston stepped aside, as did I, realizing that Ælfgar would just ride me down if I were foolish enough to try to stop him. We watched in silence as the riders disappeared out the gate. Then we heard the hoofbeats thundering away outside the palisade.

As my brother Harding said: Common people make plans; noblemen just do what they feel like.

"Well, maybe we'll go have a chat with Simon first after all?" I teased.

Winston ignored me. We walked toward the guesthouse, but I stopped abruptly when I thought of Winston's comment that we'd learned "an important piece of information" about Godfrid. I asked him what he meant.

"I'm sure you see it, right?" Winston said, teasing me back.

Great. I glared at him and thought feverishly as we strolled across the grass. Just before the door to the guesthouse, I gave up and stopped him by putting my hand on his arm.

"Nope," I admitted.

"Nope?"

"As in 'Nope, I don't see it.'"

"You don't? Why would a Viking hide in a monastery when the biggest Viking of all is king of the land?"

"Because . . . ," I began.

Winston looked up and watched another flight of geese pass overhead. He had that smug look on his face, the one that said he would give me the answer if I couldn't figure it out on my own.

"Because he'd had a falling out with the king, of course," I finally responded.

"Of course," Winston said, his voice mocking. "A Viking who'd had a falling out with the king *or* a northerner who was only pretending to be from Mercia."

"But King Cnut sent us here to ferret out whether any Mercians were plotting against him."

Winston laughed. "Godskalk said Mercia. We were the ones who assumed he meant Leofwine. But—"

"You mean maybe Godskalk and the king knew that one of their enemies was hiding in the monastery here?" I concluded.

"Exactly." Winston took another step toward the door and then stopped again. "So we've just gained yet another motive for the murder. Let's hope we can get Simon to break down and confess to the crime."

I'm sure Winston didn't think that was any more likely than I did.

Chapter 15

hile Winston and I shared a bedroom in the guesthouse with some of Ælfgar's spearmen, Edmund and Simon had a room all to themselves.

Neither Winston nor I had noticed which room the Benedictines occupied, so we knocked on the one directly across from our own to begin with. We obeyed a sleepy "Come in" and opened the door to find a drowsy-looking Wulfgar, who'd just swung his legs out of bed. He gave us a goofy grin as he rubbed his mustache.

"I figured I might as well catch up on a little of the sleep I didn't get last night," he confessed sheepishly.

We asked him where we could find the visiting monks, and he pointed diagonally across the hall. I was about to close Wulfgar's door, but Winston stopped me so he could ask Wulfgar who'd summoned him to the scene of the crime earlier.

"Alwyn came in here looking for you two," Wulfgar said. "When he told me what had happened, I figured I'd better go, too."

A movement from one of the other beds in the room caught my eye. Someone was in the bed, his broad rib cage rising and falling. I was surprised that a common spearman had been allowed to stay in bed so late, until I recognized the man, who was lying with his hands folded behind his head, staring straight up at the ceiling.

"Ulf is sleeping in here?" I asked incredulously.

Wulfgar nodded and replied, "Simon gave the order that he could stay here instead of joining the throng outside the palisade."

"Simon said that?" Winston asked, sounding surprised. "Why would he care about a disabled soldier?"

"Now that I couldn't tell you," Wulfgar said with a yawn, and scratched his crotch. "But he said that Ulf's actions during the attack on our way here ought to be rewarded."

Ulf seemed to be enjoying his reward; he gave us a satisfied look before looking back up at the ceiling beams.

"Enjoy your sleep," Winston said with a friendly nod. He knew how rare it was for a soldier to get to rest during the day.

"Well, I'd better get up," Wulfgar said shaking his head. "My crazy spearmen took advantage of being relieved from watch duty last night and drank until they were falling-down drunk. I had to go wake them all up when I got back from the church this morning." He laughed wryly. "Which was not at all to their liking; apparently they didn't think sleeping all night was enough. Now I've got to go check and make sure they're not sneaking in a nap behind the corner of some building."

We found the two Benedictines in their chamber. The prior sat on his bed with a psalter in his hands. Simon also sat, bent over with hands folded, as if we'd caught him deep in prayer.

"And now I would like an explanation," Edmund said, setting down his book and standing up.

"An explanation, Edmund?" Winston reached out and picked up the book. He studied the illumination on the page it was open to with his eyebrows raised. Then he smirked and handed it back to the astonished prior, who practically threw it on the bed.

"An explanation for the way I'm being ordered around," Edmund cried, his voice crackling with indignation.

Simon still sat in the same position as before, but I thought his eyes furtively checked on us, whereas before they had been firmly fixed on his folded hands.

"Prior Edmund," Winston said with an indulgent sigh. "A man has been murdered. Brutally slain in the most sacred place in the church, in front of the altar—"

He didn't get any further.

"This is supposed to come as news to me?" Edmund spat. "Was I not there? Did I not see it with my own eyes?"

"You found the body, yes," Winston said.

I could see Winston restraining himself, trying not to let Edmund get to him. Whereas earlier we had needed to get rid of the monks so we could work in peace, now that it was time to question them, we needed to create as collegial a mood as possible.

"You were the first person to see the awful deed committed last night. Believe me, Prior, I didn't mean to offend you, but it was important for me to work in peace."

Edmund bowed his head slightly in acknowledgment of what he took to be an apology. I thought to myself that it was a good thing that though he had a short fuse, he was just as easily placated, happy as long as he felt you pet him with the fur and not against it, like a cat.

"Well," Edmund said officiously, "now that you've had your peace and quiet, I'd like to know what you've learned thus far."

"Then I'm afraid I'll have to disappoint you again," Winston said and gave him an almost sad look.

"So you don't know anything yet?"

"Oh yes. But permit me to keep it to myself for a while longer."

Edmund may have calmed down quickly, but his rage obviously lurked beneath the surface the whole time, like someone who's not accustomed to not getting his way. "You do not have permission for that."

"Nor do I need it." It was time to fight fire with fire. Winston's voice was aggressive as he continued: "I'm here to talk to your subprior. What's up to you now is whether I will do that in your presence or if I need to ask you to leave first."

Edmund's ruddy face turned the red of a midsummer bonfire, but as Winston coolly looked on, he remained silent.

"Good," Winston said, no trace of agitation in his voice or face. "Now, Simon."

For the first time since we'd walked into the small room, Simon looked directly at us. His eyes contained what I took to be fear.

And then Winston surprised not just the monks, but me as well, by asking: "When did you recognize Godfrid?"

Simon's fear immediately gave way to confusion.

"Recognize?"

"And how about you?" Winston asked Prior Edmund.

"What is this?" Edmund shook his head. "Neither Simon nor I had seen this Godfrid before yesterday."

"You hadn't?" Winston said, and then let his question linger while he stood calmly waiting.

My eyes flitted back and forth between the two monks, and I was willing to swear that they had no idea what Winston was talking about. I saw Winston eventually draw the same conclusion. He shrugged and then gave me a look that basically said, *Ah well, it was worth a try.*

"Good," he said, like a man who'd just said good morning and was now ready to get down to important matters. "Tell me about last night."

"Last night?" Simon repeated uncertainly.

Winston nodded in response. "Did you two sleep in here alone?"

"Abbot Turold is a headstrong old man, but he knows what he owes his superiors," Edmund said, his voice dripping with self-satisfaction, answering the question that had been meant for Simon. He didn't seem to have any idea what Winston was getting at.

"Which means that you could come and go as you pleased," Winston continued. Simon saw Winston's aim with the line of questioning. "But I only left once," he said, his voice squeaking.

"Tell me about it. No," Winston's hand shot up, practically hitting the end of Edmund's nose. "Let Simon do it. Thank you."

"Edmund asked me to go to the church and pray Matins." It was hard to hear his words. "So I did."

Winston nodded and asked, "And Edmund?"

"Edmund?"

"Where was he?"

Edmund couldn't contain himself any longer. "Here! I—"

But Winston had had enough.

"Be quiet or leave! I would like to hear what Brother Simon has to say."

Edmund blinked, taken aback at the anger in Winston's voice, but didn't say anything else.

"Well?" Winston prompted.

"Edmund was sleeping when I left."

"Are you sure of that?"

Edmund's face flamed red again, but a look from Winston stifled his words.

"Yes," Simon said, smiling reluctantly. "He was snoring."

"Did you see anyone on your way to the church?"

"No," Simon's eyes wandered, which Winston and I both noticed. Our silence encouraged him to continue: "But it was dark."

I blurted out an *aha!* just as Winston said, "So pretty much anyone could have been sneaking around out there." He seemed astonished that I hadn't kept my outburst to myself.

I thought about calling Simon out on his lie. The moon had been up when I went outside to pee, but I decided to let Simon keep going. If he wanted to lie to us, why not let him really lay it on thick. Winston continued: "And then you got to the church."

"There were candles on the altar," Simon continued eagerly. It was as if the more he told us, the more his fear abated. "So I had no trouble finding my way to it."

"And Godfrid was kneeling there?" Winston asked.

Simon shook his head and said, "No."

"No?" Winston asked. I shared his surprise.

"He was lying on the floor," Simon said.

"You mean to say . . ." Winston was furious. "You said your prayers with a dead man lying there and didn't go sound the alarm?"

"No, no," Simon said, crossing himself. "He was asleep."

"Asleep? And you're sure of that? Maybe he was snoring, too?" Winston sneered.

"Yes," Simon said, nodding. "He was lying on his back with his hands folded over his stomach, snoring loudly."

So much for the nobleman monk's obedience.

"And you didn't wake him up?" Winston asked.

"I thought . . ." Simon paused.

"That you would just start arguing again, so you began your prayers instead," Winston surmised, and then turned abruptly to Edmund. "Were you awake when Simon returned?"

"No." Edmund's answer was short, perhaps to help keep his temper in check.

"Hmm," Winston said, lost in thought.

"Do you believe me?" There was a fearful plea in Simon's voice.

"Shall we say that the way things stand, I do not currently have any reason *not* to believe you?" Winston replied.

That remark did not make Simon look any more relieved. Winston turned and gave me a look of encouragement.

"It was dark, you said." I made my voice sound casual.

A nod.

"But when I went outside to pee, the moon was up. And that couldn't have been very long before it was time for Matins."

Simon's eyes widened. I saw that Edmund was about to open his mouth, so I ordered him to wait for a moment, an order he followed.

"Uh, I was wrong," Simon drew the words out, the way a person does if he's thinking while he's talking. "I couldn't see anything because I had my hood up around my head. I was cold."

I remembered that I had been shivering when I got back under the covers, and nodded.

"Maybe you should stop and think before you answer from now on," I said.

The look on his face showed that he understood what I meant.

Chapter 16

nd what about Ulf?" I asked.

Winston raised his index finger slightly; he wanted to take over the conversation.

The monks looked at each other in confusion.

"Why all this charitable consideration for him?" Winston asked, staring straight at Simon, who squirmed under the attention, but still didn't seem to grasp Winston's angle.

Maybe Edmund felt he'd been kept out of the conversation long enough. He asked who in the world Ulf was.

"Simon knows," Winston said, his eyes still on Simon.

"I don't know anyone by that name," Simon said, sounding depressed.

That fit with what Wulfgar had told me that first evening. Unlike his abbot or his prior, Simon felt that the monastery ought to care for the poor and the sick. But he was also a powerful man in his own right. Though his conscience had required him to care for the poor, mute soldier, why should he care about the man's name?

Winston was obviously in agreement, because he explained who he was talking about.

"The tongueless soldier?" Simon's eyes widened. "His name is Ulf?"

Winston clearly wanted to make some biting remark about how the least you could do was ask a man his name, but the obstreperous spark in Winston's eye died away again; in this case, there really was no point. Instead he just nodded.

"I had no idea," Simon assured us.

"But you thought he deserved to sleep in a proper bed instead of out on the village green like the other people following your procession."

"Of course," Simon said, sounding surprised that anyone would even question this. "He earned it from his contribution the other day."

That fit with what Wulfgar had said earlier as well. And yet there was still something that didn't fit. I racked my mind, trying to put my finger on it, while Winston glanced at Edmund out of the corner of his eye. Then he thanked Simon for his patience and headed for the door.

As I followed Winston, it hit me: "But why shouldn't Ulf have had a proper bed to sleep in the night before that, when we were staying at the fortification in Towcester?"

"He should have," Simon responded, annoyed. "I found him a spot all the way at the back of the hall, but he couldn't be bothered to sleep there. Instead he plugged his nose, turned his head, and just walked away."

Simon looked as if he wanted to say "without saying a word," but suddenly caught himself. I smiled to myself. Hadn't I, too, been glad not to sleep in that stuffy hall?

The sun had gained strength outside now that the morning was more than half-over. Things were quiet. Apparently the monks here didn't idle away their time lounging around out on the grass. Only a group of spearmen were visible, up to the left of the church. They had to be Edmund's, because I recognized Wulfgar, who—with his hands on his back and his chin out—drilled the men in training exercises meant to ensure that the spearmen would be ready to fall in line, lock their shield arms, and form a wall against the enemy.

However, the exercises looked somewhat laughable: the men were doing them without their spears, which they'd been forced to hand over when they entered the monastery. So the various lunges, turns, and other carefully trained skills almost made them look like they were working on some type of peculiar dance.

Winston took a few steps and then stopped with his head cocked, listening.

I tilted my own head back and gazed up at the blue sky, in which a few clouds drifted lazily by. We heard sounds from the village outside the palisade. A horse nickered. The sound blended with the bleating of sheep and the yells of men herding cattle, judging from the mooing that was increasingly drowning out the other sounds. Over all this, we heard hammer blows from the smithy and the distant barking of a dog.

In a flash I was standing back home on my father's estate. It was as if the intervening years hadn't passed or brought my father's and brother's deaths, as if I hadn't been thrown off my rightfully inherited estate. Even the soil smelled like back home.

I shook off my reminiscences and looked over at Winston, who remained still. Finally he turned to me and asked, "Did you hear hoofbeats?"

I shook my head. I hadn't expected Ælfgar to be back so soon either. Whether he had gone out riding to exercise his horse, as he'd said, or with some errand in mind, he apparently intended to show us that although he'd asked us to investigate the murder, he was still a thane and would assert his right to come and go as he pleased.

Ah well, he wasn't the first nobleman who'd pissed on us. All the same, if his fingers had swum too deep in monk's blood, he could be sure Winston would find him out, even if he were the king himself.

"We need to talk this through," Winston said, rolling his shoulders to loosen his muscles.

I didn't agree.

"There's something I want to do first," I said.

Winston raised an eyebrow.

"The palisade," I explained. "Are we so sure that no one came in from outside it last night?"

I saw the doubt in his eyes, but he eventually nodded his agreement.

"Might as well make sure. I'll go have a chat with the guards while you check it out."

He strode off purposefully, and I saw the guards by the gate straighten up when they realized he was headed for them.

I looked from the guards to the right and then to the left for as far as I could follow the palisade. It was close to twice the height of a man, and I didn't see any lower sections where the poles had been shortened or collapsed. Grass grew along the bottom of it, but even from this distance it was clear that there weren't any holes in the stakewall.

I turned around and walked behind the monks' hall. The building was far enough from the palisade that no one could jump off its roof and make it over the stakes, a precaution—I thought with a snort—which would hardly prevent monks who regretted their vows from daring to make a run for it. On closer thought, though, that would be rather dumb, since they could walk through the gate every day to work in the hospital out in the village. So the setback was probably intended to make it hard for attackers to throw a torch over the palisade and set fire to the building.

I looked at the guesthouse, the back end of which stuck out behind the hall, and saw that it was set back the same distance from the palisade. I didn't find the slightest sign of weakness in the palisade, and I made it all the way behind the church before I encountered a place where it had been penetrated.

The opening was not created by time or rot working away at the oak poles. Rather, I found a door that was scarcely tall enough for a man, and somewhat narrower than usual for that type of opening. A wooden crossbar rested in two solid iron supports on either side of it.

I grabbed the crossbar, which was almost immovable, leaned over, and studied the grass in front of the door closely, without finding the slightest trace that it had been stepped on recently. I moved on and continued my inspection all the way back around the church until I reached a spot where I had a clear view down to the gate again. I saw Winston, still engaged in a relaxed conversation with the guards.

I turned around to go back to the little door and spotted something odd. Around the apse of the church, a stone wall came up to about the height of my knee, with some sort of platform on top. I walked closer to it and stood for a bit, wondering what it was. Then I noticed a little window in the low stone wall on either side of the apse.

Now, I'm certainly not the most loyal churchgoer. I have a hard time standing still during the priests' monotonous masses. But I had kept the promise I made to my father's priest back home to take communion once a year. I had seen a fair number of churches by now, but never one with an addition like this. I followed it around from right to left and then back again to make sure there wasn't any type of door in it, which there wasn't. Only the two windows interrupted the wall, and they were both barred with a solid iron cross, which didn't budge when I grabbed hold and pulled.

I got down on my knees and peered in the one window opening without seeing anything besides darkness inside. I stood back up and made a mental note that I would have to find out what this strange addition was for.

I walked back to the door in the palisade, grabbed the heavy crossbar, and pulled up as hard as I could. At first the bar wouldn't budge; then I thought to push on the door with my shoulder and pull up on the bar at the same time. Suddenly it slid free, and I was able to remove it and lean it against the nearest pole in the palisade.

I pulled the door in toward me. It moved easily on its hinges, and my knuckle taps indicated that it was neither rotten nor worm-eaten.

From the open door I had a clear view to the west, down the hill and across the low, rolling knolls covered with fields—like small pieces of cloth in shades of green, yellow, and brown—interspersed with thickets and low woods.

Right outside the palisade was a strip of grass as wide as five of my paces, bordered by a low blackthorn thicket. I looked to both sides. A path ran along the palisade. Apparently it wasn't used all that much, because the grass in it was tall. All the same, I got down on my knees and carefully studied the area outside the door all the way over to the thicket and then off to both sides by a length about equal to my height.

As far as I could tell, no one had come this way in several days. The only sign of life was dried sheep dung.

I walked back in, closed the door, and replaced the crossbar—with less trouble than it had taken to remove it since I now knew the trick. I strolled along the west end of the church down to the gate, where the guards stood as they had before. There was no sign of Winston. I briefly considered going to look for him but brushed the thought aside.

I had told him I was going to check out the palisade, and my investigation was not yet complete.

The guards let me walk through the gate with a quick nod. They said they knew who I was and that their orders not to let anyone leave the monastery area did not apply to me.

Once outside, I walked to the right, toward an open area that ran between the village and the monastery. I followed a small creek that flowed a few paces from the palisade. Soon I had to find a way through the mud, as I reached a spot the village swine were obviously fond of wallowing in. The creek spread out over a flat area there, making it a lovely place for a pig to lie about in the muck and relax.

My detour around this area took me close to the hospital, but I didn't see or hear anything since the building faced the other direction. The palisade swung upward to my right, and I realized I'd passed the guesthouse on the other side, so I jumped over the creek and followed along the posts in the palisade until I stood on a path that must be the same one I'd discovered through the door.

It was somewhat overgrown, suggesting that it hadn't been used recently, but I wanted to be sure, so I leaned over and focused my eyes on the ground in front of me as I walked slowly up the path. I didn't see any sign that it had been used recently by anyone—other than sheep, that is; sheep dung was all over the place here, too. I reached the outside of the door in the palisade and kept going until the path ended in a clump of gorse scarcely a half spear's throw later. The gorse grew right up to the palisade and made it impossible to go any farther.

I stood there for a bit, then walked back to the village, wondering about the intended purpose of the path and the door. At the end of the path I heard a giggle to my right, coming from behind the blackthorn thicket.

It definitely came from a girl, so I stopped and sternly asked what she was doing.

"What are *you* doing?" the girl's voice responded flirtatiously.

"Come out and see," I replied.

A woman would be a welcome addition out here in the middle of nowhere, a place that so far seemed to be populated solely by relatively cranky monks.

I heard footsteps from inside the thicket, but they were not coming closer to me. Then I realized: the lass—because I could tell from her voice that she was quite young, which suited me just fine—was wise enough not to try to come through the blackthorn.

So I walked on until I came to a path leading into the blackthorn and waited there as I heard her footsteps approach.

Chapter 17

he was a disappointment. Not because of her hair, which bounced over her shoulders in blonde curls. I would have liked to run my hand through it. That wasn't the reason. She was clean, too, and although her skirt was worn and her top had seen better days, they'd been washed not too long ago. Her eyes were blue and unafraid, her lips slightly parted, and her ankles slender and tan.

My disappointment stemmed from the fact that she couldn't be any older than twelve.

"What are you doing?" she repeated, giving me a look of curiosity.

"Who are you?" I countered. I was in no mood to be interrogated by a cute little girl.

"Elvina. What are you doing?"

"Why are you creeping around in the blackthorn staring at strange men? Haven't your parents told you that can be dangerous?" I tried to look ominous.

"Dangerous?" she asked. I did not seem to have frightened her in the least. "When half the village could hear me if I screamed?" The wench put her hands on her hips and watched me, undaunted. "Aren't you going to answer my question?"

"I'm minding my own business," I replied coolly.

She made a smug snort and said, "You're not from Brixworth or the monastery, so there's nothing here that's yours."

She was really quite something. I eyed her angrily.

"All the same, my business is still my own."

"And what business would that be?" she continued.

What actual harm could it do to answer her?

"I was examining the path," I replied.

She snorted again. "I could see that. Why?"

"Tell me, do you always ask so many questions?"

"Only until I get answers."

I laughed in spite of myself. She wasn't half-bad, this little girl. "I wanted to see if it had been used recently."

"It hasn't."

"And I suppose you know all about it?" I asked with a laugh.

"No one ever uses it," the lass said with a haughty look. "You can't get through the door up there."

"Ah, and yet there is a path."

"It's there because the sheep love to graze there. The grass is sweeter there than other places."

"Ah, so you've tasted it then?" I teased her.

She didn't look haughty anymore, more like downright condescending.

"Of course not, you nitwit, but that's what Ebba says, and she knows because she tends the sheep."

That was the way of the world, I knew. After all, sheep may be some of the dumbest animals in the world, dumber than cows and certainly less clever than horses, but for some reason or other they can always find the tastiest grass. Back home there was a mound where to human eyes the grass grew just as nicely on both north and south sides, but the sheep wanted to graze only on the northern side.

"But," I objected, "someone besides sheep must have used the path at some point. There is a path there."

The lass nodded and said, "The Lady Path."

I stared at her. "The Lady Path?"

"Yes," she said, grinning, "the monks used to use it to come down and see the women in the village."

This wasn't the first time I'd heard stories about monks not being able to keep their vows of chastity. All the same, I raised my eyebrows in disbelief.

"It's true," Elvina responded indignantly. "My father said so himself."

I let it be. Monastic discipline was none of my business, plus I'd just determined that no one had used the path for lewd forays down to the village for a long time.

"So what are you doing here?" I asked. After all, she had gotten me to tell her why I was here.

"Hiding," she admitted.

Oh, she was playing a game. I looked around for other children, but it turned out it wasn't that sort of game.

"Ebba found out I'd borrowed her blue kerchief," she said.

"And you weren't supposed to do that?"

She offered an impish grin. "Sure, but I wasn't allowed to rip it."

"But isn't this Ebba out with the sheep?"

"Sure," the lass said with a nod. "But she wasn't this morning."

"So you've been hiding in here all morning?"

"Yeah," she said, her lower lip jutting out in displeasure. "Ebba had the sheep grazing right out there, so I didn't dare to crawl out."

"Well, you could have taken the path through the blackthorn thicket."

She laughed slyly and said, "Sure, but mother was doing the washing, and then I would have had to help her."

"I don't hear any sheep," I said.

"Not anymore, numbskull. Ebba led them off, but then you came."

And the lass was curious to find out what I was up to, so she had stayed.

"So you've been lying here bored?" I asked.

"Nah, I dozed a little and then I watched the birds. There's a hawk that always hunts around the thicket. And then there were the horsemen."

"Horsemen?" I stifled an exclamation.

"Hmm. They met and talked to each other down there. On the trail that leads west." She pointed through the thicket with her tan hand.

I walked over to the path the girl had come out on. The thicket closed in over it, but after I'd taken a few steps in, I could see the rolling hills and a trail that wound its way through them.

Elvina had followed me. "They met there, where the trail goes between those two hills."

Three arrowshots from us, the trail ran between two elongated ridges for the length of an arrowshot, which meant the horsemen had been hidden from prying eyes. Unless, of course, the eyes belonged to a clever young lass, who herself happened to be lying in a blackthorn thicket overlooking the trail.

"How many riders were there?"

"The three who came from the monastery and then two who came from the west."

"Are you sure they came from the monastery?"

"Where else would they come from?" The girl sounded insulted that I had cast any doubt on her report.

"Well, what do I know? There must be farms and estates around here, right?"

"They came from the monastery." Her tan foot kicked at the grass in the path. "I heard them ride the whole way through the village."

"Hmm," I said, still sounding skeptical. "What did they look like?"

"The one in front was a nobleman. The two in back were spearmen."

"And you'd know a nobleman when you saw one?"

She just glared at me and didn't respond.

"Was he wearing a sword, for example?" I pried.

Elvina nodded. Then she got a faraway look in her eyes.

"Nah, now that you mention it," she said. "He wasn't, which was strange. But he was a nobleman," she continued, certain.

And of course she was quite right. Ælfgar hadn't had his sword fetched from the church before he rode out. Either to emphasize that he acknowledged the authority he had given Winston or because he wasn't expecting to encounter any difficulties.

"That's the truth. It is!" The girl kicked the grass again.

I put a hand on her shoulder to calm her. She didn't pull away.

"Yes, I know," I said. "And the other men?"

"The ones from the west?"

"Yes." I heard a cry from a bird of prey and glanced up. A kite was soaring over us.

"Noblemen, both of them," she replied right away. "And they wore swords."

"So neither of them was a spearman?"

She shook her head in response.

"No, they rode side by side," she said.

"And then the two groups met each other, said hello, and rode on?" I asked.

"Are you stupid?" Elvina pursed her lips in outrage. "I already told you they talked to each other."

"For a long time?"

"For a while," she said with a shrug.

"And did it look like they knew each other?"

"Yeah. And the ones from the west arrived first and waited for the other people."

Maybe I ought to consider asking Winston to hire this lass. She could see *and* think.

"And then what happened when the riders from the monastery arrived?"

"Well," she said, and then thought for a moment. "The two from the west dismounted, and then when the other three arrived, the nobleman got off his horse. One of his spearmen rode on and waited, down where the trail comes out from between the ridges. The other spearman positioned himself where the ridges begin."

So Ælfgar had expected problems after all. Or maybe he was just being overly cautious. Or maybe he didn't want even his trusted spearmen to be witness to the conversation.

The girl kept talking, eager to show me how wrong I had been to question her powers of observation. "And then the nobleman from the monastery asked a few questions that the other two answered. Then all three of them talked. And then finally they shook hands and parted ways."

"And you couldn't hear what he asked?"

"No, you nitwit," she said, looking annoyed again. "But I could tell he was asking questions from the way he talked."

She was good, this little one.

"But didn't the man from the monastery ride a little way with them once they were done? Out of politeness?"

"No," she shook her head emphatically. "He waited until they were gone, and then he rode back, too."

But I hadn't encountered them or heard them coming back. No, because they had ridden right past the village and on to the north. I mulled things over, convinced that Ælfgar would return to the monastery from a ride to the north, where he would have been exercising his horse as he'd said he would.

"Thank you very much," I told her. "You are very observant."

Elvina looked at me and then said, "And you are very curious."

"Yes, I am," I said, smiling at her. "And I have my reasons. But now I have to get back, and don't you think you should be running along after your playmate, Ebba the Shepherdess, and apologize about the kerchief?"

Her response was yet another snort.

"She's not my playmate. She's my older sister."

I swallowed a mouthful of air out of sheer excitement. Now things were getting interesting.

Chapter 18

inston was displeased. No, that was an understatement. He was as sour as last year's ale. I had scarcely stepped through the gate when he popped up from where he'd been waiting, watching for my return. He had spent an inordinate amount of time looking for me, he insisted tersely, while I'd been traipsing around out there.

"Picking up girls, I suppose," he grumbled.

I had intended to yield to his anger. Instead I laughed out loud.

Ebba hadn't shown up. No, of course not. She was off with her sheep. Elvina and I had walked back through the village, until darn that lass if she didn't dart behind a wattle-fenced pigpen just as we reached the largest farm in the village.

I got my explanation when I saw a woman step out from between the wings of the farmhouse. She had blonde hair like her daughter, and a stern-looking mouth, and sharp eyes that didn't miss a thing. The woman walked over to the pigsty fence, and I wasn't even halfway to the gate before girlish squeals of protest told me that Elvina's mother had pounced on her.

"What is so funny?" Winston seethed with exasperation. "That I worry while you traipse around, unarmed, among people who may know that we're the king's men?"

I held up a conciliatory hand. As I explained myself, his face softened somewhat, but he was still indignant enough that when I paused, he hissed that I could at least have let him know I was going to continue my investigations outside the palisade.

"The guards could have told you that I'd gone out, couldn't they?" I pointed out.

He nodded sullenly. So he wasn't really angry because he'd been afraid something might happen to me. He felt left out.

"And what good was this lass?" Winston asked petulantly.

I explained what Elvina had observed.

"So Ælfgar didn't go out to exercise his horse," I concluded. "He went because he had an appointment. We'll have to ask him what the meeting was about when he sees fit to come back."

"Not necessarily," Winston said, shaking his head. "He'll just claim it's none of our business or that the meeting wasn't planned, that they just happened to run into each other. And, besides, he could just lie. Better to keep it to ourselves for a while longer."

Winston had made up his mind, so I shrugged my consent and asked if he'd spent the time we were apart doing anything besides wallowing in discontent. He looked annoyed.

"A man needs us to solve this murder, and we will accomplish that best if we cooperate."

"I thought the shire reeve was going to give us however much time we needed."

"The shire reeve?" Winston said. "What do I care about him? I'm talking about Godfrid. His behavior was repugnant, but even the most loathsome man deserves to have his murder solved."

"Have you learned anything that might help us do so?" I asked.

"Not much. The gate guards swear no one entered overnight. So we still have to assume that the murderer was someone who was inside the palisade last night."

That fit with what I'd learned. "And did anyone else have anything to add?" I asked.

Winston hadn't had a chance to talk to anyone else. All he could report was that the monks had met in the chapter house, and that he'd popped his head in for a moment. Edmund and Simon had been present, although it remained unknown whether they'd been invited or had intruded.

"But they were certainly not in agreement with the others," Winston said.

And who would have expected them to be? Apparently this time the argument was about what to do with the church.

They all agreed that it had been desecrated. But while Turold and the local monks preferred to leave Godfrid lying in front of the altar—they wanted to dress him in his grave clothes and lay him on a bier there—and not reconsecrate the church until after his funeral, Edmund demanded that the body be removed and a messenger sent to the bishop immediately. Edmund wanted the bishop to come as soon as possible so the church could be purified and reconsecrated.

"So he's still trying to act as if he's in charge here?" I asked.

"And he kept going and going, even when the good Turold all but shouted at him."

"So how did it end?"

"How should I know?" Winston said. "I had my fill and left. As far as I know they're still in there arguing."

I remembered something from the church. "If they dress him in grave clothes, they would have to remove his own clothing first, right?"

"Of course," Winston said, looking at me with curiosity. "Why? What are you thinking?"

"His belt." Winston didn't follow, so I continued: "That was no ordinary hemp belt holding his cowl closed."

"It was leather," Winston remembered. "You're right. Let's go take a look at that."

The guards at the church door snapped to attention at the sight of us but let us in without hesitation. As it approached noon, the interior of the church shimmered in the daylight, which shone through the windows and made the dust dance. The altar candles still burned, and Godfrid's body lay where we'd left it, with his head turned toward the altar, his hands folded on his chest—well, his wrist and his hand and then his other hand—and those glazed eyes closed.

Halfway down the nave, Winston turned around and walked back to the door. He asked the guards if anyone had tried to come in to where the body was after we'd left this morning. The answer was a clear no.

"Thank you," he said. "You can go now."

"There's no reason to keep it guarded anymore," he explained to me as we walked toward the altar together. "And we can also do Turold the courtesy of having the guards bring their spears back outside the palisade."

I wondered aloud that the abbot hadn't brought up this breach of the monastery's rules when we talked to him.

"He didn't know about it, did he?" Winston said with a wink.

"Yet Turold walked right by the guards twice."

"Once," Winston corrected, trying to hide his supercilious smile. "They didn't start guarding the door until after Ælfgar was fetched. And when Turold left, he had his hood up around his face."

To keep the evils of the world out, I thought. But it had probably also obstructed his view.

Winston kneeled down beside Godfrid's body. He undid the belt we had tied that morning and passed it to me while he arranged the cowl so it looked like it was still being held shut.

I examined the strip of leather carefully. It had been skillfully tanned and treated. Ox hide, I thought—but soft and supple, hardly as wide as three of my fingers.

I stepped over to the altar and studied the belt more closely in the gleam from the candle. There was no sign that it had ever carried any weight, confirming my earlier conclusion that it wasn't a sword belt.

It didn't have any stampings or other decorations, and yet something wasn't right. I studied the ends. They were worn, which wasn't odd since they'd been twisted together where Godfrid tied the belt, and one end had a tear where the holes for the buckle's prong were punched.

I noticed Winston watching me and was about to hand him the leather when I realized what was wrong.

"The buckle is missing."

Winston held out his hand and I placed the belt in it. Once he'd studied it as well, he nodded.

"It's an expensive belt," he noted. "The kind worn by a nobleman in his own home, where he has no fear of enemies and can walk around without his weapon. And you're right, you would expect a buckle."

"So where is it?"

"Your guess is as good as mine."

The door opened, and we turned to see whose footsteps were coming through the church.

The top of Brother Edgar's head shone, and if possible his tonsure was even more disheveled than on the previous evening. But his footsteps were firm and his eyes bright.

"Abbot Turold would like to know if we can prepare Brother Godfrid's body for the funeral."

"Ah, so the abbot won his argument with Prior Edmund," Winston said, his eyebrows raised.

Edgar snorted and said, "If all the saints stepped forward in a row to tell Prior Edmund that he was wrong, he would refuse to listen to them. No, Winston the Illuminator, no one won that argument, as Father Turold refused to repeat himself more than three times—which shows that he should be considered for sainthood solely on the basis of patience. Edmund refused to budge from his position, so finally a few of us escorted him and his subprior out of the chapter house."

I would have liked to have seen that. I felt quite sorry that we hadn't gone to the chapter house.

"So now the good Benedictines are cursing us to the blackest hell, but peace be to them. We do as we please in our own monastery." Edgar gave us a wolfish smile. "As I'm sure you've noticed already. But that brings me back to my question."

Winston nodded.

"Go ahead and prepare the deceased. Brother Godfrid has nothing more to tell us."

Edgar looked afraid for a moment that we had somehow managed to speak to the dead using sorcery. Then he realized what Winston had meant.

Winston continued: "But please ask the good abbot to be patient and hold off on the actual burial for a day or two until I'm sure the deceased is going to remain mute for eternity. If Turold hasn't heard from me by the day after tomorrow, he can proceed with the burial. And now, before you leave, I have a couple of questions."

Edgar nodded obligingly.

"Do the monks here have a private place to store personal items? A designated shelf or maybe just a box of mementos from one's former life?"

"Of course," Edgar responded. "We each have a box of our own possessions. We serve the Lord, but we don't deny our pasts."

"Could you show us Godfrid's box? Or tell us what it contains?" Winston asked, giving Edgar a look of encouragement. Edgar, however, seemed offended or irritated by the request.

"No, I most certainly cannot," he said. "Our shared life does not extend to our past. That is private, not shared communally. I could, however, show you to the dormitory."

"Oh, Edgar, one other thing," I said. "What is that addition built around the apse?"

Winston looked at me in surprise, and I hurried to tell him that I'd noticed it earlier.

"The ambulatory," Edgar replied, still seeming angry. "I'll show you."

He gestured for us to follow him and walked back to the chancel but then stopped and turned left toward a low door I hadn't noticed until now.

"Watch your heads," Edgar said, disappearing through the doorway. Winston and I followed.

We went down some stairs and then entered a narrow hallway that bent in an arc around the perimeter of the apse, just as I'd seen that low wall doing from the outside. The hallway was wide enough for a man to move through, but too narrow to allow two people to walk shoulder to shoulder.

When we reached what would be the top of the arc, Edgar stopped and knelt in front of a hole in the stone wall. I reached him a moment before Winston. We both knelt and when Edgar moved aside, we saw an illuminated box inside the wall.

"Saint Winfrith's holy bone," Edgar said, standing back up. "The saint's relic rests here beneath his church. Abbot Turold had this ambulatory built several years ago so pilgrims could come and be close to the sacred man."

It was a good arrangement for both the pilgrims and the monastery: for the pilgrims because their piety would be rewarded by being so close to a saint, for the monastery because those same pilgrims would no doubt generously remember themselves to the church in general and the monastery in specific.

Then another thought struck me. I apologized to Winston and Edgar and returned to the church, where I found one of the torches from the morning and lit it using one of the candles from the altar.

By the time I returned, Winston had guessed what I was planning, and we both crawled through the hallway together while Edgar watched us, wondering what in the world we were doing. The torch scattered the darkness, and we moved through the hallway in its light inch by inch. We could hear monks' sandals sliding across the floor above us, the narrow hallway somehow amplifying the sound.

When we stepped out the door on the other side of the altar, we were both sure: There were no traces or marks in the dust. No murderer had lurked in the ambulatory last night.

"Unfortunately," as Winston put it. "Because that would have explained how the murderer was able to surprise Godfrid."

I agreed, but after contemplating whether the murderer could have waited in the ambulatory, I commented that of course it couldn't have happened that way either.

"Because," I continued when Winston raised one eyebrow, "if that were the case, the murderer would have had to have arrived in the church *before* Godfrid. But no one could have known that Godfrid was going to be ordered to come."

Winston nodded hesitantly.

"And we can dismiss the other idea?"

What other idea? I wondered.

"That Godfrid was not specifically targeted." Winston said. "Maybe the killing was random? Maybe the murderer just wanted to kill someone but didn't really care who?"

Edgar cleared his throat, and Winston gave him a look of encouragement while I put the torch out in the sandbox next to the wall.

"The murderer might have known that the Benedictines would observe the canonical hours," Edgar pointed out.

"That would mean Godfrid was murdered because he was mistaken for Edmund or Simon," I said skeptically. I didn't believe that. Apparently Winston didn't either.

"The candles were lit," Winston said. "The murderer would have seen who was before the altar. And finally there's one thing that tells us that Godfrid was killed intentionally."

Edgar shook his head blankly, so I filled him in: "The severed hand. That was a message. If not to us, then to Godfrid's family or maybe his friends."

Chapter 19

m I the only one who's starving?" I asked, stopping Winston outside the church.

"No, but let's go take a look at Godfrid's box first," he said.

"Don't you monks eat lunch?" I asked Edgar.

Edgar shook his head and said, "We eat our breakfast and then maybe have a slice of bread in the middle of the day. Otherwise we wait until dinner."

So I supposed there was no hurry to get to the chapter house for lunch, but after we checked out the deceased's personal property, I was definitely going to eat.

The monks' dormitory was next to the guesthouse, behind the great hall. It did not have beds, as the monks slept right on the floorboards. Rushes and ferns covered the floorboards, and though the plants were dry, they were also soft and fragrant.

Carefully rolled-up blankets sat throughout the room, marking the sleeping spots, and although woven from thick wool, I could vividly imagine how ineffective they'd be against the cold winters.

"Why don't you use beds, so you can get up off the cold floor and away from the drafts?" I asked.

"I've never thought about that," Edgar said, looking as if my question were incomprehensible. "This is how we sleep."

He led us through the room, and I noticed boxes and small chests along the wall next to almost all the sleeping spots, but a few of the monks apparently wanted to forget their pasts so much that they hadn't kept anything from their former lives.

Edgar stopped in front of an unadorned alderwood box held together with dowels.

"This is an inexpensive box for a man we believe was a nobleman before becoming a monk," Winston said.

"He didn't bring anything with him when he arrived that he couldn't keep in a small bag," Edgar said, turning his back. "Abbot Turold had the cobbler who makes our wooden shoes make him this box."

Winston and I exchanged glances. The nobleman wanted to bury his past, and yet he still accepted a box in which to keep mementos. Curious.

Edgar was already walking away when Winston's voice stopped him. "Doesn't Abbot Turold need to know if we remove anything?"

"No," Edgar said, shaking his head. "Brother Godfrid left his past behind when he came here. It is not our place—any of us, his brothers—to nose around in it."

Winston had one more question. "What did Godfrid call himself when he arrived?"

"Godfrid was the name he gave us."

The door closed behind Edgar.

Winston nodded to me, and I raised the lid of the box. A quick glance at the closest boxes and chests showed me that none of them bore locks.

"The monks trust that their secrets will be respected," I commented.

"And surely not without reason," Winston said, and peered down into the box, which still smelled faintly of wood. My eyes followed his.

There was one item in the box: a small bundle. I reached down and picked it up, unwound the cloth, and stood there holding two metal objects in my hand.

The first object was an attractive, and old, belt buckle. The buckle plate was made of gilded silver, inlaid with garnets and framed with gold leaf. An inlaid pattern graced the middle of it, and the hoop and the prong were of silver.

I turned the buckle over and showed Winston the runes engraved on the back: ERIK.

A Viking name so common that in some parts of the Danelaw you couldn't spit without hitting an Erik on the back of the head. I pointed that out.

"True," Winston said, "but don't forget, both Turold and Edgar mentioned that the good Godfrid spoke like a Viking who'd learned Mercian English."

In other words, possibly the first hint that we were getting at the murdered man's past.

Winston nodded at my hand, and I handed him the other object, a pewter plate.

It wasn't ostentatious and bore no gold foil or semiprecious stones. It was simple and slightly bent.

I carefully flattened it out. One side was glossy, and two words were engraved on the other side. The runes were deep, as if the person who'd used the stylus had pressed hard out of anger: ERIK NITHING.

"Well," Winston said, signaling to me with a nod that I could put the things back, "now we will eat and talk."

By the time we finally found our way to the kitchen at the south end of the hall, it was empty apart from one young brother who was busy scrubbing a solid worktable with sand.

When we asked about food, he shook his head and said the scullery and larder were closed.

I tried in vain to convince him, and just before I hit the guy, Winston grabbed my arm and started pulling.

"Let's go try the village," he suggested.

It was well past midday by the time we walked out the gate. I turned to the right down toward the path I'd explored earlier, followed by Winston, who hadn't said a word since we'd left the sanding monk.

The rabble that had followed Edmund's procession north had settled down to our left. A quick glance showed that most of the tradesmen had moved on, more interested in reaching marketplaces to the north than worried about traveling without protection.

Unlike all the poor slobs who were left. They were clustered together on the patch of the village square they'd been allotted, far too fearful to stray farther from the soldiers' protection, and lacking the peddlers' keen focus on the profits awaiting at the marketplace.

I had no idea where I was going, just that I was willing to pay quite a bit to get some food into me. It felt like it had been days since we'd enjoyed ham and bread in the abbot's chamber.

We passed Elvina's farm—with no sign of either the jaunty lass or her mother—and turned onto the lane between it and the neighboring farm. We just barely managed to avoid being hit by a bucket of kitchen slop that a plump woman was tossing into a small fenced area—we hadn't seen her where she'd been hidden, in the shadows between two building wings. Myriad chickens, ducks, and geese instantly descended on the scraps with a tremendous clucking, quacking, and honking.

The woman glanced at us and was about to go back inside when I stopped her to ask if we might get a hunk of bread and a bit of ale.

Her response was a condescending look from eyes that were half-hidden beneath rolls of fat. Warily, she outstretched her hand, and Winston quickly gave her a coin.

With a rusty sounding "Wait here," the large woman disappeared through the carriage gate. The instant she stepped into the chipstone-covered yard, she started yelling for someone named Gudrun.

We waited patiently and were rewarded with rye bread that smelled of sourdough and a small cask, handed to us by a filthy woman with no front teeth, presumably Gudrun. She silently handed us the goods, then instantly turned on her heel and disappeared back into the farmhouse.

I took the bread under my arm while Winston carried the cask and led the way down to the path and the thicket where I'd met Elvina. Soon we sat comfortably in a spot with a view of the road between the hills—the same road where Ælfgar had held his meeting.

The autumn sun shone down on us as we sat in the lee of the hill. No hint of moisture filled the air. The bread was filling, the ale refreshing, and we ate and drank in silence.

Eventually Winston wiped his mouth with the back of his right hand, burped, and said, "Well, I suppose we'd better talk, too."

"I presume we agree that his name was Erik?" Winston asked.

I nodded. "And that he was running from his past."

"At least he wanted to hide it well away. Would a man like him run away?"

"Maybe," I said, raising the cask. It was half-full. After I took a drink, I continued: "But probably not."

"So it wasn't fear that made him hole up in the monastery," Winston said, and took the cask.

"Shame seems more likely," I said. "Given the second word on the pewter plate. Hard to think of a worse insult for a man. A *nithing* is someone who's broken a code of honor. A coward, a villain, someone who would be publicly scolded, stigmatized. It would not make you afraid. It would make you ashamed."

"A nobleman like yourself would know more about that than me," Winston said.

Let him tease. I remembered what my brother Harding had said: The nithing is the most wretched of men.

"How would someone become a nithing?" Winston asked.

I shrugged and said, "Killing someone dishonestly, surrendering your master in the face of the enemy, fleeing from battle . . ."

Winston added to my list, his eyes half-closed as he brainstormed. "Letting down a friend, abusing women or children, breaking his word . . ."

"Yup," I agreed, taking another drink. "Well, that certainly narrows it down."

Winston heard the sarcasm in my voice and smiled. "Well, we know one thing about what he did."

"It cost him his life."

"Yes, presumably," Winston said. "But that's not what I was thinking of."

I thought it over.

"His hand," I said.

"That too," Winston said, sitting up. "His right hand, his sword hand."

"He deserted in battle," I said with a nod and then continued: "Which cost someone his life. He *did* run, and his flight from the battlefield meant that someone—his chieftain?—fell. How many chieftains have fallen in recent years? And of them, how many were let down when the enemy grew too strong by men who broke their oaths?"

"Hundreds of hundreds," Winston said. "But that's not what I was thinking of. His name!"

"Erik? The Eternal Ruler? Well, he certainly was full of himself, but I don't see what you're getting at."

"No," Winston said, shaking his head. "The name he chose."

"Godfrid? God's Peace? You mean he was seeking peace with God." Now I was following.

"Yes, many men who seek out a monastic life do that. But this Godfrid was already calling himself that before he arrived. Edgar confirmed that."

"So a villain atones with God and seeks peace in the monastery, but he gets killed anyway? And why would he hide the pewter plate and the belt buckle?"

"The buckle I understand," Winston said. "Even a man who wants to bury his past often feels a need to hold on to one thing, something that can tie him to his history like a thread, for when he misses his past more than he wants to forget it. But why the pewter plate?" Winston paused.

"Maybe," he continued after a bit. "Maybe he knew himself and knew he would have days when he felt he had already atoned not just with God, but with mankind. And on those days, he would take out his plate to remind himself of his crime."

"Which was so bad that he didn't think he could find peace, at least not with mankind." I said. "And maybe not with God either. Maybe you're wrong. Maybe he chose the name Godfrid not because he'd already atoned with Our Lord, but because he was seeking that atonement."

Winston nodded and picked up where I'd left off. "And then his past caught up with him last night. Someone didn't want to make up with him."

"Yes," I said and flung my arms up. "So all we have to do now is find out who this was. Could it have been Simon?"

"I doubt it," Winston said. "He doesn't seem like a killer. But if he did do it, I think our original idea might have been right: that it was because of the way Godfrid made the sign of the cross."

"What about Edmund?" I suggested.

"The nobleman who became a prior?" Winston stuck out his lower lip. "More likely. For the same reason, but maybe he also thought that Godfrid would put up the most opposition to him and his own abbot and their designs on the Brixworth monastery."

"And he can tell a lie," I pointed out.

"That he can. He was there when the body was found. The best explanation he could give would be that he had just found the man dead. The question is, then, whether he or Simon would break their monastic vows and commit murder."

"Maybe they got someone else to do it?" I suggested.

"Wulfgar, yes, their spearman," Winston said, narrowing his eyes at me and then nodding. "Would he kill for them?"

I thought it over. I remembered what he'd said that first night.

"Definitely not," I said. "He doesn't care much about the comings and goings of the nobility or prominent monks. Besides, he would hardly use another man's sword."

"Unless he knew how to hide his tracks. Actually, though, I agree with you, but for a different reason. Edmund and Simon are both too haughty to entrust such an act to a common soldier."

"How did the murderer manage to avoid making a mess in all that blood?" I asked. This question had been bothering me.

"Godfrid was unconscious. Of course his arm jerked around in spasms of pain, but if the murderer just stepped well back after chopping off his hand, it shouldn't have been much of a problem."

Maybe. I would keep an eye out for any bloodstained clothes we might find tucked away . . . although everyone we'd talked to this morning was wearing the same clothes I'd seen them in last night.

"And then there's Ælfgar," I said.

"Hmm," Winston said. "The jarl's thane, who may be aware that we have an ulterior assignment. He's a nobleman from Mercia, who could easily have recognized Godfrid as the man who had failed some mutual friend or chieftain. Ælfgar is a man who would kill without hesitation and who has evaded our questions. But he will have to come back and answer them soon."

Chapter 20

e strolled back through the village to the fat woman's farm and returned the empty cask to Gudrun, who still didn't say a word to us. Then we loafed along, because—as Winston had put it as he put the birch stopper back in the empty cask—it wasn't like we were in a hurry. We had to wait for Ælfgar to come back.

That the village was prosperous was evident in part from the well-maintained farmhouses and outbuildings, with their fully thatched roofs and freshly tarred post-and-plank walls. The grain stacks in the crofts were taller than a man, each individual sheaf carefully positioned and the stack top-dressed against the rains, which would come sooner or later.

As we passed in front of Elvina's farm, I scanned the area around the buildings and saw the lass standing by a tabletop placed atop a couple of sawhorses. Her mother stood next to her. They both wore coarse aprons and were busily plucking a couple of chickens, so that feathers billowed around them like fog. Other birds lay on the table in front of them, still unplucked, so apparently Elvina was paying for taking the whole morning off.

Their backs were to me, so I pointed the lass out to Winston with my index finger. I stopped in surprise when rather than simply accept the information, he turned and started walking toward them.

Neither of the women noticed him, preoccupied as they were. So he walked around the makeshift table, with me following him. The mother didn't look up until we were right in front of her.

"May God lighten your work," Winston said politely.

Elvina looked at me out of the corner of her eye, and I grinned at her, but it was her mother who responded to Winston's greeting with a brief thank-you.

"You're slaughtering chickens at this time of year?" Winston asked, blowing on an errant feather.

At first I didn't think the woman was going to answer him. Then she explained that these were last year's laying hens, who were now past their prime, having served as brood hens and hatched this year's chicks.

"And now they have to die so they won't take feed away from the chicks," Winston stated. He seemed quite knowledgeable about raising poultry. "My name's Winston. I'm a manuscript illuminator."

I could tell that the woman didn't have the slightest idea what that was.

"I'm currently staying up at the monastery," Winston went on.

The woman raised her shoulders ever so slightly, obviously too polite to say that she didn't give an autumn herring about where he lived.

"My man here spoke with your daughter this morning."

Finally he got a reaction. The woman raised her head from her work and glared at me. I tried to adopt my most appeasing look, flashing her my best smile.

"A grown man, keeping a young girl from her work!" she chided, her voice not exactly pleasant, but at least not angry.

I was about to defend myself and point out that when I met the girl, she was already well along with shirking her responsibilities, but Winston brushed me aside.

"I'm afraid the good Halfdan takes kindly to others who are fond of idleness," he said, stifling any objection I might have made with a stern look. "But I would really appreciate it if I could ask your daughter a question."

The woman turned the now-plucked bird over and flopped it down on the table before thrusting her right hand into its rump and pulling its innards out. I turned my head away from the stench of dead chicken, but Winston was apparently unaffected.

"Do you mind?" he asked.

The mother responded with a shrug.

"Elvina," Winston began. "It is Elvina, isn't it?"

The girl pouted at me and then nodded at Winston.

"You told Halfdan about the nobleman you saw meet some men on horseback. Had you ever seen him before?"

The mother stiffened and raised her bloody right hand toward her daughter.

"Nobleman?" she squawked. "What is this about you and noblemen?"

"Nothing," Elvina mumbled, sounding annoyed. "It's not like I could do anything about him riding out in the open where I could see him."

"And that was all?" The mother's voice was sharp as a newly sharpened sickle.

"Yes," came the girl's sulky response.

"Well, then answer the man."

"I didn't recognize him," Elvina said.

"And you're sure of that?" Winston asked.

Elvina nodded irritably.

"We don't rub shoulders with the nobility," the mother added.

"Of course not," Winston said placatingly, and then continued: "I never caught your name."

"Huh?" the mother grunted, her lips opened in surprise. "I gave you my name, and my husband's."

"No," Winston pointed out.

The woman pulled herself together, perhaps realizing how impolite she'd been.

"I'm Estrid. My husband's name is Ribald."

"He's obviously a talented farmer," Winston said, admiring the many buildings belonging to the well-maintained farm.

"The best," Estrid said arrogantly and straightened her back. "Abbot Turold always wants to talk to him."

"Yes, Turold mentioned that to me," Winston said. He can be a very convincing liar.

"Ah, but I'm forgetting my manners," Estrid said, drying her bloody hand on her apron. "Elvina, go fetch a cask of mead and two cups for our guests."

I stifled a snort. Winston is always accusing me of using my wiles on women when it suits me, as though he would never do anything like that.

The mead was strong and sweet, and we each drank two cups before we said good-bye and walked on, leaving the farmer's wife in a somewhat better mood than when we'd arrived.

At the section of the village square where our retinue's followers had settled, a haze of smoke lingered over the grass, from the cooking fires of the ones who could afford to buy food requiring cooking. Laundry hung everywhere from poles and the strings stretched between them. The riffraff were making full use of the good weather and the time they had to spend waiting to pound the worst of the filth from their clothes.

We saw the smithy across the square, its smoke rising straight up. A couple of men chatted in front of the stone building. This village was so rich that the blacksmith's shop could be built of fireproof material. We heard hammer strikes from inside and shouts as the blacksmith gave his apprentices instructions about how to tend the bellows.

I tilted my head back and thought again that I could have had a life like this. I could have been walking through the square of my own village, listening to my own blacksmith working with iron and celebrating the harvest my own farmers had reaped.

Winston walked along at my side whistling, something I'd noticed him doing when he was very relaxed. When he abruptly stopped whistling and inhaled deeply, I stopped.

He responded to my surprised "Hmm?" by pointing with his chin. I looked in that direction and saw a redheaded woman come riding into the square. I scanned the area behind and around her. "She's riding alone!" I said, shocked.

Winston was already at a run. He accidentally toppled a toddler, who fell on his bottom howling. Then he jumped over a cooking fire and reached the woman on horseback before I'd even gotten the child back up onto his feet.

By the time I reached them, they were in a tight embrace. The horse calmly tossed its head, not having budged a step from the moment Alfilda slid off into Winston's arms. Someone had trained that animal well.

"What in the world are you doing here?" Winston asked, after he had relaxed his arms around the alewife. He held her out away from himself to look at her.

"Looking for you," Alfilda replied.

"Well, yes, but—"

"I'm hungry and thirsty," she interrupted him.

For once my master was at a loss for what to do. He looked around, dazed.

"Perhaps," I suggested, "we could coax a little ale and bread from Estrid."

"Estrid?" he repeated, staring at me blankly.

"The farmer's wife," I reminded him. "Elvina's mother."

"Oh, right. Yes, of course."

I led the way, leading Alfilda's horse by the reins, followed by those two, who walked hand in hand.

There was only one chicken left on the table. When Estrid heard our plea for food and drink for Alfilda, she nodded obligingly and left the plucking to Elvina, who stuck out her pointy tongue at me. I responded in kind and then tied the horse to a solid iron ring built into the wall of the farmhouse.

Alfilda sat down on the bench next to the farmhouse door, which was wide enough so Winston could sit next to her. I rolled a firewood log over in front of them and sat down on it.

Estrid soon brought ale and bread. While Alfilda chewed, the rest of us drank the sweet, malty ale, since the farmwife had been shrewd enough to bring a pitcher and three birchbark cups out with her.

Winston looked as if he were sitting on needles, and as soon as Alfilda swallowed her last mouthful of bread, he asked her again what she was doing in Brixworth.

"Well," she replied, "I sold the inn and came looking for you."

"Sold the inn?" Winston's eyes grew wide and he looked at me, dumbfounded. For my part, I noted that when she said *you*, she meant *him*.

"Why?" he asked her.

Winston was a smart man. He certainly noticed a lot of things before I did. But this was a man who did not understand women, despite his having quite a way with them. I gave Alfilda a look of approval.

"Why?" Winston repeated, wondering what the look I just gave Alfilda was supposed to mean.

And then the cat suddenly seemed to get her tongue. She raised her cup and hid behind it but eventually had to lower it. Coy woman that she was, she still didn't answer his question but instead asked where he was heading once he was done with his job for the king?

"Where I'm . . . how in the world would I know that?" Winston said, flinging up his hands in a gesture of utter cluelessness.

"You don't know because there will be a new job, which will send you somewhere else. And that place . . ." Alfilda gave me a pleading look.

I got the message. She wanted me to make up some excuse and leave them alone, but I'd be darned if I was going to do that. This was way too much fun.

"That place . . . ?" Winston shook his head, not understanding. "What do you mean 'that place'?"

"That place won't be Oxford," Alfilda said. Then she stood up abruptly and walked away from us. Obviously her courage had failed her at the last moment.

Winston stared from me to her and back again. I looked right back at him, raising my eyebrows and smiling widely. And my master, who always liked to point out that if you could make out the details, you could envision the bigger picture, sat there opening and closing his mouth like a fish on land, staring again from her to me.

"Do you understand any of this?" he finally asked.

For a moment I toyed with the idea of saying no to see if Alfilda would find the courage to just tell him point-blank how she felt about him. But ultimately I took pity on them.

"If you went somewhere other than Oxford," I explained, speaking slowly as if to a simpleton, "that would leave her waiting for you in Oxford in vain, Winston."

"Waiting in vain . . . for what?"

Yet again I raised my eyebrows, but I remained silent, as I enjoyed watching the wheels turn in his mind. When he finally figured it out, all the color drained out of his face. Every muscle in his face went slack. His eyes seemed to stop working and his lower lip quivered.

I smiled at him encouragingly but might as well have been sitting on the moon for all the notice he took of me. He had eyes only for Alfilda. She stood a little ways away with her back to us, her shoulders drooping.

People say that young love is beautiful and innocent. Well, these two weren't innocent, and beautiful wasn't the first word that came to mind when I thought of Winston, but they were cute, standing there lost in their embrace, the rest of the world long forgotten.

I noticed a movement at my side. It was Elvina, who was apparently done with the last chicken.

"Are they in love?" she asked.

"I think that's safe to say, yes. Listen, sweetie, do you think you could fetch us a little more ale?"

The pitcher foamed over with ale. Estrid wasn't being stingy with us, thanks to Winston's little lie. All the same, I managed to finish the entire pitcher before they tore themselves loose from their embrace and returned to the bench.

"So you rode up here protected by the armor of love," I said innocently, my eyes on Alfilda. She asked me what I meant.

"You rode alone through a region that is plagued by bands of robbers," I explained.

But no, it turned out she'd joined a division of housecarls who were bringing a message to the king's consort, Ælfgifu, in Northampton.

"Although," she said, "I did ride on alone from there, when I was told you'd come this way. I didn't think I'd catch up to you two until Peterborough, but then I saw you come walking across the square."

Winston didn't say anything. He just sat there holding her hand. So I pointed out that we had better find someplace for Alfilda to stay, since it would hardly go over well if we tried to sneak her into the monastery.

I looked around and spotted Elvina, who hadn't gone far. She sat on an overturned bucket. We were way too exciting for her to want to miss anything.

"Do you think your mother has a room we could rent?" I asked her.

And that was that. Alfilda received room and board at the farm for a reasonable price, and she was already chatting away comfortably with Estrid by the time I dragged a reluctant Winston back up to the monastery. We'd heard horse hooves at last, telling us that Ælfgar had returned from his ride.

"Well, there is one thing you can be happy about," I told him as we walked in through the palisade gate.

He gave me a questioning look.

"I found the Lady Path, so you won't need to sneak through the gate tonight."

Chapter 21

e spotted Ælfgar's man Alwyn as soon as we set foot on the monastery's lawn. We walked straight over to him and asked where his master was.

"In his chamber," Alwyn said.

Winston politely asked him to inform the thane that we wished to speak to him.

It was news to me that Ælfgar had a room of his own. Not that I was surprised; as a nobleman, he could insist on not having to share sleeping quarters with snoring and snorting men, but the information was not insignificant. Unlike the rest of us, he would have been able to come and go as he pleased without necessarily disturbing anyone else.

While we waited, I teased Winston, who leaned against the corner of the building, lost in thought.

I'd known that his and Alfilda's relationship was serious enough; he had sometimes openly referred to her as "my woman." Still, I was surprised by her display of feelings for him.

It had obviously surprised him, too.

She was a stout-hearted woman, our Alfilda. Widowed at a young age, she'd inherited the inn and tavern from her husband. Alewife was not an occupation for faint-hearted women—our stay at her inn during the Witenagemot in Oxford had made that abundantly clear to me—but she made it look easy.

She was a woman of action, too. I suspected she'd sold her property decisively—and probably not cheaply—the moment she had decided to burn her bridges and wager her future on my master. She was a mature woman, who clearly had not hesitated to set her course north, toward unknown territory, to find Winston.

And now I knew she was a woman of stamina. She must have ridden from Oxford to Northampton in one day. The whole time we were in Oxford, I never saw her on horseback. And yet she'd managed to keep up with a platoon of housecarls, who were not out for a little casual trot around the park. When they'd reached their destination, she continued riding on her own, not even knowing how far she'd have to go.

Finally, she was a shy woman. A woman who—despite all her years as an alewife and her age of nearly forty—still had not been able to just tell Winston outright what I had guessed she wanted to say as soon as she opened her mouth.

Are they in love? Elvina had asked.

Alfilda was. That much was clear. I had no doubt that Winston also was, the way he stood there with that dopey, dreamy look on his face.

As Harding had put it: Rotted wood burns hot once it finally takes.

When Alwyn reappeared to bring us to Ælfgar, I cleared my throat to wake Winston from his reveries. Winston shook the cobwebs out of his head, looked at me with clear eyes, nodded, and said, "Well, it's time to tackle yet another nobleman."

I laughed, glad to see him back to his old self now that work called.

Ælfgar had changed his clothes after his ride. Over dark-gray breeches, he now wore a yellow kirtle with embroidery around the neck. A thin gold chain hung across his chest, and a silver belt circled his waist. He didn't wear an arm ring, unlike his man Alwyn. Instead, he demonstrated his nobility and the rewards of his bravery through his style of dress.

A bed sat against the wall. Late autumn sun shone through the window onto an elegant table and four chairs.

A silver pitcher and four goblets of the same metal sat on the table. The thane invited us to take our seats, and Alwyn filled the goblets, passing the first to his master and then one to each guest before taking the last one for himself and sitting down.

I glanced at Winston, whose mouth curled into a faint smile. He, too, had noticed that they found emphasizing rank more important than displaying hospitality.

"I hear you haven't apprehended the murderer yet." Ælfgar's voice did not sound as deep here in the room as it had the evening before in the chapter house.

"Then you have not been told a lie," Winston replied. His words and his tone indicated he was not in a subservient mood.

"And yet the case seems quite straightforward to me," Ælfgar said.

"Really?" Winston said, leaning back in his chair, which, like the thane's, was equipped with a backrest. "How so?"

"One man challenges another and pays with his life," Ælfgar said, a bite to both his words and his tone.

"So Simon is the murderer?" Winston asked.

"Who else?" Ælfgar said, making a sweeping gesture with his hand.

"I thought you might be able to help me with that," Winston said, leaning forward a bit.

"Me?" Ælfgar said. "I have nothing to do with the monastery."

"You're staying here."

"Because the monastery is obligated to provide my master with hospitality."

"And your master is Leofwine," Winston said.

"My master is Leofwine of Mercia, yes," Ælfgar confirmed. Both men were aloof but polite.

"And your business here?" Winston inquired.

"Is for Jarl Leofwine," Ælfgar replied.

"Leofwine uses the Danish title of jarl, not the Saxon title of ealdorman?" Winston asked.

"He goes by ealdorman to some," Ælfgar replied, his cool look matching the chill that had crept into his voice.

"But he calls himself *jarl*?" Winston continued.

Ælfgar shrugged dismissively.

"Ælfgar," Winston said, leaning forward again. "I assure you, I just want to solve the murder, as you yourself have asked me to do." As I mentioned, Winston could lie quite adeptly when it suited his purposes. "Are you convinced that nothing having to do with your business may have resulted in the murder?"

Ælfgar stared, his mouth open.

"To do with my business? For the jarl? I can assure you, Winston the Illuminator, that that could in no way interest a foul-mouthed monk."

Winston gave me a half wink, an unnecessary signal.

"You didn't like him?" Winston noted.

"My feelings on the matter are irrelevant. I do not concern myself with monks."

"But you found him impudent?"

Ælfgar shrugged. "Didn't we all? He interrupted his abbot and swore at one of the monastery's guests. Even Abbot Turold, who is among the mildest of mild-mannered men, felt obliged to do something to punish the man."

"True enough," Winston said. "And you knew him?"

"Knew him?" Ælfgar said. "I'd never seen him before."

"You hadn't? But you know Turold?"

"This isn't the first time I've made use of my master's entitlement to hospitality."

The questions and answers followed, each in rapid succession without so much as a heartbeat's pause in between.

"So you must have run into Godfrid before?" Winston asked.

"Not that I know of."

"But I was told that he'd been here at the monastery for a good year. When were you here last?"

Ælfgar cocked his head and looked at Alwyn, who until now had sat stiffly and silently in his chair.

"Shortly before midsummer," Alwyn said.

Ælfgar nodded.

"And you didn't meet Godfrid then?" Winston asked.

Ælfgar shook his head.

"But what about Erik?" Winston inquired.

"Erik?" Ælfgar looked around, as if he were expecting to find a fifth man whose presence he had not been aware of.

"Godfrid's name was Erik before he became a monk," Winston explained, leaning back again.

Ælfgar was silent. He tilted his head back and closed his eyes halfway. Winston and I both watched him, but I also noticed that Alwyn was watching Winston.

"Wasn't he a redhead?" Ælfgar eventually asked.

Winston nodded and Ælfgar continued: "I've known a fair number of people named Erik, but none of them were redheads as far as I recall. Alwyn?"

Alwyn slowly shook his head; then his eyes opened a little wider.

"What about Erik Sigurdson?" he asked.

"The thane from Jutland?" Ælfgar asked skeptically. "But he died at Ottanford."

"Oh, right. I forgot," Alwyn said quickly.

Alwyn's response was fast. So fast that he might have been given a sign. Surely Winston wasn't the only one who could tell a lie.

"And his property went to the monastery in Ramsey," Ælfgar continued. Then a teasing look came into Ælfgar's eyes. "That is no farther than a day's ride from here. Send your servant over there, Winston, and you'll have it confirmed for you."

Servant! I glared at him, which did not go over well.

Winston looked down at the floor as he tugged on his nose. His shoulders tense, he paused a bit, thinking, before deciding to pry into the thane's business.

"Who were those men you met with today?" Winston asked.

And to think he had just claimed he was only interested in solving the murder.

The thane was furious. His cheeks flamed, but the look he gave Winston was icy. Ælfgar slowly turned to look at me.

"Did you have your man eavesdrop on me?" he asked accusingly.

"No one's been eavesdropping on you," Winston said, calmly shaking his head. "But I know you met two men who came from the west. From Mercia?"

Ælfgar's mouth was a bitter line.

"You rode out without your sword, Ælfgar. So it wasn't someone you feared. Friends perhaps?"

Ælfgar stood up.

"I rode today to the shire reeve, who approved my suggestion that you should investigate Brother Godfrid's murder. Don't let me regret that choice, Winston the Illuminator."

Ælfgar gestured with his head toward the door, signaling that the interview was over. Alwyn promptly obeyed his master and opened the door to show us out. I saw Winston hesitate, but then he stood up, and we left the room. In the doorway Winston turned and said, "In a murder investigation, even noblemen have to put up with answering uncomfortable questions, Ælfgar. If you do not accept that, you will regret having asked me to take the case. Would you like me to withdraw?"

Ælfgar struggled to control his breathing. His chest heaved and his eyes never left Winston's. Finally he shook his head.

"No," he said. "But understand that I will only answer questions that pertain to the investigation."

"As long as we both agree that *I* decide what pertains to the case," Winston replied calmly, and turned to leave.

Chapter 22

t must be acknowledged that the monastery set a generous table. The tongueless Ulf got to sit with the youngest of the monks at dinner, and as far as I could tell from my place between Brother Edgar and Wulfgar, he was provided for every bit as well as the rest of us.

He clearly had a hard time eating. He cut his meat—a fatty lamb steak, which made the whole room smell like rosemary—into very small pieces with his dagger and placed them one by one on equally small pieces of bread. Then he worked on each mouthful with his molars, his jaws tense. Then he swallowed, which was obviously difficult without a tongue to help him.

Winston didn't eat with us.

After our conversation with Ælfgar, we returned to the church, where the body had been duly dressed and laid out on a bier before the altar. It was dark in the cold stone building, now that the afternoon was more than half-over, and the altar candle had been put out to reflect the church's desecration. The candle would remain dark until the bishop found time to reconsecrate the church.

Winston and I stood on either side of the great arch with our backs to the rock wall. The stones felt cool through my shirt, and a dry smell of lime hit my nostrils and made me sneeze.

"What are they going to do with him?" I asked, gesturing toward Godfrid's body with my chin.

"Bury him," Winston said in surprise. "That's what people usually do with the dead."

"Yeah, yeah," I said, hiding my irritation. "But can they do that from here in the church if it's been desecrated?"

"Ah well, I don't know. At any rate, what do you think about our nobleman?"

"He seemed like most noblemen," I said with a laugh. "Cooperative until we started asking him about the really interesting stuff."

"Was he lying?" Winston asked.

"Ugh," I said with a shrug. "Of course he was lying. About something or other that we can't see yet. Maybe he was lying just to keep quiet. Maybe he knows something he thinks we shouldn't know about."

"And his business that had to be kept secret?" Winston asked.

"He thinks it's none of our business," I said. "Or maybe it's just the kind of—possibly shady—business we suspect. But how are we going to find out?"

"Well," Winston said with a snort, "he was very quick to finger Simon."

"Of course. Simon is the only one who openly made an enemy of Godfrid. So for everyone who was present, it is obvious to finger him."

"But if you were the murderer," Winston said, "then Simon would also be an obvious person to finger, to keep the suspicion off yourself."

"Ding! You rang the bell," I said, nodding supportively.

Winston gave me a curmudgeonly look, then leaned his head back to rest against the stonework. We both stood there in silence until Winston abruptly straightened up.

"Enough of this," he said. "I'm going to go see Alfilda."

That came as a bit of a surprise, but I wisely suppressed the smile that came to my lips.

Darkness had begun to fall outside. A warm, golden dusk bathed the monastery buildings in an autumnal glow. A group of spearmen walked out the gate. Ælfgar's, I noted. So they had probably been ordered to go find food and lodging in the village, as the monastery was obligated to provide only one night of hospitality.

I accompanied Winston to the gate.

"Should I expect you back tonight?" I asked.

He didn't respond.

For a moment I toyed with the idea of walking with him so that I could take a peek at Elvina's sister, Ebba, but I pushed the thought aside. The chances that her father would let me anywhere near her were too small, so although I would have gladly taken a closer look at what she was hiding behind her blue kerchief, I refrained.

On my way across the grass to the hall, the thought of her kerchief stayed with me. There was something about it that bothered me.

Ælfgar still sat in the place of honor in the hall. Regardless of what the monastery was or was not obligated to provide the jarl's soldiers, the rules of politeness dictated that the brothers offer certain things to a visiting noble-man attending to that same jarl's business.

Neither Edmund nor Simon were present, and when I politely asked the brother waiting on my table, he explained that the Benedictines had asked for permission to remain in their chamber, where they would spend the time praying for the deceased.

"How nice of them," I mumbled to Edgar, who scratched his red ring of hair, but otherwise remained silent, concentrating on his lamb.

Wulfgar sat across from me, not next to me as on the previous evening. There was more room at the table now that the thane's spearmen were absent. Wulfgar had a healthy appetite, presumably because he'd drilled his men all day.

The monks who had eaten at our table the previous night were absent, too. I asked Edgar if some of his brothers had been told to fast. He looked at me, puzzled, so I explained.

"No," Edgar said, spitting a piece of bone into his hand. "They're tend-ing the sick."

Then he went on to explain that he and Brother Hubert, the stocky monk who had been pointed out to me earlier as an attendant to the ill, were in charge of the monastery's hospital. Edgar examined the ill, decided how they should be treated, and measured the medicine for them, while Hubert was in charge of actually administering their care. The other broth-ers who didn't have duties in the kitchen or the large garden all took part in a cleverly designed watch schedule so that someone always attended the ill, day and night.

"And you're also the prior?" I asked.

Edgar looked at me blankly.

"Since you were at the abbot's side today."

"No," he said, shaking his head. "No, we don't need a prior. I was with Turold during your talk because I just happened to be with him when you arrived this morning."

I pretended that I believed him and looked back over at Wulfgar, who pushed himself back from the table, patted his belly, and gave me a satisfied smile before reaching for the ale pitcher.

"So," Wulfgar said with a sigh, once he'd filled his tankard. "This is really living like a lord, for a soldier."

I knew what he meant: sleeping with a roof over your head, in a bed and not under a hay wagon, and eating solid meals several times a day. He was surely not accustomed to that.

"It seems to agree with Ulf as well," I said.

Wulfgar turned and glanced at Ulf. "Looks like it. It must be a long time since he's eaten so well."

"Is he good company?" I asked.

"Well, at least he's not a chatterbox," Wulfgar said, and then tipped his head back and laughed. "I guess I don't know any more than that."

"You said you went to the church when the body was discovered because Alwyn came by looking for us."

"I did, and he did," Wulfgar said.

Something here didn't add up. I thought it over. Edmund had found the body, but did we know what he did next? We know that at some point he went to Abbot Turold's chambers, but what did he do before that? I couldn't remember that any of us had asked him, and I bit my lower lip in annoyance.

"Why Alwyn?" I asked.

"What do you mean?" Wulfgar asked, looking at me in surprise. "Did you expect the thane to come get you in person?"

"No, I mean, why did Edmund notify him when he found Godfrid dead? You're in charge of Edmund's spearmen. Wouldn't it have made sense for Edmund to have notified you?"

"Oh yeah, I can explain that," Wulfgar said, but then didn't say anything.

"Alright, let's hear it," I urged.

"Well, I wondered the same thing, you know? So I asked Edmund earlier."

I swore to myself that this spearman had thought things through further than we had.

"And what did he say?"

"That Alwyn happened to be walking across the grass when he came out of the church."

"What?" I stared at him, dumbfounded. "What was Alwyn doing there?"

"Now that I can't tell you," Wulfgar said with a smile that basically said he could see why I was bewildered.

I looked around. Alwyn had eaten at our table yesterday. Today I couldn't see him. I decided to change the topic.

"Do you think Simon could be the murderer?" I asked.

"I don't think so," Wulfgar said, suddenly serious. "He's pretty hot-headed, that's for sure, but to kill someone in cold blood? The hell if I know."

"You mentioned to me that he's not a nobleman by birth. Have you ever seen him with a sword in his hand?"

"Never," Wulfgar said, shaking his head. "But . . ."

"Yes?" I encouraged him.

"Nothing."

The Benedictines were his employers, and he was too smart to say anything to put them at a disadvantage. I understood. I was going to have to say whatever he was thinking.

"Not that it takes much skill with a weapon to knock a man down from behind and chop his hand off with a sword," I said.

Wulfgar nodded.

"Simon had a motive," I continued.

"So did several other people. As far as I've heard, this Godfrid was known for his rude behavior."

I realized it would be impossible to break through Wulfgar's loyalty unless I had some firm evidence of Simon's guilt. So I turned to Brother Edgar instead, only to discover that someone had come and occupied the seat next to him while I'd been talking to Wulfgar.

"Alwyn," I said by way of greeting. "You're late to the table."

Alwyn finished chewing his mouthful before he responded that he'd been out on an errand for the thane.

"A long ride?" I asked.

He didn't respond, and I made a note to go to the stable and check if his horse had been ridden.

"And last night?" I asked.

Alwyn took a bite of meat.

"Last night?" he mumbled as he chewed.

"When Edmund ran into you outside the church. Were you doing an errand for the thane then, too?"

"Oh, that," Alwyn said with a wide grin, exposing his teeth. "No, that was more like an errand of my own. I was answering the call of nature."

I pointed out that the outhouse was behind the stables in the other direction from where Edmund had seen him.

"Yeah, but I usually do a perimeter check every time I wake up at night."

If Alwyn was the kind of seasoned, ever-vigilant soldier I took him to be, that made perfect sense.

"How was he?" I asked.

"What do you mean?" Alwyn was struggling with his slice of bread, which had come apart after soaking up the juices from the meat.

"Edmund. How was he when you met him?"

"Oh. He was . . ." Alwyn's face took on a contemplative look. "Surprisingly calm, actually, considering that he'd just found a dead body."

Edmund was able to keep a calm head, I knew, remembering back to how he'd acted during the attack along the road. All the same, most people would be shaken to find a man murdered in a church like that.

"What did Edmund say?" I asked.

"Say?" Alwyn thought about it. "I'd taken a stroll down past the gate and exchanged a few words with the guards when I saw the door to the church open. I didn't think any more about it. These monks are always going in and out, but then Edmund called out to me. He came walking out the door of the church."

"You recognized him?" I decided I should talk to the guards who were on duty last night.

"Of course. It was a moonlit night. He said . . . he said something terrible had happened in the church."

"Something terrible? He didn't say a man had been murdered?" I asked.

"No," Alwyn said shaking his head. "'Something terrible.' That's what he said."

"Hmm," I said.

Wulfgar cleared his throat to draw our attention.

"That is exactly what a man like Edmund would say after coming upon something desecrating a church," Wulfgar said.

He was right. *Such a gruesome act in the house of the Lord*, the prior had called it, before he'd said that it was terrible no matter who'd done it. Not the murder itself, maybe, but the fact that it had happened where it had.

"Did he mention Simon?" I asked.

"His subprior?" Alwyn asked. Then he shook his head. "No, but then he wasn't in the church."

I let that remark pass without commenting on it.

"And then what did you do?" I prompted.

"I went into the church, and after I saw what had happened, I woke up two spearmen and ordered them to guard the church. After that I woke Ælfgar, who accompanied me to the church. After he saw the body, he told me to go get Abbot Turold and you."

"Why not go get the abbot first?"

"Before getting the guards?" Alwyn said. "I thought it was important to seal off the church. The dead man could obviously wait a few minutes."

"Who did the church need to be sealed off from?"

Alwyn opened his mouth but then just stared at me, surprised. A few moments later he smiled slightly.

"You know what? I actually have no idea now. I just thought that's what should be done."

I smiled back at him. That's how people are when they're in command. The first thing they do is put their soldiers to work. Maybe later they start thinking about why.

I thanked him and stood up. The refectory had gradually emptied out. Only a few monks who'd arrived late were still seated, leaning over their bread trenchers.

In the stables a one-eyed, stooped stable hand told me Alwyn had come in on horseback a little while ago and had left his horse in the man's care. And at the gate I was lucky to find that one of the guards had had the night watch the previous night as well. He confirmed Alwyn's story. The guard had also seen Alwyn walking the whole way over from the outhouse, past the gate, and he had then watched Alwyn go around behind the church and back.

"There wasn't much else to do," the guard said by way of explanation. I asked whether he'd found Alwyn's behavior odd, but he just shook his head and said, "I'm sure the thane's man just wanted to check with his own eyes that everything was as it should be."

In other words, the guard approved of Alwyn's leadership and wouldn't have minded serving under a man like him. I thanked him and walked back across the turf.

Wulfgar sat on a bench outside the guesthouse, a pitcher and two tankards next to him. He waved to me jauntily and called out, "There's always a use for a pitcher of good ale, right?"

So, like brothers, we spent the evening in pleasant conversation, emptying the pitcher of strong, sweet gale–flavored ale.

Chapter 23

was alone when I woke up. The spearmen might grumble that the lodgings they found in the village were worse than at the monastery, but as far as Winston was concerned, he was certainly better bedded than he'd dreamt he would be even as recently as yesterday morning.

I found Alwyn and his master in the hall, dressed to go riding. They both spared me a nod, but that was all.

I sat down at the other end of the hall and hungrily ate the breakfast porridge, which I poured plenty of honey over. I washed it down with weak ale as I contemplated what I ought to do if Winston didn't show up soon.

Which he didn't.

I had no trouble deciding who I should talk to after my chats with Alwyn and Wulfgar the previous night.

Simon answered the door. He looked pale, but not particularly torn up. The corners of his mouth were slick with ale, and behind him I saw Edmund at the little table, busy with a loaf of wheat bread, cold food, salted salmon, and a pitcher of ale. The Benedictines were certainly being treated well.

"Oh, it's you," Edmund said.

"Indeed," I said, directing my most winning smile at Edmund. "I have a couple of questions, Prior Edmund."

"You're still working on that?" Edmund licked the salmon fat off his fingers. Then he furrowed his brow. "Where is your master?"

"He had another engagement," I said. I wasn't sure that an honest response would be the best choice.

The brow furrows grew deeper. Edmund apparently felt that discussing anything with me was beneath him, and he was about to tell me that it would be far more suitable if we were to wait until Winston could be present. But before Edmund managed to open his mouth, I'd asked my question:

"After you discovered Godfrid's body, you left the church. Why?"

"Why?" His gray eyes looked surprised. "To sound the alarm, of course."

"Of course. To whom did you sound it?"

Edmund's eyes widened farther, and he gave Simon a nervous glance.

"I, uh . . ." Edmund flung up his hands, flummoxed. "I don't actually know."

"No, I don't suppose you thought that far through it." I smiled reassuringly. "But what actually happened then?"

Edmund's forehead wrinkled up again as he thought about it. Then it smoothed out again and he said, "I met a spearman."

"And that was . . . ?" I prompted.

"The one who's in charge of Thane Ælfgar's men."

"Alwyn?"

"Yes, him," Edmund said with a vehement nod.

"What was he doing in front of the church in the middle of the night?" I asked.

The look on Edmund's face was no longer just surprised. Now it was also completely mystified.

"Now that, I really couldn't tell you," he admitted.

"Maybe he had just come out of the church?" I asked.

"Out of the . . . ? Of course not." Edmund's voice was beginning to regain its customary authority, so I hurried to confuse him further.

"Is it really such a matter of course, Edmund?" I badgered.

He seemed startled.

"Prior Edmund," I corrected myself. "Is it, Edmund?"

His ruddy face blushed, but when I refused to back down, he became angry. I heard Simon's foot scraping against the floor behind me.

"Of course the prior would have noticed it if this Alwyn fellow had been in the church," Simon said.

"Were you there?" I asked, not even bothering to turn my head to look at Simon.

"You know I wasn't," Simon said haughtily.

"Then be quiet," I told him. "Well, Edmund?"

I could see in Edmund's eyes that I'd won this power struggle. He turned a bit, ran a hand over his stubbly scalp, and mumbled that as his subprior had so rightly stated, he would certainly have noticed if there had been a person present in the nave.

"You would? In the dark?" I kept my eyes focused on him.

Edmund nodded his head, bit his lower lip, and then his eyes widened triumphantly.

"He came from over by the gate!" he exclaimed.

So Alwyn had told the truth. I contemplated the likelihood that Alwyn had been inside the church, killed Godfrid, and sneaked out while Edmund was on his way in, only to then hurry over to the gate guards so that someone could corroborate his story. Not very likely, I thought, although I decided to present the possibility to Winston whenever he decided to show back up.

I turned to Simon and asked, "How handy are you with a sword, Simon?"

A shiver ran through Simon's chiseled face. I raised my eyebrows encouragingly.

"I'm no swordsman," he confessed.

"I know," I said cheerfully. "That's why I asked how good you are with a sword."

"I'm . . . I'm not good. I've never trained at using weapons."

"Never held a sword in your hand?" I asked.

"Never." He seemed to have found a reserve of strength from somewhere.

"Maybe as a boy? Before you put on the habit?"

"Never."

Well, well, like I'd told Wulfgar the evening before, it doesn't take much skill to chop a man's hand off.

"And you still claim Godfrid was alive when you left him?" I asked Simon.

Simon's self-confidence slipped away, like a cloak falling on the ground, and I saw tears gleam in his eyes.

"Yes, I swear by the living God," he said.

Based on what Wulfgar had told me about Simon, I was inclined to believe his solemn oath.

Chapter 24

I returned to our room and found no sign of Winston or any indication that he'd been there, so I decided to go down to the village. It was one of those clear, crisp autumn days when the sky is as blue as a jarl's cloak, the air cool without tearing at your lungs, and the sun on the verge of regaining its strength. You could tell the harvest was drawing to a close. People walked around calmly, without the urgency typical of farmers when they're struggling to bring in the grain before the weather turns.

All the same, the square and the lanes were busy.

A lanky boy drove an oxcart away without needing to poke the animals' hindquarters with his hazel switch. The bullocks patiently shook their crooked horns and bellowed back at the boy, who gave me a friendly greeting, and then they calmly lumbered away. A lass with wispy hair walked right across their path with her flock of geese without causing the bullocks' heads to even tug at the yoke, not even when the honking, hissing birds darted between their legs.

The boy blew the girl a kiss and then urged her to meet him "at the stile, you know," an offer she responded to by sticking out her tongue.

I laughed. The cheeky boy gave me a wink, and the girl rolled her eyes. I watched her contentedly as she drifted away, sashaying her hips, following her squawking gray flock. Eventually she had to step aside to make way for a creaking cart, which squeaked its way along behind a nag whose head drooped so far it almost touched the grass along the dusty lane.

When I reached the farm where Alfilda was staying, I found a corpulent farmer putting a new handle on a shovel. He was about thirty, with a flat face and hands that were each twice as wide as my own. He was attaching the handle to the blade with an iron bolt.

"Ribald."

He looked up, thus indicating that I had guessed correctly.

"I'm Halfdan. I'm looking for Winston the Illuminator. Is he here?"

Ribald responded with a headshake.

"How about Alfilda, who's staying here?"

Same response.

"Do you know where they are?"

He raised the shovel, inspected his work, and gave me an obtuse look, which I responded to with an obliging smile.

"The hospital," he said, then turned and walked off around the corner of the building. A man of few words, apparently. I wondered how Abbot Turold succeeded in "always talking to him."

A movement by the farmhouse door caught my attention.

The girl who stepped out onto the worn millstone doorstep and glanced over at me could have been Elvina in about five or six years. Light-blonde hair fell softly around her face. Her eyes were blue like the kerchief around her shoulders. Her bosom pushed against her gray top. And her calves—which were visible below her skirt—were tan and inviting.

"You must be Ebba," I said, walking over to her.

Her eyes widened slightly.

"I'm a friend of Elvina's." I could claim that, right? "You're not out with the sheep." Let it not be said that I'm an unobservant person.

The girl wrinkled her nose but remained silent.

"My name's Halfdan." If I kept talking, eventually she'd have to say something, right? "And I'm looking for Winston. He's the man who slept with Alfilda, who's staying here."

Now I was rewarded with a smile.

"We work together," I added.

The girl wrinkled her nose again and was just about to open her mouth when a woman called to her from inside the house. I recognized Estrid's voice and hollered in that it was me, Halfdan.

Estrid stepped out the door and gestured with her head that Ebba should get back inside, which the girl obeyed with a sidelong look at me.

"And what do you want?" she asked me.

"I'm looking for Winston—and Alfilda," I added.

"They're not here."

"No, I understood as much from Ribald. They're at the hospital." I smiled affably.

"So if you're looking for them, what are you still doing here?"

That was a question that I could have answered, but I thought it wisest to simply nod and go on my way.

I pictured Ebba as I walked through the village. I let my thoughts dwell on the curve of her breasts and her tan calves, but I kept being distracted by that kerchief that had been around her shoulders. There was still something about it that bothered me.

It had been big, I remembered. It covered both her shoulders. Finely woven, too, as far as I could tell from a distance. And sky-blue.

Blue! That was it.

The hospital sat off to the side of the village square, where the square opened onto a wider grassy plane. It was a post-and-plank building with a sod roof. The structure was as long as the church, but naturally not as high. My head was about even with the edge of the roof. A door, the upper half of which stood open, stood more or less in the middle of the building's long southern side. The hospital had no windows but had a smoke hole at each end, from which gray smoke rose straight up on this windless day.

I pushed the half door open and ducked into a long room, which was divided into smaller areas by woven hangings suspended from the ceiling. The air inside was nauseating, thick with human miasmas. I heard throaty gurgles, sighs, and muffled groans of pain from every direction. A couple of monks carried a limp form, wrapped in a roughly patched-together cloth, through the room and out the door. They turned right and headed up toward the monastery gate.

I stood for a bit, letting my eyes adjust to the darkness. I heard rustling around me and squinted. I discovered that I was looking at a stout monk leaning over a bed. The protective drape had been pulled aside.

"Brother Hubert?" I thought I recognized his blotchy face.

The monk glanced up, but continued doing what he was doing, so I stepped over to him.

"I'm Halfdan."

"I know who you are. Here, hold her."

I looked down at the patient, a wizened old woman, who was gasping for air. Her breath sounded like dry peas rolling across a kitchen table.

"I'm looking for Winston the Illuminator."

"I said, 'Hold her.'"

I reluctantly obeyed. I took hold of the old woman's upper arms and slowly pulled her into a sitting position. She moaned and complained, clawing at the coarse cloth beneath her with a crooked hand. As soon as her torso was free of the bed, Hubert thrust his hand under her and turned her, revealing a skinny rump. There was a large open sore on one of her buttocks.

"There you go, my dear." The monk's voice was gentle. "Now I'll ease your pain.

"Stay!" he said to me, in a hoarse voice. I watched with my hand over my mouth and nose as he applied a stinking salve to her bleeding butt cheek. "It burns now, my friend, but it will start helping soon."

The old woman put up with the treatment, making that rattling sound while lying with her face buried in the covers and her arms limply at her sides. I saw her buttock clench as the salve touched it and smelled the unmistakable stench of a cabbage fart waft up from her.

Brother Hubert kept steadily applying the salve, finishing by leaning over and inspecting the other buttock. He apparently found it to be satisfactory, because he set the jar of salve down with a grunt.

"Now just lie back, my friend, while the salve soaks in," he instructed her.

The old woman made a sound—half sigh, half moan—and the monk got up without further ado and pulled the drape closed again.

"So, you're looking for your master," Brother Hubert said, moving on to the next bed.

My eyes had adjusted to the darkness, and when I looked down the length of the building, I saw other monks leaning over beds or kneeling in front of them.

"Yes. Do you know where I can find him?" I scanned the room, trying to spot his or Alfilda's characteristic heads of hair.

"Yes," Hubert said. He flung the next drape aside, revealing a legless man, whose fleshy paunch drooped off him to both sides like butter melting in the heat. "Now, Grandfather, let me take a look at you, my friend."

"My dear," "grandfather," and "my friend" were apparently his names for the sick.

"Where?" I asked impatiently.

"He left," Hubert said, holding up one leg stump.

"Left? Alone?"

"No." Hubert apparently approved of the red flap of skin at the end of the man's leg, because he moved on to the other stump, which caused him to shake his head in disapproval. "Listen, my friend, this is infected."

He gave the sick man a reproachful look and then turned to me and said, "Hold here."

I wanted to object, but he just took my hand and positioned it in under the stump before walking away from us. The cripple lay very still, staring at me with either pain or fear in his eyes. I couldn't figure out which.

Hubert came back with a steaming pot in one hand, a stone mortar and pestle in the other, and some rags hanging over his arm.

"Now just hold tight," he told me, when I indignantly pointed out that I had other things to do besides stand here. He placed the steaming pot on the floor, dropped the rags into it, and then started grinding with the mortar and pestle. As the pestle went up and down, I noticed a sharp odor. The monk dipped a finger into the mortar and pulled it back out, inspecting his now yellow fingertip. "Hmm."

Another couple of tamps, yet another fingertip inspection, and then he nodded. He pulled a steaming rag out of the pot, dipped it in the mortar, and spread the foul-smelling bandage on the man's leg stump.

Another three rags were dipped and applied to the wound. Then he nodded at the old geezer, who stared at him, wide-eyed.

"There, Grandfather. That ought to help."

"He left with Edgar," Hubert told me by way of explanation.

I got out of there before he compelled me to saw the arm off of some poor old woman.

Chapter 25

he morning was drawing to a close as I stood outside the hospital once again. I was happy to breathe in the crisp autumn air after the fetid smells of the ill, and happy to leave the muffled cries of pain behind me.

The sun had gained strength. A hazy heat lingered over the farms and buildings. The nobleman in me was glad for the farmers and the monastery that the autumn would soon be dry enough to bring the sheaves in to the threshing floors and haylofts, where the grain would ensure everyone ale and bread for the winter.

It was a good year for farmers and noblemen alike, and even the country's poor would reap the rewards of the bountiful harvest, because, as Harding put it: A full man is willing to share.

I heard a deep voice from across the grass, over by the road to the south. A soldier was putting eight spearmen through their paces. They obeyed his shouted commands willingly, and I stood contentedly in the sun, watching the well-trained soldiers drill.

The leader released them a short while later, warning them not to cause any trouble in the village, but to remember that it belonged to the monastery, to which they owed their respect. He ended by assuring them that if any farmer accused them of vandalism, he would come down hard on the culprit.

I'd recognized the leader. It was Alwyn, who apparently hadn't noticed me. He set off walking across the grass toward the village's public house, a sod-roofed cottage with a green branch over its door and a couple of benches out front.

Alwyn sat down heavily on one of the benches and nodded to a stooped man in a leather apron, who went inside and came right back out carrying a foaming barrel-stave tankard.

I let Alwyn empty half his tankard before I strolled across the green and stopped in front of him.

"Is the ale good, Alwyn?" I asked. When he looked up in response to my voice, he had the sun in his eyes.

"Oh, it's you," he said, shielding his eyes with his hand. "Yes, it's splendid. Flavored with sweet gale the way I like it."

"Hmm, maybe I'll have some," I said and sat down next to him. The stooped man must have been keeping an eye on me from inside his nook, because he came out right away and asked in a creaky voice what I'd like.

"I'll take a tankard of ale," I said and then glanced over at Alwyn's tankard and raised my eyebrows to ask if he wanted more. "Actually, make that two."

Alwyn finished his tankard and handed it to the proprietor, who left us with a slight bow.

It *was* good ale. The sweetness was balanced by the bitterness of the wormwood, without overpowering the taste of the malt. We drank in silence, watching the green in front of us. I think we both enjoyed sitting in the sun and listening to the sounds of village life.

Eventually Alwyn cleared his throat and said, "Well, I suppose I ought to buy you a tankard. Or did you have your sights set on some other form of payment?"

"Payment?" I pretended not to understand him.

He stood up without a word, took my tankard and walked over to the door, where he handed the tankards in to the waiting proprietor. He brought us two more tankards shortly thereafter.

I let a little time elapse before I repeated my question: "Payment?"

"The day before yesterday you wanted to pump me for information. Then a murder was committed, and my master asked you and *your* master to solve it. Which gives you even more reason to want to question me. So, I'm puzzled that you considered last night's answers sufficient."

I chuckled agreeably. This man wasn't dumb.

"I thought you might like to answer me today?" I tried.

"Ælfgar wants the murder solved," Alwyn said with a shrug.

"Then tell me what business he rode out on."

Alwyn looked at me sharply.

"You can ask me about the murder."

"Good." I bit my lower lip. "Do you have anything to add to what you told me last night?"

He shook his head in response. He'd guessed that I was more interested in Ælfgar's business than the murder. All the same, we both still had to play the game.

"Ælfgar said he didn't meet Godfrid when you were here at the monastery before midsummer. Was that true of you as well?"

"Definitely," Alwyn said.

"So you'd never seen him before?"

"Not here at the monastery anyway."

"But . . . ?" I looked at him in surprise.

"I can't say for certain," Alwyn said, hesitating, "but after your master's chat with Ælfgar, I've been thinking a lot about it. I might have seen him before, but it's hard when you see a man lying dead to try to picture him alive."

He was right about that. Especially, I pointed out, if you had met each other a long time ago. He nodded.

"And you suggested he had only been a monk for a year. So he wouldn't have had the tonsure. That makes it even harder."

"Picture a fiery, redheaded soldier," I said, trying to help.

"But Erik Sigurdson fell at Ottanford, as Ælfgar said."

"And he's the only one you remember?"

"Yes," Alwyn said, looking serious. "Believe me, I'm being candid about everything I say about the murder."

I appreciated that. Ælfgar probably honestly wanted the murder cleared up. I tried to find another way to coax Alwyn to open up.

"What was the reason for your visit here last summer?"

"What in the world does that have to do with the murder?" he asked, narrowing his eyes.

"Probably nothing. But we're fishing in the dark, you understand." I made my voice tremble with honesty. "We're starting from scratch with this murder. Your master and you are innocent, we understand that. The same is true of the Benedictines, I believe. Who does that leave? So I'm trying to gather as much information as possible. Most of it will probably turn out to be insignificant, but we won't know that until we have our hands around the murderer's neck. And so I'm asking you, and I hope that you will understand why it might be important for you to answer."

Alwyn watched me, but then he looked out over the green. His eyes widened for a moment, and I looked to see why. Ebba was walking across the green, hips swaying.

"A beautiful lass," I said, winking at him.

"Indeed, as farm girls go. In a few years she'll be worn to a shadow from popping out babies."

I supposed you could look at it that way. Something in his voice made me study his facial expression, but it seemed quite neutral. He noticed me looking at him and quickly looked away, only to look back again.

"My master is highly trusted by the jarl," Alwyn said.

I didn't say anything but nodded encouragingly.

"And often rides on his business. That is what we were doing last summer as well." Alwyn shrugged. "But why should I remain quiet about what any monk can tell you? Ælfgar was meeting with someone at the monastery."

"Someone who doesn't want his name known?" I asked, raising an eyebrow.

"If so, he was behaving foolishly. Which wouldn't be the first time." Alwyn shook his head dismissively. "My master was supposed to bring him back safely."

"Back to the jarl?" I asked. Now he really had my attention.

"To his father, yes."

"Was it Leofric?" I couldn't stop myself from whistling.

But that didn't make any sense. Godskalk told us that Leofric had been named by his father to lead the fyrd. The leader of the fyrd wouldn't hide in a monastery and wait to be brought home to his father like some bedraggled puppy.

And Alwyn's response showed that I was right.

"Eadwin," Alwyn said, "who is the second oldest of Leofwine's still-living sons."

I heard the bitterness in his voice, presumably at the loss of Norman. Here sat a man who was loyal to the core and of one mind with his masters.

I thought so hard my brain practically creaked. I had claimed I was fishing in the dark as far as the murder was concerned, and it was true—I actually had no idea which direction to cast my net. Then I began to see the daylight.

"Eadwin wasn't satisfied with Leofric's promotion," I guessed.

"Eadwin is not satisfied by much," Alwyn muttered, staring into his tankard dejectedly.

I stood up and walked over to the door. Why was he suddenly being so talkative when he and his master had otherwise put up such a fuss the moment we inquired about their business? I had found a potential answer by the time the proprietor set the tankards in front of us.

"He behaved foolishly, you said. Was the meeting supposed to have been kept secret?"

Alwyn nodded.

"But Eadwin insisted on using his own name so that he would receive the monastery's finest treatment, and when we arrived, everyone already knew who he was."

As he'd said: *Why keep secret what any monk could tell me?* The next question was obvious. "And what was his offense?"

But here I reached the limit of Alwyn's willingness to share. He had told me what he knew couldn't be kept from me if I just asked the right person. He clammed up about everything else.

Still, he had told me something important that might help with our actual assignment: Leofwine's family did not see eye to eye on all matters.

Chapter 26

 shadow fell over the table where I'd sat alone for the few minutes since Alwyn had left. I looked up. It was Winston and Alfilda, of course. Since Alwyn had left, I had been wondering how to go about finding Winston. And now here he was, holding his girlfriend's hand, with a contented, goofy look on his face.

"About time you showed up, Winston."

"Yes, here *we* are." It was subtle, but it was there. Winston was asserting Alfilda's right to take part in things.

"I've been looking for you guys," I said. I figured I'd better make it clear that I'd gotten the message.

"We went for a walk," he said.

He seemed purely amused by the angry look on my face. This was no time to play lovey-dovey! We had a murder to solve and a job to finish.

"By the Lady Path," he added, just as I was about to give him a piece of my mind. "Not that I thought you'd overlooked anything. Just to take a look for myself and form my own impression."

"And?"

"No one has been up that path for a long time."

Alfilda hadn't said a word, and now she sat down across the table from me. I caught some movement over by the door out of the corner of my eye and saw the proprietor looking at us. I nodded in response to his unasked question.

"Have a seat," I told Winston, as the proprietor served our ale. "We need to talk."

They listened as I recounted my morning. Alfilda kept her hand on Winston's arm, her gray eyes half-closed. Winston drank in small sips as he listened to me.

"You were at the hospital?" I finished by asking.

He nodded.

"I wanted to see if the abbot was telling the truth," he said.

"The truth about what?" I didn't understand.

"The monastery spending its money to benefit the maimed and the sick."

Hmm, it hadn't occurred to me to doubt the venerable Turold's words.

Winston turned his arm so that Alfilda's hand slid down into his upturned palm.

"So you believe Simon?" Winston asked me.

"He is a disagreeable and self-righteous fart of a monk, but I highly doubt he's a murderer," I said.

"I agree," Winston said with a nod.

"There is one thing I've been thinking," I said, although that wasn't exactly true. The idea had only just occurred to me that moment. "The hand. Maybe Godfrid making the sign of the cross didn't have anything to do with his hand being cut off."

"As long as you're also right about Simon not being the murderer, you're probably right about that." Winston gave me an almost sarcastic look. "Well, you've told me what didn't happen. What have you decided *did* happen?"

"It was his right hand," I said, and paused. Maybe it was foolish of me to pretend I'd thought through the case.

"Which you would hold out to someone in friendship," Alfilda suggested.

She was on to something.

"Which you would use to steal from someone," Winston pointed out.

He was also right.

"Which holds your sword," I said, wanting to get in on the action.

"Which caresses a woman."

"Which puts silver into the hand of a shopkeeper."

"Which you raise when you take an oath."

"Which you hold to your heart in greeting."

"Which shakes the spear at your enemy."

"Which brings the food to your mouth."

"Which pulls the arrow and the bowstring back to your ear."

"Which slaps the slave."

We all looked at each other. We knew we could keep going with this list, but also that this wasn't getting us anywhere. We had no idea why the hand had been chopped off, just that it was a message of some kind.

Winston released Alfilda's hand and leaned over the table.

"So, Alwyn let the cat out of the bag and told you what they were doing here last summer," he said.

"Bringing Eadwin home to his father," I replied.

"What do you know about this Eadwin, son of Leofwine?" Winston asked.

"Not much," I said, thinking it over. "He's a thane with some land out west, I believe, so actually I don't understand what he was doing here."

"He wanted to be close to his father, the jarl," Alfilda suggested, leaning forward like Winston.

"And his brother, who'd just been promoted," I pointed out. After all, I had a brain, too.

"I've been thinking about that," Winston said, and then cleared his throat. "Didn't you say that Alwyn's words were, 'Eadwin is not satisfied by much'?"

"Yes," I said, thinking back on it.

"Interesting wording," Winston mused. "Not satisfied by much, not, not satisfied with his brother's promotion?"

I had found that interesting, too.

"Alwyn tipped you off," Winston concluded, pausing to bite his lip for a moment. "Leofwine's decision to transfer command of the fyrd to Leofric was not what caused Eadwin to hide here in Brixworth."

"I suppose not," I said. "Maybe it was his father making peace with Cnut?"

"Is this Eadwin a hothead?" Winston asked.

"Not from what I've heard."

"Then he would realize that the only way forward for his family goes through Cnut," Winston said.

"But," I added quickly, before I lost the thought. "That way forward goes through a swamp of Danish jarls."

"Leofwine's jarldom really is quite surrounded by Danes and Vikings," Winston said, nodding.

"Leofwine isn't the one who's scheming against Cnut," I said. I could see it now.

"No, it's Eadwin. That's why Ælfgar was sent to bring him back to his father—so Leofwine could return him to the proper path."

Winston's and my eyes met, but it was Alfilda who asked the uncomfortable question. "If you're right," she said, "how will you two prove it?"

"We may not be able to," Winston replied. "Maybe Ælfgar will talk if we show him we've figured it out. Or maybe we don't need to prove it. If we're right, Eadwin has been helped to see the wisdom of his father's point of view—and his brother's."

"Which means that if we don't find any indications of trouble brewing in Mercia, we can report to Cnut that the jarl is keeping his word," I said, leaning back in satisfaction.

All three of us were quiet. The proprietor appeared in the doorway looking hopeful, but I shook my head.

"So you want to go straight to Ælfgar?" I asked.

Winston hesitated. "No," he decided. "We'll start with Turold. It will be easier to get him talking than Ælfgar. Turold has no reason to be on his guard against us when it comes to questions about Jarl Leofwine and his family."

"Ælfgar knows we're Cnut's men," I said with a nod.

"Well, he's certainly guessed that we're not here just to draw pictures for Edmund and his fellow monks," Winston said, standing up. But my upheld hand made him sit down again. "Yes?" he said.

"How much blue clothing do you own?" I asked, directing my question to Alfilda.

Winston muttered something, surprised by my question. Alfilda's eyes widened.

"Clothing?" she asked, puzzled. "Blue? What?"

I nodded.

"A dress, maybe? A skirt or a top?" I asked.

She shook her head. Winston watched me warily.

"I don't follow your train of thought," Winston said.

I smiled at him and then quickly smiled at Alfilda as well.

"No, I suppose not. Because you know as well as I do that even if Alfilda could afford such expensive clothing, it would hardly be worth her while to show off her wealth that way."

"I had a blue hairband once," Alfilda said with an apologetic look at Winston. "It was my betrothal gift from my husband."

Whom she never talked about—at least not when I was around. The only thing I knew about him was that he'd left her the inn and tavern in Oxford when he'd died several years earlier.

"Who demonstrated his esteem for you," I said. One glance at Winston's icy face had caused me to avoid using the word *love*. "By giving you something made of the most expensive color there is." I didn't bother to point out that maybe the point of that had been lost since he'd only given her a hairband.

She nodded, still not understanding where I was going. "And what's your point?" she asked, allowing Winston to take her hand again.

"There's a farm wench here in the village who wears a blue kerchief, quite brazenly," I said, doing my best to sound scandalized. I leaned back, satisfied with the look on their faces as they slowly grasped what I was saying.

"A farm wench," Winston said, rubbing his chin.

"The daughter of Ribald, whose family you're staying with, Alfilda," I added.

They looked at each other.

"Well, he's not exactly the poorest man in the village," Alfilda said pensively.

"His wife was quite overt that he's the best farmer in the village," I pointed out.

"But he's hardly a man who would buy his daughter expensive clothes," Winston said, staring at me. "What are you getting at?"

"Someone gave her that kerchief," I said. They both nodded, so I continued: "Someone with some power. Someone who knows how to reward people with expensive gifts."

"A nobleman," Winston declared.

"Exactly. And what do noblemen usually reward pretty farm girls for?" I asked, avoiding looking directly at Alfilda, which she acknowledged with a gently mocking snort.

"For spreading her legs," she said indulgently.

"Exactly." I flashed her a winning smile. "And as a rule, the gift is given once the nobleman has gotten what he wanted, when he wants to move on."

"You mean—" Winston sat up straight now.

"That a nobleman bedded Ebba and thanked her with a gift. I wonder if it was one of the two noblemen we know have stayed here in the village?"

"You might be on to something," Winston said, cocking his head and studying me. "And I suppose you thought you might go ask the girl who gave it to her?"

"Yup, while you're with Abbot Turold," I said with a nod.

"Good," Winston said, rising. "No doubt you'll use the same means of persuasion employed by this unknown nobleman before you."

I hid my chuckle. He knew me well. I do indeed have a way with the ladies. But that wasn't the only reason I smiled to myself. I relished the thought of Edmund bumping into Alfilda on her first visit to the monastery.

The good prior's fear at finding himself face-to-face with a comely woman would be surpassed only by his subprior's horror.

Chapter 27

inding Ebba turned out not to be so easy. First I went to the thicket where Elvina and I had run into each other the day before, assuming the sheep would probably follow the same pattern today that they had yesterday. But there was no sign of the girl or the flock entrusted to her care.

Swallows twittered above me, a curlew whistled sadly over the banks to the west, and somewhere in the village a dog barked, but I didn't hear the tinkling of the bell around the bellwether's neck or the calls of the shepherdess.

Off to my right, a few hundred paces up the Lady Path, stood a wide oak tree, its lowermost branches at about shoulder height. I wrapped my arm around one and pulled myself up, with difficulty, swinging my leg up over it and struggling until I was standing on top of it. From there, it wasn't hard to climb high enough that I had a clear view of the foothills between the village bank and the hills that rose in the west.

No woolly creatures and no blonde wenches to see.

I scanned the horizon. The church and the monastery area were behind me. A few men in cowls moved around on the grass, but I saw no sign of Winston or his lady friend, so they were probably in the abbot's chambers.

Outside the palisade I had a good view of the center of the village, including the hospital. Narrow lanes extended out from the village green between the various farms. Smoke rose from the smoke holes in most of the roofs and from the smithy. Two barelegged boys drove a herd of pigs down a clayey street with a great deal of hullabaloo. Even from my lofty perch, the boys appeared to be crawling with lice.

My eye stopped at a fold on the other side of the village, where I spotted gray sheep jostling each other behind a wattle fence. Either Ebba had chosen to graze her flock for just a little while today, or she'd been asked to do some other job.

I climbed back down to the lowermost branch, then slid back to the ground, where I slipped on a decaying mushroom. I heard an unmistakable giggle as I landed flat on my back.

"Are you shirking your work again already?" I asked. I rolled over and got up on all fours, and from there, back to standing.

"Aren't you too old to be climbing trees?" Elvina asked, popping her head out from behind the tree trunk.

"Well, maybe to be climbing back down from them." I smiled at her. "What work are you avoiding today?"

She stuck her tongue out at me in response.

"I'm not avoiding anything. Can't you hear that?"

"Hear what?"

"The swarm," she said, her tan hand pointing up the path. I looked where she was pointing and saw the brown mass before its buzzing reached my ears. "It's from my father's best hive, so I'm supposed to follow it, because he doesn't want to lose his hardest-working bees yet."

"But autumn is upon us," I pointed out.

"My father is a good beeman," she explained nonjudgmentally, "who makes sure his bees stay in the hive. This is the first swarm of the year, and as I'm sure you know, the hardest-working bees are the ones who follow the queen."

I had no knowledge about such things, so I just nodded.

"So you're going to bring the bees back?" I asked. I decided not to mention that her father obviously wasn't good enough to actually keep the bees from running off in the first place.

"Of course not," she said with another long-suffering glance. "My father will take care of that. I just have to tell him where the swarm is."

So I had some company as I walked back. Elvina skipped along happily at my side, chattering away incessantly, and I let her talk while I waited for the right time for my question. My moment arrived when she swallowed a fly and had to stop talking in order to cough.

"That's what happens when your mouth runs on like a water mill," I teased as I thumped her on the back.

She was gasping for breath and had to make do with giving me an angry look.

"And your sister?" I continued before she recovered. "Is she off chasing bees today, too?"

"Why are you asking about her?" she said, looking irritated.

"No particular reason." I shrugged. "I was just wondering. I mean, you can't be the only one in your family who has to slave away."

She didn't respond, so we walked on in silence, which she didn't break until we stood in front of her father's farm.

"Ebba's tummy hurts," she mumbled with a pouty glance. "If you know what that means."

I refrained from smiling. Elvina herself had probably not known the meaning of that for very long, but I was glad that whichever nobleman her sister had lain with, it hadn't had any consequences.

But apparently their mother did not consider their monthly bleeding an excuse for shirking their duties. Although Estrid hadn't made Ebba take the sheep on a rigorous countryside trek, she apparently hadn't allowed the girl to be idle all day. We eventually found Ebba sitting on the bench next to the farmhouse door, where Winston and Alfilda had sat yesterday. Her blue kerchief lay carefully folded at her side as she bent over the drop spindle, which spun beneath her hands.

Elvina pouted at me when I headed toward her elder sister, who didn't look up from her work. Elvina stomped off, presumably to find her father and tell him where to find the swarm of bees.

Without any invitation, I sat down next to Ebba, who acknowledged my presence with a subtle nod of her head, but conscientiously continued her spinning.

I leaned back against the wall, stretched out my legs, and yawned loudly. The lass stole a glance at me, so I apologized and added that I'd had one too many tankards of ale.

"It makes me drowsy, it does, the good ale you folks brew here," I told her.

No response. Apparently this was going to take more than me flattering her village's brewing abilities. I casually let one of my hands fall to the bench so that it touched the kerchief, which I absentmindedly picked up and examined more closely. It wasn't just the color that made it an expensive gift. The fabric itself was finely woven of soft wool.

"What a beautiful kerchief," I said, setting it back down.

The lass blushed a little, but her hand didn't stop the spindle from twirling on its axis.

"It's not from the village here, is it?" I continued, making small talk. "Was it a gift?"

The redness spread from her cheeks down her neck.

"From a man of means, I would imagine. Your betrothed?" As if I didn't know the answer. No farmhand could have afforded such an expensive betrothal gift.

Ebba quietly shook her head.

"Oh," I said, putting my hand on her arm. "Maybe you don't have a fiancé?"

She shook her head again.

"A beautiful girl like you?" I said, leaving my hand resting on her soft arm. "But it *was* a gift, right?"

She nodded.

"From a man of means, as I said?"

Just then the door opened. I turned and saw Estrid eyeing me with suspicion, a look I responded to with a friendly nod.

"Good day, Estrid. I was just admiring Ebba's kerchief."

Estrid looked sharply from my face to my hand, which was resting on her daughter's arm. I gently removed it.

"It was a gift, I understand. From a nobleman." I looked Estrid in the eye. "No doubt as thanks for some big favor."

"What are you . . . ?" Estrid began, her eyes narrowing.

I snuck a glance at Ebba, who was quietly spinning away.

"I'm sure all three of us know what I'm implying."

I said it coolly. I wanted to show them that I, too, understood how Ebba had earned this token of appreciation.

Ebba's response was to bend over farther, becoming even more engrossed in her spinning. Her mother, on the other hand, came over and stood in front of me with her hands on her hips.

"No, we don't," Estrid said tersely.

"A gift like that?" I said, raising my eyebrows at her. "From a nobleman? Come now, Estrid, we both know what noblemen are willing to pay pretty farm girls for."

No sooner had the words left my mouth than I realized my foolish mistake. It didn't take Estrid's angry outburst, either. I'd already realized my stupidity before she unleashed her torrent of abuse.

Of course I'd been wrong. Of course I should have realized it before I fired off my foolhardy, bullheaded remarks about farm girls. Ribald, the best and therefore also the richest farmer in the village, would never allow his daughter to wear a token showing that she'd been a nobleman's whore. What was I thinking?

He might have had to put up with Ebba allowing a nobleman between her legs—rarely can a farmer do anything to stop a thane who wants to claim what he considers to be his due. But he would never allow her to publicly wear the evidence of her shame.

I held my hand up to fend off Estrid's rain of anger, as I thought like crazy. Could I get myself out of this pinch? I hadn't actually said the name of whore, thereby branding the girl. I had to try.

"Stop, my good woman," I pleaded. "You've misunderstood me."

The "good woman" continued her angry outburst, making it clear that she wasn't convinced.

"I didn't mean who you think I meant," I said, standing up and putting on what I hoped was a sorrowful expression, "and I apologize if you took it that way. I would never have dreamt of implying that your Ebba could do something like that."

Estrid had stopped scolding me, but the anger was still blazing in her cheeks and her eyes.

"I meant," I quickly continued, soothingly, "that noblemen are always willing to pay a farmer for his silence. Well, yes, I said pretty farm girls, but I'm sure you understand that that was just because I wanted Ebba to know that I find her pretty. Believe me," I drooped sadly. "I would never think something like *that* of your family."

"Think what?" Ribald asked.

None of us had heard or seen Ribald coming. Elvina stood next to him, glaring from her mother to me. I swallowed a mouthful of air at the arrival of the burly farmer.

"Nothing," I hurried to say. "A stupid misunderstanding. I just want to know who gave your daughter this kerchief, and why he needed to buy her silence with it."

Estrid's bosom still rose and fell in angry heaves, but she didn't say anything. It was unclear, but also unimportant, whether she believed me or was just scared stiff of angering her husband by telling him what I'd implied. All that mattered to me was that she didn't say anything.

I had to seize the conversation, before it was too late.

"Ebba, who gave you the kerchief?"

I might have convinced her mother, but I could tell from the look Ebba gave me that she did not believe me. She wasn't just hurt, but angry and offended. She stopped her spindle without a word, raising it and the finished yarn in one hand. She picked up the basket of carded wool in the other and walked past me, flashing me a taunting look.

I planned to stop her by putting my hand on her arm when an *ahem* from Ribald made me think better of it.

Ebba went into the farmhouse and closed the door behind her. I turned to her parents.

"Then I will have to ask you," I said.

They exchanged glances; then Ribald nodded to the door. Estrid went inside and Ribald followed her, pulling their youngest daughter in behind him.

Elvina turned around in the doorway and stuck her tongue out at me.

Chapter 28

swore at myself, banishing myself to the darkest pits of hell. How could I have been so dumb? Obviously Ebba could never have so flagrantly shown off something she'd earned through whoring. And the realization stung that I'd actually known this before I rolled out my "I'm sure all three of us know what I'm implying." If only I had held my tongue, I was convinced Ebba would have told me the truth about the kerchief.

I asked after Winston at the monastery gate and learned that he and Alfilda were with Turold, so I headed for the hall. The monastery was completely peaceful—no spearmen to be seen. The only sign that soldiers were staying at the monastery came from Ulf and Wulfgar, who sat side by side in the sun in front of the guesthouse.

I greeted them on my way to the hall, where I stepped into Turold's chamber after a quick knock on the door was followed by a quiet "Come in."

Once inside, I stopped in surprise. Winston and Alfilda weren't the only ones present. Brother Edgar was there as well, which didn't surprise me, because I hadn't bought his assurance that he wasn't the abbot's trusted man. But I was taken aback to see that the two Benedictines were in the room, too.

Apparently I'd walked in on yet another monastic squabble, judging from the way the four clergymen were looking at each other.

Edmund—breathing heavily, the back of his neck bright red—leaned over in front of Turold, whose lips were pressed together into a line. Edmund was so focused on whatever Turold had just said that he didn't even glance up when I stepped in.

Simon was just as pale as Edmund was red, but I suspected that wasn't just due to the argument. Simon was not merely leaning on the wall. He seemed to be pressing his body back *into* the wall in an attempt to get as far away from Alfilda as possible.

I smiled at him cheerfully and then at Winston, who threw up his hands, shook his head in disgust, and said, "Allow us to leave you to your business."

Winston shot me a look and then spun on his heel and headed for the door, followed by Alfilda, who I noticed made no effort to leave space between herself and Simon as she walked past him. She stopped and thanked Turold for his time, and then I followed her out of the room.

Once we were well clear, Winston glanced across the grass at Ulf and Wulfgar, who didn't look up from their one-sided conversation. Even in a case where only one of them could actually speak, off-duty soldiers always felt an easy sense of camaraderie with each other as men who have known fighting and danger. I hurried after Winston, who headed for the gate.

Soon we were once again seated on the bench in front of the village's little public house, each with our own tankard of ale.

"So what was the argument about this time?" I asked, in no hurry to explain my stinging defeat with Ebba.

"You have to admire Turold's patience," Winston said, shaking his head. "Can you imagine: those two louts barged in without so much as a knock on the door, interrupted our conversation, and demanded to know how long they were going to have to wait until Turold was ready to travel."

"Ready to travel?" I looked from Winston to Alfilda. Did the monks not understand that no one would be allowed to leave the monastery until we'd completed our investigation? Then I realized that they had never even dreamt that the travel ban applied to them as well.

"Ready to travel," Winston repeated. "You remember that first night? They demanded that Turold go to Peterborough with them so they could convince him that this monastery is a daughter to their own?"

"I remember, but Turold rejected that rather forcefully," I said with a nod.

"And you think that settled the matter?" Winston asked rhetorically. "That the two parties agreed to disagree? Edmund doesn't see it that way. He believes that if he just keeps pushing his perspective, eventually Turold will concede. It's like a lie: if you get enough people to repeat it, it ends up being accepted as the truth."

"What did our hosts tell him?"

"Told him to go to hell," Alfilda said with a chuckle, "which almost made Simon the Subordinate open his mouth, but then he saw me—he had otherwise been avoiding looking at me—and he clammed up."

"So did you get to talk to Turold?" I asked.

"He willingly discussed Eadwin's stay here," Winston said. "Thane Eadwin arrived unannounced but was of course welcomed since he's the jarl's son. However, after hosting him for three weeks, Turold decided it was time for Eadwin to move on."

Things obviously hadn't gone the way Turold wanted. And sure enough, Winston continued, "An opinion Eadwin loudly dismissed."

"So the monastery sent a messenger to the jarl?" I guessed. That would have been the normal thing to do.

"Who immediately dispatched Ælfgar to come retrieve Eadwin."

"And Eadwin obeyed?" I asked.

"Absolutely," Winston said.

We looked at each other, and I could tell we were thinking the same thing: only Ælfgar could tell us both why Eadwin had felt compelled to stay at the monastery for so long and what had been said to get him to come back home.

"And this Erik?" I asked.

"Godfrid, as he's still called here. Yes, he and Eadwin spoke to each other quite a bit. Turold claims he doesn't know what they had to talk about."

"Claims?" I said.

"I'm sure Turold knows more than he's admitting," Winston said, tugging at his nose, "but I'm also sure that we'll never get him to open his mouth about it."

"The confessional?" I guessed.

"Turold is an honest man who would rather die than break the sanctity of the confessional," Winston said with a nod.

We sat for a while in silence, and then Alfilda asked if I'd had any luck with Ebba.

I pouted at her, but when she just looked back innocently, I shrugged and told them what had happened.

They listened in silence, but I saw the crease appear between Winston's eyebrows as my account proceeded, ultimately ending with my admission of how dumb I had been not to see how things fit together sooner.

"Dumb?" Winston said, his voice thick with anger. "Damn foolish is what you were."

"Well, if I was, it's not like I was the only one," I sulked. I looked at Alfilda and said, "You said yourself that noblemen pay farm girls to spread their legs."

"Yes," she said with a nod. "You and I think the same way."

At least she wasn't making excuses.

"Well, what's done is done," Winston said with a sigh. "Now the question is what the devil we do next."

Chapter 29

suppose you've considered his name?" Alfilda asked, pushing her half-emptied tankard away and leaning in over the table. I was about to answer that there were as many Eriks in the Danelaw as there were sheep, but then I realized what she meant and nodded.

"He was seeking God's peace, hence the name Godfrid. Yes, we've considered that," Winston said, picking up Alfilda's tankard and drinking.

"Or he'd found it," Alfilda said, snatching her tankard back.

Which Winston had also implied. Men who run away from their past, sinking into monastic amnesia, are usually struggling to come to terms with that past. Or, as Harding used to say: The monastery is where remorseful men or those lacking influence seek refuge.

Although of course a person who feels he has already made up for his sin could still choose to live among silent brothers to make sure he remains at peace—or to keep from sinning again.

"Not that it matters," Winston said with a yawn, scratching at his scalp.

"Doesn't it?" Alfilda said. Something in her voice got our attention.

"The abbot said Eadwin and Godfrid talked to each other quite a bit," Alfilda said, her elbows propped on the table and her hands over her eyes, as if she needed a moment alone with her thoughts in order to express them. "Let's suppose they either knew each other in the past, or Eadwin recognized Godfrid, whom he had once known by the name of Erik . . . Actually," she said, taking her hands off her eyes briefly, "it might not matter which."

Neither Winston nor I spoke. We both waited as she covered her eyes again and continued.

"What matters is that they didn't just exchange a polite word or two," Alfilda said, "but 'talked quite a bit with each other'—that was how the abbot put it, you recall. In other words, the jarl's son knows that Godfrid is the same as Erik, so he must also know what drove this Erik to the monastery. Do you agree?"

We both nodded. What she was saying made sense.

"And that knowledge could have been dangerous for Godfrid," Alfilda continued. "If Godfrid *had* made his peace with God, Eadwin could have threatened to reveal his true identity. Maybe his sin was so great that the monks would have wanted to kick him out. Maybe the threat was that Eadwin would tell the victim of the sin where Godfrid was."

"But," I objected, "surely Godfrid would have just said that nothing could threaten the peace he felt in God?"

"Maybe," Alfilda said, "but would it be the truth? Although you're probably right. But, maybe Eadwin realized that Godfrid *hadn't* reconciled with Our Lord. If that were the case, Godfrid would die in sin and be robbed of his chance at salvation. Then the threat of revealing him would carry more weight."

"Revenge would have lain him in his grave without atonement," Winston said, "ensuring him all the agonies of hell—if the sin was as serious as we're assuming."

"Exactly," Alfilda said, finally removing her hands from her eyes and leaning back with a satisfied smile. Then she suddenly bit her lip and looked at us despondently. "Aside, of course, from the fact that it's a bunch of hogwash, which can't be important after all."

Winston and I exchanged puzzled looks, but then he nodded.

"It's hogwash because Eadwin wasn't the one killed," Winston said.

"Exactly," Alfilda said, her mouth twitching in exasperation.

I leaned over in annoyance and rested my forehead in my hands. Aside from that, her idea had made so much sense. I heard ducks quacking mixed with geese cackling and saw the wispy-haired goose girl out of the corner of my eye, driving her flock across the green. Above me a kite cried shrilly, and a small bell rang somewhere in the monastery. It must be time for Vespers, which made sense given how empty my stomach felt.

"But," I said, groping after the thought that had flitted through my mind. "But . . . maybe you *were* on to something after all. Maybe we just need to look at the whole thing the other way around?"

They both looked at me.

"Eadwin recognized Godfrid," I continued eagerly. "We all agree that's how it started. And then Eadwin left the monastery when he received a message from his father, whereas Godfrid stayed behind. A few months later, we find Godfrid murdered. There's got to be some kind of connection."

"Sure," Winston said, reaching his hand out and stroking Alfilda's cheek. "Eadwin told someone where Godfrid was."

"Either because he made good on his threat, or—if we're wrong, and he didn't threaten the monk—maybe purely by accident," Alfilda said, and then sat up straighter.

"Yes, that's it," Winston said. "So now we just have to find out who Eadwin talked to in the last few months."

"We were supposed to have a little chat with Ælfgar next, weren't we?" I said with a smile.

Winston turned to Alfilda and said, "If it's alright, Halfdan and I will see to that. Will you try your hand with Ebba?"

Alfilda nodded in agreement.

"Good," Winston said, standing up. "Vespers will be over soon; then the monks will head to the refectory for dinner. We'll do the same and see if we can get a seat close to Thane Ælfgar. I wonder if you couldn't convince Estrid to let you dine at her table?"

Alfilda thought that would probably work and left us with a promise from Winston that he would come find her as soon as we were done with Ælfgar.

When we arrived at the refectory, the monks were already seated around the long table. Edmund and Simon had found seats next to Turold, possibly because Turold wanted to emphasize the polite obligations of a host despite their failure to see eye to eye.

Ulf and Wulfgar sat at the only other table in the room. Ælfgar and Alwyn had taken seats at the other end of that table, so Winston headed for them. Without an invitation, he simply sat down next to Ælfgar and nodded for me to take the seat across from him, so that I ended up sitting next to Alwyn. Neither of them looked up when we sat down.

The food was good: roast pork and root vegetables fried in fat on thick slices of bread. The ale that went with it was hoppy and strong.

I ate in silence, waiting for Winston to take the lead. When he eventually finished chewing, he just said flat out, "So you had to bring Eadwin home by force."

"What in the world—" Ælfgar said, his head coming up with a jerk.

He didn't get any further, because Winston held up a hand to silence him.

"Spare me," Winston said. "I know that Leofwine's son stayed here this summer, and I also know that you came to get him. What had he done to his father that made him need to hide out here for so long?"

"It's none of your business," Ælfgar said with a scowl.

"Oh yes it is," Winston replied calmly, "if it has anything to do with the monk's murder."

"Nonsense," Ælfgar said.

"Eadwin knew Godfrid," Winston said. He spoke calmly, as if he were discussing the weather. "They talked together, and then shortly after Eadwin left the monastery, Godwin was murdered. And I know what he did."

"Impossible," Ælfgar said, looking right at Winston.

"So you admit he committed an offense," Winston said, a smile playing on his lips. "He was trying to foment opposition to King Cnut."

Alwyn moved in his seat next to me, caught off guard, but Ælfgar's eyes had already told me that Winston had hit the nail on the head.

"Eadwin has not forgiven Cnut for his eldest brother's death and doesn't care if there was good reason for the king's actions," Winston said, still speaking very softly and calmly. "Which is why Eadwin sought to consult with other disgruntled thanes."

Ælfgar pressed his lips together, which caused Winston to lean in over the table in confidence.

"I wonder," Winston wondered aloud, "what Cnut would pay for information about his jarl colluding with his enemies?"

I had to admire the way Winston avoided revealing that we were actually here on assignment from Cnut. His words could be interpreted as any man's musings over what the king would pay for information.

"You would lie?" Ælfgar said grudgingly.

His voice was hoarse and hardly as toned down as my master's. I looked up, but it was clear that no one was paying any attention. The monks kept eating in silence, and Wulfgar had apparently accepted responsibility for entertaining the tongueless man, because Wulfgar was leaning forward and running on at the mouth, but keeping his voice quiet. Presumably he was taking a cue from Winston, guessing that Winston was speaking softly to avoid disturbing the other diners.

"So my guesses about Eadwin are correct?" Winston asked.

"Come with me," Ælfgar said, nodding.

We followed him out of the hall and across the grass to the church, where he continued on around the building and then walked over to the palisade. Here he sat down in the grass with his back against the posts so that he had an unimpeded view of the monastery grounds. We sat down next to him while Alwyn walked down to the door to the Lady Path, which I'd opened yesterday. He pulled it open and positioned himself in the doorway so he could be sure no one was on the path outside.

"Do not think that I haven't guessed that you ride on the king's business, Winston the Illuminator," Ælfgar said, eyeing Winston gloomily. "Take him the truth."

"Which is?" Winston inquired politely.

"That your guess was wrong." Ælfgar sounded certain. "Leofwine and his sons realize that Norman deserved to die by Cnut's order. And none of them would dream of opposing the king. They realize that Cnut is the only one who can secure England against harrowing feuds and wars and also ensure their power as ealdorman and thanes."

"So what was Eadwin doing here in the east?" I could tell from Winston's tone that he believed Ælfgar.

"Eadwin is young and hotheaded. When his brother Leofric was promoted to lead the fyrd, Eadwin demanded an equivalent promotion, which of course his father had to refuse him."

"Of course?"

Ælfgar nodded.

"There's only one fyrd. Besides, the jarl is of the opinion—an opinion he made no attempt to hide from his son—that Eadwin is a little too young to be promoted. But he promised that on the very day Eadwin was old enough, he would reward him the way he had rewarded his brother."

"And when Eadwin ran off in a sulk like any boy who hadn't gotten his way," Winston said with a smile, "that proved that Leofwine was right."

"And when Eadwin realized that the road to power led through his father," Ælfgar said, "he was too proud to go straight home with his tail between his legs like any puppy. Instead he came and hid himself away here at the monastery. And that is the truth."

"Why is this all so secret?" I asked, stifling a yawn.

"Because Leofwine, like other people, prefers to keep his family's squabbles behind closed doors."

"I believe you," Winston said, rolling his shoulders. "But then why lie about Godfrid?"

"About Godfrid? I haven't lied about the monk."

I leaned over and pointed at Alwyn.

"Your man claimed that he hadn't seen Godfrid here when you came to fetch Eadwin."

"That's the truth," Ælfgar said. "We didn't."

"But he was here," Winston said, his brow furrowed. "We know that Eadwin spoke to Godfrid quite a bit."

"Yes, you said that before." Now Ælfgar's brow was also furrowed. "But Alwyn is right. We didn't see him."

I caught Winston's attention and stood up.

Turold still sat at the long table.

"Abbot Turold," I said in a polite voice.

He looked up.

"You told my master that Eadwin Leofwineson and Godfrid spoke to each other quite a bit this summer. And yet neither Ælfgar nor Alwyn saw Godfrid when they were here. Where was he?"

"I'm sure you can imagine," Turold said with a sigh.

I could? Then I laughed to myself. His violent temper, of course.

"He was sent to the church to atone for inappropriate conduct?" I guessed.

"He had scolded our guest most rudely," Turold said with a nod, "so I sentenced him to three days' penance before the altar."

"Scolded? About what?"

But here the abbot had only an apology. All anyone knew was that the two men had stood next to each other during a service, which was suddenly interrupted by a stream of invectives from Godfrid's mouth.

So he had offended both a guest and God's house of worship.

"And how did Eadwin react?" I asked.

"He just laughed and asked Godfrid to remember who had the upper hand," Turold said, his eyes filling with tears. And that was all Turold could—or would—tell me.

When I returned to the palisade, Winston and Ælfgar stood up.

"Ælfgar says that Eadwin has been all over the place since he left the monastery." Winston shook his head apologetically. "His father wanted to show him he trusted him and sent him to ride out on a number of business matters."

So it would be nearly impossible to find out whom he'd revealed Godfrid's secret to. I told Winston what I'd learned from Turold, that whatever Eadwin had threatened Godfrid with, it had been enough to make Godfrid lose his temper.

"So Alfilda was right when she suggested Eadwin recognized Godfrid," I concluded.

"Yes," Winston said with a nod. "I've learned that that's often the case."

Chapter 30

he next morning it threatened to rain. Clouds had come in overnight from the west. Now in the early morning they towered over the hills, and in the distance stripes of rain cut through the sky below them.

I woke up alone; Winston hadn't slept here last night either. After my morning pee and a look at the weather, I returned to our room, lay down flat on my back, and stared at the ceiling.

I thought back to the night before. Winston hadn't let Ælfgar off that easily. He had asked him if he'd be willing to swear that what he'd told us about Eadwin was true.

"Gladly, if giving you my word is not enough," Ælfgar said. A wrinkle in his brow made him seem less willing than his words.

Winston let his demand slide. He knew better than to provoke a thane who insisted on his word being enough. I had urged Winston to put some pressure on Ælfgar about his *current* visit to the monastery, but Winston pretended not to understand what I wanted. After we had parted from Ælfgar and Alwyn, I asked him why.

"Based on what he said, I doubt his business here has anything whatsoever to do with Godfrid. And," Winston had added, glancing at the gate, "there's no point in pressuring him to answer a question we know he doesn't want to answer. Better to let him leave as our friend, convinced that we believe him."

With that, Winston had nodded and walked off toward the gate, leaving me on my own.

I shivered under my blanket. A draft came in from the window, and I listened to the morning sounds of village life: the sharp cock-a-doodle-doos of a rooster; sheep bleating to their lambs; and a distant cow, mooing to make people aware that it wanted to be milked.

The spring calves were separated from the cows now, and it was time to make the cheese that would last through the winter, or else be paid to the thane, jarl, or king as tax. Soon the grass and feed would run out, the milk would dry up, and the cattle would be put into the stables for the winter.

I heard a delicate bell and then the monks' feet scuffling through the grass outside on their way to Matins, which meant breakfast wouldn't be on the table for another hour.

I swung my legs out of bed and shivered in the morning cold. I walked out to the water trough, where I managed to wash—trembling from the cold— before rubbing the warmth back into my body with a clean horsecloth.

I ate breakfast alone and in silence. Then I set off for Ribald's farm, where I found a contented Winston sitting next to his woman, both of them eating their sweet bolted rye bread. They washed it down with ale so malty that just the scent of it made my nostrils quiver pleasurably.

Apparently Winston and Alfilda had managed to smooth over my affront from the day before, because Estrid offered me a tankard. I nodded in thanks. I had to smack my tongue in appreciation, the brew was that good.

We chatted about the weather as my companions finished eating. It wasn't until we were out on the street that I asked whether Alfilda had had any luck getting anything out of Ebba the previous evening.

Alfilda looked up at the dark clouds, shook her chestnut locks, and apologized. The girl had been willing enough to talk to her, but as soon as they approached the question that Alfilda was actually interested in, the girl clammed up.

"And now?" I asked, my eyes following the path of a low-flying swallow.

The answer surprised me.

"Turold wants to see us," Winston announced, and I looked at him in surprise.

He hurriedly corrected himself and clarified that actually just *he* had been asked to come. I had suspected Turold might finagle a meeting to see Alfilda again. But when and how had the message been passed on, and what did Turold want to discuss?

"Well," Winston said, putting a hand on Alfilda's shoulder. "A monk came awhile ago. But it remains to be seen what Turold intends to discuss."

So we were going to the monastery.

But no. The invitation was for Winston. And where he went, Alfilda followed.

"What about me?" I asked, annoyed.

Winston had already turned toward the monastery. He turned back around to face me and shrugged.

"I suppose we'll have to wait and see what I get out of the good abbot," he said.

He and Alfilda disappeared up the lane, leaving me seething at being left out.

I grumpily kicked a clod of dirt, looked up at the ominous clouds, and walked aimlessly up the lane, too angry at being left out to think clearly.

At the end of the lane, I heard a girl calling my name and turned around, hoping it was Ebba, then realizing in annoyance that it was just her little sister.

"Go away."

"I don't think I want to," Elvina told me with a defiant look.

"Get lost. I'm not in the mood to play with little kids."

"This is my village, and I'll walk where I please." She put her hands on her hips and stood in the middle of the alley in front of me.

I stifled a smile. This wench certainly did not lack a fighting spirit.

"Fine, you walk whichever way you please, and then I'll choose another way."

"I came to help," she said, looking disappointed.

"I doubt you can help me," I said, already walking away from her. I felt the first raindrops landing on my hair. Glancing up, I accepted that it was just a matter of minutes until it started pouring.

I looked around. A little farther down the street I saw an unwalled hayloft. If she'd been her big sister, I would've gladly invited her to share this aromatic berth with me, convinced that my hands, lips, and sweet words could get her talking.

I strode over to it, yanked a stack of hay down from the hayloft, allowed my backside to slide down into it, and heard the rain start drumming away on the bark roof above me.

Through a veil of rain I saw the girl standing in the lane, and I took pity on her.

"Come in out of the rain!"

She stood there for a long time, seemingly unaffected by the drops soaking her clothes. Eventually she shrugged and joined me, sliding down into the hay and jabbing me in the side with her fist.

"And here I thought you wanted to know what my sister won't tell you."

I gaped at her. She gave me an impish look back.

"Did your sister tell you?" I asked.

She shook her head so her hair splashed water droplets onto my face.

"Then you don't actually know," I said.

"I do, too." She poked me in the side with her index finger this time. "So there."

"How could you know if she hasn't told you?" I said, shaking my head at her, doubtful. "Did your father or mother tell you?"

If that were the case, Winston would no doubt prefer I direct my questioning to them. But I wasn't Winston.

"Of course not, you simpleton," she said. "I was there."

"You were there?" *Where*? I wondered. Where Ebba had earned her blue kerchief?

"In church, of course." The lass leaned back and gave me a cunning look.

I inhaled.

"Good. Please excuse me for my stupidity before. I would very much like to hear what you know."

"That's better," she said, now flirting outright. "If you give me a kiss, I'll tell you."

"A kiss!" I scoffed. "You're a child."

"A child who knows something you want to know," she said, crinkling up her nose. "Well?"

I glared at her and then looked around. It was still pouring, and the lane was deserted. They were probably all sitting inside with full ale tankards in front of them. I leaned over and kissed her cheek.

"No," she giggled. "Here."

I looked from her puckered lips to her inviting eyes, sighed to myself, and leaned over.

Her lips were warm and dry, so I felt it when they parted and a small tongue slipped between my own. I pulled back, startled.

"No, stop it," I ordered.

Elvina gave me a disappointed look.

"Calm down. I just wanted to know why Ebba and her friends always find it so fascinating to talk about. And that was it. It didn't even taste good."

That wanton little minx! I wanted to tell her that many a young maiden had sighed beneath my lips, but then I noticed her mocking look.

"It didn't taste bad, either," she laughed, "but I don't see the appeal."

"Good," I said, exhaling. "Well, now you've received your payment. So let's hear it."

"Ebba was in love with our neighbor's son, a stupid lad, who luckily didn't want anything to do with her. So she went to church to pray to Saint Winfrith." Elvina pushed herself back up in the hay until she sat upright. "Stupid girl. As if some old saint could help her with that. I followed her."

I noticed she was shivering. The rain had cooled the air, and I pulled my tunic over my head and passed it to her.

"Thanks." She almost disappeared in the garment. "Ebba is deathly afraid of rats, and it's such fun to tease her, since I'm good at squeaking the way they do. I let her go down into the ambulatory"—Elvina had trouble with the odd word—"first and I waited for a while. Then I went down through the other door. I heard her mumbling, but before I could start my rat squeaks, I heard footsteps in the church above, and two men started talking."

She was a good storyteller, this lass, and had my full attention.

"I recognized the one voice. It was the monk that got killed. The other voice I'd also heard before, but it took me awhile to recognize it. It was the son of our jarl."

"But I don't suppose they were talking loud enough that you could hear what they said?"

"Yes, I could. You can hear super well down there in that passageway."

I had noticed that myself when I'd been down there, so I nodded.

"Go on," I told her.

"The jarl's son threatened the monk. The jarl's son was going to send a messenger to someone up in Northumbria, someone who wanted to take revenge on the monk."

That sounded credible.

"Revenge? Did he say for what?"

"Yes," Elvina said, nodding eagerly. "He said Godfrid broke his oath when he led Uhtred to his death."

I sat bolt upright. Uhtred was the ealdorman who had been murdered after King Cnut had agreed to a formal exchange of peace between them. How long ago had that been? I thought about it. A couple of years at the most.

We had determined that the monk's name had been Erik. And now I knew who he was. Everyone had heard of Cnut's thane, Erik, who gave his oath-bound word that the king had promised Uhtred and his men safe conduct, that they would ride in peace. But he led them to their deaths. And this Erik had not been seen or heard from since the killings.

"Does that help you?" Elvina asked, watching me.

"A lot," I said with a nod. "Then what happened? They must have found you two."

"The two men argued for a long time; then the monk said he would reward the jarl's son for not saying anything."

"Reward him? With what?"

"The jarl's son asked that, too," Elvina said with a shrug, "but the monk just said he would think of a way. And then they left."

"They left?" I said. That didn't add up. Why buy Ebba's silence if they didn't even know she'd been listening?

"Well, that's what I thought," Elvina said. "So then I started making my rat noises, and Ebba totally lost it and ran back up into the church."

Ah. I understood.

"But Brother Godfrid hadn't left yet?" I said.

"No, I think he was still kneeling in front of the altar. At least that's what Ebba told Father and Mother."

"So he bought her silence with an expensive kerchief," I concluded. "Did he figure out that you were there, too?"

"No. I'm not that dumb! I waited until they'd left before I came out."

No, she was far from dumb, this girl. But there was one thing I still didn't understand.

"Brother Godfrid is dead. Why is Ebba still keeping this all secret?"

"How should I know?" Elvina said, shrugging her shoulders melodramatically. "He made her swear that she wouldn't say anything. My sister believes in keeping her word."

Unlike the murdered thane, I thought. I leaned back and thought for a moment. Then I asked where Erik had gotten the kerchief.

"Well, obviously he didn't have it there with him in the church," Elvina said, looking at me as if I were an idiot. "But he promised her something nice if she would swear to keep her mouth shut about what she'd heard. And then he brought it back from Peterborough with him one day when he'd been up there on monastery business."

The rain had let up by now, so I stood up. Elvina pulled my tunic over her head, and I put it back on, my mind elsewhere. Now I knew who Godfrid was and why his hand had been chopped off. As for who the murderer was, Winston and I would find that out together.

I hesitated, still grumpy about being excluded by Winston and Alfilda. And yet, as long as Winston paid me, it would be his wishes and not my own that stipulated the conditions of my employment. Presenting my newly acquired knowledge to him was my only option.

"Was it worth it?" Elvina asked, tugging on my arm.

"Most definitely," I said with a laugh.

I hesitated at the drip line from the eaves. The rain had turned the street to mud, but the sun had come out and now the mud was steaming. I glanced back at Elvina, who was once again shivering from the cold in her rain-drenched clothes.

Oh, what the hell. Had I not just said that she had most definitely earned her salary?

She watched me wide-eyed as I leaned in, took her face between my hands, and put my lips to hers. When my tongue opened her mouth, it was met by her own. She tasted fresh and young. I drew the kiss out until I heard her stifled sigh. Then my lips released hers and I gently stroked her cheeks.

Her eyes, which looked right into mine, were bright.

"Now you've been paid," I said with a smile. "And this will not happen again."

Chapter 31

inston and Alfilda stepped out of the abbot's chamber just as I had raised my hand to knock. Winston could tell I was excited.

"You have news?" he asked.

I nodded.

"News that can be discussed here?" he asked.

I looked around. There was no one in the small hallway outside the abbot's chamber, but monks could presumably walk by at any time, so I shook my head.

"Let's go to my room," I suggested.

Winston didn't comment on the fact that I now referred to the room as mine instead of ours. He merely proceeded calmly, holding Alfilda's hand. On our way, I casually asked if they could fill me in on what Turold had wanted.

"Permission to bury Brother Godfrid, since the corpse is starting to smell," Winston said.

"Surely the abbot could have just decided that on his own?" I said, peering over at Winston distrustfully.

"He did, but he's a polite man, the good Turold, so he wanted to know if we still needed access to the deceased." Winston pushed the door to my room open.

Once inside, Winston and Alfilda sat down on the bed that had been Winston's while I made sure the door was closed all the way and then took a seat on my own.

"Well?" Winston said expectantly.

I recounted my conversation with Elvina. As I spoke, they sat leaning together, Alfilda with her eyes half-closed, Winston watching me attentively.

"So I think the murderer is very clear," I said. Godfrid's true identity was my first piece of news. My second was the identity of the murderer. I waited to give them a chance to guess this for themselves.

"Ælfgar?" Winston suggested, tugging at his nose.

"Who else? He's the only thane who was staying in the monastery the night of the murder. None of us know his family, but I wonder if he won't turn out to have kin from north of the River Humber? After all, they marry for power, influence, and silver, these noblemen."

Winston grinned at me in amusement.

"I was born a nobleman," I said, gesturing theatrically with my right hand. "I do know how they work."

"But Ælfgar was willing to swear," Winston said, shaking his head thoughtfully.

"No," Alfilda replied, shaking her head more vigorously. "He was willing to swear that what he said about Eadwin was the truth."

"Exactly," I said, sitting up straighter in excitement. "And no one asked Ælfgar what he didn't say. Think about it, Winston! Ælfgar is Jarl Leofwine's trusted man, who's sent to the very edge of the jarl's territory to fetch the man's son Eadwin back home. That same son has discovered that a man who is trying to hide behind a cowl, Brother Godfrid, is actually a nithing, none other than the man who led Uhtred to his certain death even though he'd sworn him peace and safe-conduct. And furthermore, Eadwin knows that the thane he rides home with, Thane Ælfgar, is related by blood to Uhtred, the victim of the betrayal. It makes perfect sense that Eadwin would share what he'd learned with Ælfgar as they rode back home."

"And then Ælfgar asked us to stand in for the reeve and investigate the murder?" Winston objected skeptically.

"Maybe that was a diversionary tactic. Or lust for power," I suggested. "Both of them afflictions noblemen are known to be susceptible to."

"But," Alfilda said. She stood up, walked over to the window, and looked out. "There *is* another possibility."

Winston and I turned to look at her.

"Prior Edmund. He's noble-born, isn't he?" Her gray eyes looked from Winston to me.

I nodded grudgingly.

"Wulfgar told me he was from the North, that his family has owned land up below the Scots for many generations."

"Northumbria, in other words," Alfilda said.

"But Edmund's family is Saxon," I said. "Uhtred was an Angle."

Winston gave me an almost pitying look, and then I remembered Wulfgar's words: *Noblemen are first and foremost noblemen. Only after that do they become Saxons or Danes.*

"Edmund is conceited and hot tempered, but a murderer?" I said. I just didn't believe it.

"He *was* alone in the church with Godfrid," Winston said.

"After Godfrid was already dead," I said.

"Or so he claims," Winston pointed out.

He was right about that. We had only Edmund's word that he'd found the monk dead. We had to concede that the case wasn't solved yet.

"We're going to have to talk to them both again," Winston said, getting up off the bed.

"Who do we interview first?" I asked, looking from Winston to Alfilda.

"Whichever one we encounter first," Winston said.

He opened the door and we made our way back out into the daylight. The storm clouds had passed and it was sunny once again. The brightness felt refreshing after the rain.

The question of whom we would interview first was answered when we saw five men coming over the grass toward the monastery hall.

Ælfgar and Alwyn both wore their traveling clothes and walked with their legs spread slightly, the way even seasoned riders find relief right after a long ride. They walked side by side in silence. Thane Ælfgar never found it necessary to emphasize his rank or authority by walking ahead of his spearman.

Edmund and Simon walked just to their left, following a tall monk I'd seen in the refectory but hadn't paid any attention to. Edmund's round face was scrunched up in rage, an emotion also evident in Simon's sharp eyes, which—the way the sun hit them—looked black.

No one noticed when we joined them. When they reached the door of Turold's chamber, which the tall brother opened for us, we followed them in as if we also had been summoned by the abbot.

Which, it turned out, was indeed why Edmund and Simon were there. To their immense consternation, Turold had summoned them.

The door had scarcely swung shut behind us when Edmund proclaimed—his voice trembling with indignation—that he was not in the habit of allowing himself to be summoned by any old novice. His outburst earned him just a brief nod from Turold's head.

Simon noticed us and lurched back—to get away from Alfilda, who had positioned herself right next to him—only to discover that he was then very close to Ælfgar, which seemed to make him suffer as much as if Alfilda had put her hand on his arm.

It couldn't be easy, I thought, being equally afraid of women *and* noblemen with elfish names. For a moment the thought remained with me, but then Turold started talking, and it drifted out of my head again.

"I will not apologize for having guests summoned when it suits me in my own monastery," Turold said. On previous occasions I had thought Turold sounded like a weak old man, but he surprised me again by speaking firmly, as someone who doesn't brook contradiction.

All the same, Edmund opened his mouth, presumably to protest that he wasn't a guest. Turold raised his hand and stopped him.

"I asked you to come to my chambers once and for all to quash this laughable claim that we should be subject to Peterborough," Turold said.

I heard the two Benedictines gasp for breath, but Turold's hand silenced them again before they could speak.

"We've known for a long time that your alleged document, on which you base your claim, is a forgery, but we couldn't prove it until today," Turold said.

The two monks looked at each other, dumbfounded, apparently too shocked to even respond.

"This summer we expressed our grievance to Jarl Leofwine's man, Ælfgar, who promised to help us if he could," Turold said, and then turned to Ælfgar. "Perhaps you'd like to take this part yourself?"

Ælfgar stepped forward.

"Although it is well-known that the church prefers to handle its own matters," Ælfgar said, "my master, Jarl Leofwine, became concerned when I told him about the dispute between your two institutions. Just as kings and noblemen should keep the peace for the benefit of the land, so too should the church strive to maintain peace in its own house. And as the jarl is obligated to restore the peace in his jarldom if someone breaks it, so too is he responsible for rehabilitating justice when it is trampled underfoot. And when the church is in dispute with itself, it falls to he who wears the sword in the king's name to reestablish the peace, when the church's own magnates fail to do so."

Edmund was about to say something, but one look from Ælfgar stopped him.

"So I sent men out to scour the land and investigate, hoping to track down someone who could give a definitive answer to the question of whether the document you Peterborough brothers refer to could be authentic. Word reached me a few weeks ago that you could be proven wrong. I returned to Brixworth as soon as I could."

I heard a half-stifled gasp from Simon, but Edmund managed to compose himself enough to speak first.

"This is outrageous," Edmund spluttered.

"No," Ælfgar said, calmly shaking his head and reaching into his tunic. "Here is a letter from Archbishop Wulfstan, which reached me today from Hampton. If you would be so kind as to read it."

He handed the document to Edmund, who irately noted the wax seal at the bottom. I looked from Edmund to Ælfgar, trying to put my thumb on my fleeting thought from before—there was something about the mention of the archbishop—but to no avail. Edmund pressed his lips together tightly as he read and then passed the letter to Simon, whose head was boiling red.

I thought like crazy, trying to fathom what Leofwine's interest in this conflict was. Then Winston whispered in my ear. "Peterborough is not in the portion of Mercia that belongs to Leofwine."

Now I understood. It was in Leofwine's interest to protect the monasteries that were in his jarldom, to show he could take care of everyone who fell under his power.

It was a trivial added bonus that he happened to be driving a wedge between a competing jarl and a monastery under that man's dominion.

"Do you accept the archbishop's letter?" Ælfgar asked gently.

"The archbishop is the head of the church, not the monasteries," Edmund spluttered, panting like a man on the verge of flinging himself into a fistfight.

"Just read the letter again." Thane Ælfgar spoke calmly. "As Wulfstan writes, Brixworth monastery was founded by King Oswig with the clear clause that it was a free, independent monastery, which could invoke the archbishop's protection if anyone encroached on it. I don't know much about church matters, but I've been told that this is a rare, although not unheard of, setup."

Ælfgar looked pointedly at Edmund and asked, "Am I right?"

"You . . . that's . . . ," Edmund stammered, licking his lips.

"Am I right?" Ælfgar asked again, emphasizing each word.

"This arrangement has been seen before," Edmund confirmed grudgingly.

"And you accept the archbishop's statement that such is the situation with Brixworth?" Ælfgar inquired.

The two Benedictines exchanged glances.

I almost pitied them. They were in somewhat of a predicament. Even the most powerful head of a monastery would have to think twice before going up against the Archbishop of York, King Cnut's lawgiver, the pope's representative in England, and the king's most trusted man beyond his circle of jarls.

The reason for Archbishop Wulfstan's enthusiastic support of the monastery in Brixworth was brilliantly clear, even to me. Like other churchmen, he eyed the conceited conduct of the Benedictines with concern, and an opportunity to assert the church's overlordship was too good to let slip through his hands.

"Do you?" Ælfgar repeated with a hint of sarcasm in his voice.

Edmund bit his lip. Simon shuffled his feet but then stood still again.

"Yes," Edmund eventually said with a slight nod.

"And we won't be hearing any more about this matter from either you or your abbot?" Turold asked.

"The matter is dead," Edmund said, looking like someone forced him to drink vinegar.

Simon shuddered with barely suppressed rage and took a step forward until he bumped into Ælfgar, which caused the monk to stiffen. I leaned over to Alfilda and whispered to her that in Simon's eyes it must be darn near the work of the devil that Abbot Turold was receiving assistance from the elves.

She had no idea what I meant.

"Ælfgar," I explained, "his name means Elf Spear, or Protector of the Elves."

Her eyes grew wide as she contemplated this. Then understanding slid over her face, finally allowing me to put my finger on my previous errant idea. I turned to Winston, who was just explaining that the Benedictines would unfortunately have to stay a little while longer.

"No, Winston," I said, "just let them go."

"But . . ." He looked at me, perplexed.

"We were wrong, Winston," Alfilda told him.

"Yes," I continued, feeling confident now. "It's not Ælfgar or these little monastic farts we need to talk to."

Chapter 32

 thought only Winston would hear my remark, but in my excitement I forgot to muffle my voice, so everyone heard me describe the Benedictines as "monastic farts." Edmund—who was quite obviously thirsting for some outlet for his suppressed rage, now additionally fueled by humiliation—erupted and demanded that I apologize.

I was inclined to ignore him, preoccupied as I was with the idea taking deeper and deeper root in me. As memory after memory popped into my head, I became more and more convinced it was true. To think I hadn't seen it before!

I bit my lip in disappointment at my blindness and was on the verge of shoving Edmund, who had stepped right up against me. Edmund stammered for a second time that I apologize. Winston's voice stopped me. He sharply ordered me to apologize for my choice of words.

I wanted to shrug the whole thing off, but one look from Winston made me think better of it. Plus, compared to what lay ahead, an apology was so profoundly trivial. So I bowed my head in feigned remorse to Edmund and apologized for having called him and his companion names that were not suitable for use where others could hear them.

For a brief instant he looked like he might demand I take it back altogether, but then he shook his head, turned back to Turold, and bid him farewell.

"We shall no longer strain the hospitality between our two monasteries," Edmund declared, attempting to sound superior, and then he left, followed by Simon, who was green with bile. Edmund turned around in the doorway and gave us all one final poisonous look. Ælfgar seemed puzzled.

I suggested to Winston that he, Alfilda, and I should withdraw. Turold nodded to us and we headed for the door. I half expected Ælfgar to try to stop us, but he remained calm, and we reached my room without either him or Alwyn running after us and demanding to know what was going on.

Once back in my room, Winston sat down and stared at the floor. Alfilda and I exchanged glances, and then she said that we knew who had murdered Godfrid.

Winston looked at me, and I nodded.

"I should have seen it a long time ago," I said. "Meanwhile Alfilda, who hasn't had the same experiences I've had, caught it right away once she realized what the names meant."

"So you're both sure?" Winston asked.

Alfilda and I didn't even need to look at each other, both simultaneously blurting out our yeses.

Winston leaned back but found nothing to support his back, so he scooted all the way back against the wall, wiggled his backside comfortably into the mattress, and then looked at me.

"Do tell," he said.

I peeked at Alfilda, who had walked over to the window. She stared out, so I looked at Winston.

"The names are the final proof," I said, "but I should have suspected them much sooner."

"As should I, I suppose," Winston mumbled. "If it's as obvious as all that."

"It's not obvious until you see it, and even then you have to put a number of small details together to see the big picture," I said, winking at him. One of his favorite claims was that, unlike mine, his career had taught him how to look at all the fine details and put together the big picture. "Besides, unlike me, you haven't spent hours talking to Wulfgar, although there is one thing you should have noticed, as should I."

Winston looked puzzled. I gave him some time, and then he suddenly nodded.

"He wears a sword," Winston said.

"Exactly," I said. "He's not a thane. He's a spearman, and yet he wears a sword."

"As does Ulf, the tongueless man," Winston said, looking over at Alfilda, who was still looking out the window.

"We don't know the first thing about Ulf," I pointed out. "He could actually be a thane, but it's not so unusual for a common soldier to win a sword in battle and wear it. Well, as long as he doesn't need the money he could make from selling it. But Wulfgar wears the sword as part of his regular attire. That is something thanes do, not spearmen."

"So he's a thane?" Winston asked.

"Yes, his comments about noblemen notwithstanding," I said with a nod. "Or maybe I should say specifically because of them.

"On that first night when he and I spoke, I said, 'Noblemen are like that.' And he said, 'If you say so.' A common spearman would have agreed with me and added a few observations about how arrogant thanes can be. Wulfgar's response was that of a man who doesn't want to talk about it."

"Go on," Winston said, his brow furrowed.

"After the attack, when I blamed Ulf for not sparing the life of that last outlaw, I was mad at having lost the chance to question the outlaw," I recounted. "Wulfgar, however, who had actually given Ulf a direct order to save the guy's life, seemed strangely resigned. That is not the reaction you would expect from a leader who had just been disobeyed by a common soldier. Insignificant when taken by itself, but in hindsight definitely striking. And finally, they're good friends."

"They probably became friends because Simon let Ulf bunk with Wulfgar," Winston said, not sounding entirely convinced.

"That was an extremely lucky coincidence, I admit," I said, shaking my head. "Which they knew to use to their advantage so we'd all think they'd become friends because they were suddenly sharing a room with each other."

"Coincidences," Winston said, leaning his head back and resting it against the wall. "Coincidences and guesses."

"Yes," I admitted. "But put them together and you have a picture. And I remember when Godfrid interrupted the conversation between Turold and Edmund that first night here. I interpreted Wulfgar's surprise, like my own, as being due to the voice of a man I hadn't noticed. But that's where I was wrong. He was surprised because he had suddenly heard the voice of the man he'd been pursuing for the last two years."

"So Wulfgar didn't *know* his quarry was here?" Winston asked.

I thought it over.

"Maybe," I said, "but if so, he must have looked around for him and not found him. Then he was surprised to suddenly hear his voice. Also, think about Ulf's sword."

"Ulf's sword?" Winston asked, looking up.

"When we asked him . . . in the church," I added, thinking back. "We asked if he had been taking revenge when he took this sword from Eadwulf."

"He said no," Winston said in surprise, thinking back. "Or actually, he shook his head."

"He did," I said. "But first he hesitated. And not for the reason we thought. We assumed he hesitated because it didn't have anything to do with revenge. Well, it *did*, but it turns out it wasn't about getting revenge against Eadwulf. No, Ulf hesitated because the sword he carried had belonged to Jarl Uhtred, who was double-crossed and murdered in Wiheal two years ago."

"Uhtred?" Winston eyed me keenly. "But the sword says Eadwulf."

"Yes, it does. And who was the first ealdorman of Northumbria?"

From the corner of my eye I saw Alfilda turn her head. Then she looked back out the window again. Winston sat up and watched me, his brow furrowed.

"I'm sure you're about to tell me it was Eadwulf."

"You're quite right," I said, outright grinning at him. "I heard many songs about the noble Eadwulf growing up. At my father's estate we used to eat to the sounds of heroic epic poems: songs about my own family, but also other people's—kings, ealdormen, and powerful thanes. That was how we learned to navigate the family tree, to know who we were tied to through blood and marriage, to whom we had sworn allegiance from olden times, and who were our enemies. And yes, Eadwulf—which means Powerful Wolf—was the first high reeve of the House of Bamburgh, a dynasty whose seat was Bamburgh Castle. The most recent scion of that family, Uhtred, was slain through treachery on the king's orders."

I could see that Winston was almost convinced.

"And what about the names?" Winston asked.

"Yes," I said. I glanced over at Alfilda, but she made no move to take over, so I continued. "What Alfilda realized in the abbot's chamber is something I should have seen ages ago: Ulf and Wulfgar. *Ulf* means Wolf in Danish, and *Wulfgar* means Wolf's Protector or Wolf's Spear in Saxon. So Wulfgar is Ulf's protector, the Powerful Wolf's Spear. In other words, it's up to him to strike back on behalf of Eadwulf's family."

"But," Winston objected. "Wulfgar and Ulf slept in a room with several other spearmen. And none of those other spearmen have sworn any oath of allegiance to Wulfgar. He's just their paid leader. Why would the spearmen keep quiet about Ulf and Wulfgar leaving the room in the middle of the night to walk over to the church and murder a monk?"

I laughed out loud.

"Because they were asleep," I said. "We have Wulfgar's word on that. They were staggering around drunk and slept the deep sleep of drunken men. I can't tell you if he contributed to their inebriation with a friendly keg of ale or not, but their drunkenness certainly suited his purposes."

"I'm not completely convinced," Winston said, "but at any rate we'll have to talk to the spearmen who stayed with them."

Just then there was a knock on the door. We opened it to find Ælfgar's slender form.

"You don't want to speak to me or the monastic farts?" Ælfgar asked, eying Winston. "You still suspect me?"

I glared at Winston, who didn't say anything, so I was forced to respond: "We have considered many suspects."

Ælfgar nodded angrily, but then he seemed to digest what I'd said.

"Considered?" he asked, noting the past tense.

"Yes," Winston said, getting up off the bed. "We need to go speak to Wulfgar now."

"He and Ulf just went into the church," Alfilda announced, turning away from the window.

I swore aloud. Hadn't Edmund said something about them wanting to leave?

"Into the church," Winston murmured. "Actually, that might not be the worst place to have our conversation."

Chapter 33

eaving the guesthouse, Winston and Alfilda started across the lawn toward the church. Ælfgar held out his hand and stopped me in the doorway.

"You need to speak to Wulfgar?" he asked.

I was far more concerned with the procession of men I saw in the grass between us and the church. Abbot Turold was in the lead, followed by Brother Edgar. Behind them came a half-dozen monks with their heads bent and their hands folded. They were on their way to church, I realized, presumably to bury the dead.

I watched Winston walk up to Turold and take him by the arm. They spoke together for a few moments, and then Turold turned to Edgar and gave a quiet order. Edgar then turned to the other brethren, who looked at each other in puzzlement before withdrawing back to the monastery hall.

Turold and Edgar remained where they were. Turold said something urgently to Winston, who listened with his head cocked. Then Winston gestured with his hand and proceeded toward the church with Alfilda at his side and the two monks following close behind him.

"You need to speak to Wulfgar?" Ælfgar repeated.

"Follow me," I said. It seemed like Jarl Leofwine's man had as much right as the head of the monastery to witness the case being solved.

So six of us entered the church through the westwork to meet Ulf and Wulfgar, who were walking back down the aisle holding their sword belts. Both had apparently decided to show the proper respect for the abbot's wishes by waiting to put their belts on, probably until after they exited the gate.

It must have been clear that our entry was not the beginning of a funeral procession, because as soon as they spotted us, both abandoned any attempt to show respect for the church or monastery. They took a step apart from each other and stopped. Each held his sword sheath in his left hand so the hilt was centered by his waist and the sword could be drawn quickly.

I bit my lip at the sight and glanced at the altar behind them, realizing it was way too far for me to dream of making it to my weapon. Ælfgar had the same thought, judging from the way I saw him first tense and then relax his muscles.

We stood only a few steps from the two soldiers. The bier, from which a nauseating stench billowed, was off to the side behind them. Winston was to my left and had pushed Alfilda behind him to shield her with his body. Turold and Edgar stood to Alfilda's left, breathing with their hands over their noses. Ælfgar and I stepped forward. Wulfgar stood just in front of me, with Ulf to his left, facing Ælfgar.

Wulfgar watched us calmly, seemingly relaxed, but I could see the muscles in his right forearm quivering with tension. The tongueless Ulf kept his head bent slightly like a bull considering charging.

I gave Winston a questioning look. He shook his head imperceptibly and took a half step forward.

"Are you leaving?" Winston asked the men.

"Prior Edmund would like to return home to Peterborough," Wulfgar said, his voice calm.

"I'm part of the prior's retinue, and I was not informed," Winston replied.

Wulfgar shrugged as if to imply that the prior must not think Winston was all that important. Wulfgar was simply obeying orders.

"But of course I suppose I could receive word any time," Winston continued, watching Ulf. "So, you're riding together?"

"Edmund decided, at Simon's suggestion, to accept Ulf as one of his soldiers," Wulfgar said. His voice didn't so much as quiver.

"Ah, Simon, right. He's really showing quite a bit of support for this tongueless soldier," Winston said, looking straight at Wulfgar. "At your request, perhaps?"

The response was yet another shrug.

Ulf pushed his left foot forward a little. Starting position for a sword-fight. I heard Ælfgar inhale abruptly and signaled to him with my eyes. He nodded in response. We were both ready.

"What's your name?" Winston asked.

I guess Alfilda and I must have convinced him after all. He had obviously decided to put an end to this farce.

"Wulfgar," the soldier said, still standing with his feet at ease.

"Not the name you gave us," Winston said, shaking his head, "the one your father gave you."

Wulfgar looked to his left and his eyes locked on to Ulf's. Ulf drew his hilt out half a hand's width. This caused Ælfgar to bend his knees, but when Ulf allowed his blade to slide back into his sheath again with a clang, Ælfgar relaxed again.

Ulf's gesture seemed meant to give Wulfgar permission to answer the question.

"My name," Wulfgar said calmly, "is Ealdred. My father was Ælfred. I was a Northumbrian thane and Jarl Uhtred's sworn man."

"Uhtred, who was killed by Thurbrand," Winston stated.

"Uhtred, who took the king at his dishonest word and was then cut down, unarmed, along with his thanes, my peers," Ealdred said, his voice trembling now.

Winston lowered his head and said, "Truly a dishonest act. And Ulf?"

"Is Ulf, Uhtred's man."

"And you both survived."

Wulfgar—Ealdred—winced.

"My master sent me to do an errand before he rode the final leg to the hall where he was murdered."

"So you weren't in Wiheal?" Winston asked.

He shook his head in response.

"And Ulf?"

"Ulf didn't follow the jarl into the hall. At Uhtred's command, Ulf took up position outside with his sword at the ready. If there was any sign of treachery, he was to kill one of the Danish prisoners."

I could picture it. Both sides had provided hostages to assure their good faith—hostages who would guarantee with their lives that no treachery would take place. Two groups of men whose fates would rest in the hands of others.

"We've heard what happened there," Winston began.

Ealdred shrugged his shoulders in a gesture that said, *Who hasn't?*

"Inside the hall," Winston continued. "But outside? Did you kill your hostage, Ulf?"

We all looked at the soldier, who looked down in silence. His face blushed with shame.

"As soon as the doors to the hall closed behind the last of Uhtred's men, those nithings struck against our hostages." Ealdred's voice was hoarse with suppressed hatred. "Ulf had no chance to strike. Instead he was clubbed on the back of the head with a spear staff and fell to his knees. He wasn't knocked unconscious, but he was stunned and had to watch helplessly as his sword was taken from his hand and his comrades' heads were chopped off with axes. The bastards had hung up their swords, but their axes lay hidden in the grass."

"And his tongue?" Winston asked.

Ealdred glanced at Ulf, who calmly nodded.

"Ulf tried, dazed as he was, to get to his feet and help his companions, but then he was completely knocked out by an ax, which must have been turned the wrong way, because he was hit by the butt end. When he came to, the whole thing had been over for a long time. Everyone from our side had been killed, and Thurbrand's bloodthirst slaked. He had Ulf's tongue torn out so he couldn't tell anyone about the atrocity."

"But we all heard what happened," Ælfgar said, adding his voice to the conversation for the first time.

Ealdred nodded harshly and said, "Everyone knew that the king had guaranteed Uhtred safe passage, so Thurbrand decided to broadcast news of the killings himself—with the rumor that our companions had grabbed their weapons first."

"And Ulf couldn't contradict that," Winston surmised.

"Oh yes," Ealdred said with a bitter smile. "Ulf knows his runes."

Winston had once explained to me that the reason men write things down is to remember our past. Turns out it also makes lies harder to conceal.

"Some of the men who participated in this atrocity," Ealdred continued, "did not see it as the act of treachery it was but boasted that they'd wiped out a powerful enemy."

"And Erik?" Winston asked.

"Was the ratbag who gave Uhtred the king's word and then vouched for it with his own oath," Ealdred said, and spat on the church floor.

"Therefore the hand?" Winston said.

"The nithing hand that swore the deceitful oath, yes."

A silence came over all of us. Winston seemed reluctant—with a reluctance I shared—to bring these men to justice. They had merely taken revenge for one of the cruelest acts of treachery the world had known. And in our land, we'd seen quite a few in recent years.

"So you decided to avenge your master." Ælfgar stated a fact we had all understood. "Why not go after the king? Or Thurbrand, who wielded the sword that day?"

"The king set the trap," Ealdred said, "as kings do, but he didn't force Uhtred to stick his head into it through dishonorable perjury. And Thurbrand?" He bared his teeth. "His time will come. Uhtred's brother and sons will find him and his family. But I was there when Erik swore his oath, and it was only because Uhtred trusted that man's oath that he gave me leave to return home to take care of another matter." So it was Erik's fault that Ealdred had not fallen at his master's side.

I thought it was about time to remind them of my presence. "So you went looking for Erik?" I asked.

"And found him," Ealdred said. "Always protected by at least a dozen soldiers, never unarmed, and never alone. He was impossible to get close to."

"Instead you sent him a message," I said.

Ealdred looked up at me, surprised.

"A pewter plate engraved with the words *Erik Nithing*," I said.

"Oh," he said, his mouth hanging open slightly. "He kept that? Yes, I let him know that he could hide behind armed men, but we knew where to find him, and one day we would strike. But he ran, that bastard, and hid here."

"No," Turold said.

We all turned to look at him.

He continued: "He wasn't running away from you. He was running from himself. Godfrid—forgive me that I still call him by that name—repented his sin even before he received your message. That was just what drove him the last bit of the way. He realized that he deserved death for his betrayal, but he so fervently wanted to die having atoned with God. He had already decided to come here; he just became more driven."

Turold broke off and swallowed before continuing. "Yes, I am revealing things that were confided to me in the confessional, but the man who said them is dead, and I owe it to his memory to tell you that he regretted his part in this act.

"He knew you were on his heels, and he prayed sincerely to the Lord for a sign that he was forgiven. Truth be told, he occasionally forgot why he was here, particularly when his nobleman's sensibilities were provoked, and our agreement was that I would remind him of that when necessary."

To my surprise, I saw Winston smile.

"By sending him over to the church?" Winston asked.

"Yes," Turold continued eagerly. "Like the other night. Of course I never stated the actual reason I was sending him, as that would have given him away. But, believe me, his final hours were spent in prayer. Not to be guided in how he should behave toward the Benedictines, but in honestly pleading for forgiveness."

I was glad that Simon wasn't here to point out that Godfrid had actually spent that time sleeping.

Turold watched Ulf and Ealdred for a moment and then said, "He died at peace with the Lord."

"But not with me." Ealdred's lip twitched.

"You killed him with your master's sword," I pointed out, wanting to get back to the case.

"Which Ulf took with him from Wiheal, yes. And which he has guarded constantly since. I swallowed my pride and became leader of the

Benedictines' spearmen because I thought it would be easier for a common soldier to get close to Erik once we finally found him. I figured a rich monastery like Peterborough would have plenty of business throughout the land, which proved to be correct, because I've traveled widely with them and always kept my eyes and ears open for any news of Erik the Nithing."

"How *did* you find him?" Winston asked. He went to take a step forward but was stopped by Ulf, who placed his right hand on his sword hilt.

"Ulf found him," Ealdred said. "He was traveling around like I was, just on his own, and he reached Jarl Leofwine's estate the same day the jarl's son returned home. The convenient thing about being mute is that people think you're blind and deaf, too, so they speak freely around him.

"Eadwin talked about what he'd learned. The men who heard told others, and so it reached Ulf's ears. He came and found me, and you know the rest."

"Not quite," Alfilda said. She had stepped forward to stand next to Winston and remained there, although he was trying to push her back behind him again. "He must have recognized you."

"Recognized Ulf?" There was no joy in Ealdred's laughter. "Like a powerful Danish thane would even notice a simple soldier!"

"But if you traveled with Uhtred, he must have seen you at some point before Wiheal," Alfilda said, brushing aside Winston's hand.

"Oh yes," Ealdred said. "He saw me as a Northumbrian thane with a trimmed beard and fancy clothing. If he saw me again in the monks' hall the other day, he saw a man in common soldier's clothes and a Saxon mustache. No, he didn't recognize me, not even when we came looking for him here."

Turold moaned suddenly and exclaimed, "Oh no! I sent him to his death."

"No, Father Abbot. His death was his own doing," Ealdred said, glancing over at the bier, and then suddenly laughing wryly. "If anyone helped us, it was Simon, who came up with the idea that Ulf should share quarters with me and some of my men. That saved us from having to go visit each other. While my men stumbled around dead drunk, we agreed to strike right away. But in any case, Turold, he was going to be dead before we left the monastery, I can assure you of that."

"He didn't resist?" Winston asked, having finally managed to maneuver his girlfriend back behind him.

"He asked only that we do it quickly," Ealdred said, his eyes growing serious.

"Is that why you knocked him out first?" Winston asked, looking back and forth between Ulf and Ealdred.

Ealdred shook his head.

"He offered his chest to our swords, but when he realized we wanted to chop off his hand, not run him through with the sword, he went on the offensive and tried to overpower me. Ulf knocked him out with his sheath."

"But you hewed off his hand while he was unconscious," Winston said with a furrowed brow. "Didn't you want him to suffer?"

"Oh yes," Ealdred said bitterly. "But we were afraid he would cry out. We didn't know how well sound would carry through the church windows, and the gate guards weren't that far away."

"And then you just watched him die?" Winston asked.

Ealdred nodded to Winston.

"Ulf had conked him so hard that he just twitched a little when we cut off his hand, and then as the blood flowed out of him, he just kicked his legs a few times."

I saw Turold cross himself. Maybe because he was grateful the deceased hadn't suffered.

"Which of you cut off the hand?" Ælfgar asked, as if the question were important.

"One of us guided Uhtred's sword, but it was Uhtred himself who struck the blow to achieve his revenge," Ealdred said, looking at Ulf, who nodded. "And now I ask that you step aside. We are bringing his sword home."

My muscles tensed, and I saw my own sword over Ulf's shoulder, leaning against the altar. I thought that if Ælfgar and I both started running at the same time, one of us might be able to reach them.

"No, Halfdan," Ealdred said, shaking his head in warning. "None of you will be able to catch us."

They both drew their swords and held them at the ready in hands that seemed quite calm.

I heard Ælfgar exhale through his mouth. Then he flung his hands up in the air and ordered, "Step aside, Halfdan."

I looked at Winston, who nodded, and I stepped aside.

The two men walked calmly back down the length of the church, reached the door, and pushed it open. Then they stepped out into the daylight. Cursing under my breath, I raced up to the altar, grabbed my own and Ælfgar's swords and ran back to catch up with the others, who were already halfway to the door.

Ælfgar took his sword, slid the baldric over his shoulder, and walked out the door ahead of me. The others were already outside.

We all stopped in front of the church and stared across the grass to the gate. Alwyn stood in the gateway. He was armed with his spear, and six spearmen stood behind him, all with their weapons lowered. Five paces ahead of them stood the two murderers with their swords drawn.

Chapter 34

inston!" I cried, but didn't wait to see if he heeded me and managed to push Alfilda behind him again. I moved toward the murderers, who were back to back now, their sides facing us and the gate.

Ulf's quiet snarl didn't stop me. I heard the slow scratch of a sword against the lip of a sheath and sensed more than saw that Ælfgar was keeping step with me as I moved through the grass.

Four paces from the two criminals, Ælfgar's order—"Stop!"—caused me to slow my steps, but I kept going until I was so close to them that I could have reached them with my sword in half a step if I needed to.

Ulf made another growling noise in his throat.

"You make your own choice, Halfdan, whether you live or die," Ealdred said sharply.

I glanced at Ælfgar, who had stopped by my side. I moved to the left, my eyes locked on Ulf's. When I was a little lad, and Harding would drive me around in the thick sand on our practice ground with his wooden sword, he would say: The eyes, Halfdan, the eyes will tell you where and when your opponent will strike.

All four of us breathed heavily. Ulf was bent slightly at the waist, his torso tilted forward and his sword slightly downward, but I wasn't fooled. I'd seen him fight and knew he could swing a deadly blow in less time than it took to inhale.

Then a silly thought occurred to me: maybe my chances would have been better if I had been facing Ealdred instead of Ulf. Sigh. Maybe Ælfgar had had that same thought, but I staunched that line of thinking. I didn't take my eyes off Ulf, so I had no idea how Ælfgar was faring with his opponent.

Everything was totally quiet around us. We could hear Turold quietly saying prayers, that was all. Whether they were for the man who was already dead, for those who would soon be dead, or maybe for liberation from the sense of guilt he still no doubt carried around with him, I couldn't tell you. He mumbled in Latin, not Danish or English.

Ulf's eyes narrowed. I raised the tip of my sword slightly, which caused a cold smile to slide across his lips. I placed my right foot firmly on the ground and was ready to begin when Ælfgar's voice broke the silence: "Alwyn!"

Over Ulf's shoulder, I saw Alwyn take a step forward. The two murderers didn't even look at Alwyn or his spearmen. They kept their eyes focused on us.

When the tips of the spearmen's weapons were a hand's width from the two murderers' shoulders, Ælfgar barked and his men stopped advancing.

"Alwyn?" Ælfgar prompted.

"I went to the church to find you and heard the discussion," Alwyn said, sounding very much like a man who knew he was about to be given the order to attack. "And I thought I'd better secure the monastery exit."

"Good thinking," Ælfgar said, sounding pleased.

A tense silence settled over us again. Ulf's eyes hadn't strayed from my own, and I had to admire his show of courage even in the face of certain death. I clung to the hope that it wouldn't be left to me to kill him, that he would be gored by a spear.

I heard footsteps in the grass behind me, and suddenly Abbot Turold appeared in my field of vision. The aging abbot's shoulders drooped, but his pace was steady as he proceeded, right hand raised.

He stepped between Ælfgar and myself, stopped, and straightened his stooped form as best he could.

"Concede," he advised Ealdred and Ulf. Although his voice was gentle, there was a force to it, which made the words strike the two men like arrows on armor.

"Never," Ealdred replied, his voice containing a touch of disdainful superiority.

"There is no shame in conceding to a superior force," Ælfgar said, joining the conversation.

"Shame?" Ealdred's voice suddenly sounded almost cheerful. "Our shame was cleansed in the church the other night. Now all that's left is for us to die, as we should have done defending our master."

Ulf's eyes narrowed again, and I prepared myself for his lunge.

But again the fight was delayed, this time by the arrival of Edmund and Simon, dressed in their traveling clothes.

"What are you doing to my man?" Edmund thundered angrily once he realized what was going on.

"Your man has blood on his hands," Ælfgar summarized, apparently not in the mood to go into long-winded explanations.

"Wulfgar?" Prior Edmund's legs swayed. "That's not true."

Ælfgar didn't deem this worthy of a response, and it got quiet again. A quiet that Simon interrupted when he realized what Ælfgar had just said.

"Wulfgar is a murderer?" Simon said. "*He* murdered Brother Godfrid?"

The only response was silence.

"Then you truly deserve to die, you who have desecrated the Church itself by shedding blood in this hallowed place," Simon said, half choking on his words, overwhelmed as he was by rage.

This time all he received in response was a growl from Ulf.

"You have offended against the most powerful law of all and sullied the sanctuary itself," Simon said sanctimoniously.

"Shut up, you monastic fart," Ealdred growled.

I smiled in spite of myself.

"There are laws," Ealdred continued, "that are older and more sacred than those you know."

Out of the corner of my eye, I sensed Ælfgar raise his head.

"Laws . . . ? Such as . . . ?" Simon spluttered, but he was interrupted by Turold.

Turold once again raised his hand to the killers, made the sign of the cross to Ulf, and loudly proclaimed: "*Ego te absolvo.*"

Simon sounded as if he were choking.

"Impossible!" Edmund said, scandalized. "There's no excuse for this defilement."

Apparently Turold didn't hear him, because he turned to Ealdred to absolve him. But before he'd managed to raise his hand, Simon had stepped over to intercede, grabbing hold of his hand.

"Never, never!" Simon cried, horrified.

Ulf's eyes had widened in surprise at being absolved of his crime. I thought about seizing that opportunity to start swashbuckling, but he wasn't distracted for long. In an instant, he was alert again and ready to fight. He didn't even glance at Turold and Simon struggling silently, Turold to raise his hand to absolve Ealdred and Simon to keep Turold from doing so.

Suddenly Winston stepped up behind Simon, grabbed him around the waist, and pulled him, squirming and twisting, away from Turold. Without another look at Simon, Turold crossed himself and conferred the Church's absolution on Ealdred.

Ealdred stood silent for a bit, then nodded to Turold. Then he tightened his grip on his sword hilt.

"Thank you, Father," Ealdred said. "Now step back."

I saw a twinkle in Turold's eyes as he walked by me. Once again I found myself eye to eye with Ulf, who appeared every bit as determined to die as I'd ever seen any man.

I slowly exhaled, the way you do to clear your mind and your muscles before an imminent battle. I relaxed my grip on my sword a little and then once again grabbed firm hold of the hilt and set the ball of my right foot hard on the ground.

"Raise your spears!" Ælfgar ordered Alwyn.

I saw a shadow pass over Ulf's face. Edmund emitted an exclamation of astonishment and savagely ordered Simon to stand at his side. Then Alwyn raised the tip of his spear, followed by his six spearmen.

"Step aside," Ælfgar commanded, calmly sheathing his sword and looking at Ealdred. "There is your path."

"No!" Simon exclaimed, his voice sounding like a pained shriek.

"Shut up," Ælfgar thundered. "As Ealdred said, there are laws older and more sacred than those you know. Go," he continued, addressing the two murderers. "With my peace."

Ealdred looked at Ælfgar in surprise, then bowed his head in a gesture of respect. He resheathed his sword and turned toward the gate, which now stood open. Ulf followed his example, and only once the two of them stood side by side did I put my sword back in the scabbard and realize what a hard time I was having breathing calmly.

Ulf and Ealdred walked on, surrounded by the spearmen. They reached the gate and then stopped suddenly. Ealdred turned to Ælfgar and said, "I arrived on horseback."

Ælfgar looked at Alwyn and nodded, who gave a quiet order that immediately caused two spearmen to hand their weapons to their comrades and walk off toward the monastery's stables.

We all stood there in silence while we waited. The silence was broken only by the two Benedictines' labored breathing. But not a word was exchanged before the spearmen returned, each leading a horse by the reins.

Ulf held Ealdred's horse for him while he climbed into the saddle; then Ulf swung himself up onto the mount provided and rode off in the lead, out the gate in the palisade. Once they were clear of the monastery gate, Ealdred turned his horse, looked Ælfgar in the eye, and raised his right hand.

"Hail to thee, Thane Ælfgar," Ealdred said. "My life is yours."

"I shall hold it as the sheath holds the sword," Ælfgar said, bowing his head.

"But first," Ealdred continued, his horse flinging his head, longing to run after days in the stable, "first I must satisfy the oath I took to my master, which he took with him to the grave."

"You can only pledge your allegiance to one man at a time," Ælfgar said, raising his right hand. "And in time I may draw that sword."

They looked into each others' eyes for a long time; then Ealdred finally turned his dancing horse toward the village square and quickly rode off.

I felt my shoulders relax and saw Alfilda lean against Winston, who had his arm around her shoulder. I gave Ælfgar a nod of approval, and he responded with an enigmatic smile. Abbot Turold raised his hand to Ælfgar and made the sign of the cross, which Ælfgar received with a bowed head.

Now only we and the Benedictines were left. Simon's eyes seethed with rage as he took a step toward Ælfgar, who just raised a hand to him in warning and then walked right past him without so much as a glance.

Instead, Simon turned to Winston and said, "You laid a hand on me, a servant of the Lord. All agreements between us are annulled."

Chapter 35

I yawned.

For the fourth straight week, I sat idly around at Peterborough while Winston spent his days the way he loved, bent over his drawings. If Alfilda or I disturbed him while he worked, he would look up at us in annoyance and then return all his attention to the parchment before him. We soon learned to leave him be from the time he left us in the morning until he returned in the evening.

Simon's threat that all agreements were thereby annulled hadn't stood. For two reasons: the first was obvious; the second was understandable if you knew how powerful men think.

The monks were very concerned that their book about Seaxwulf should be exquisite. They'd sought out Winston for good reason, and they'd agreed to his demand for one and a half pounds of silver in addition to room and board. Consequently they were not really of a mind to make do with mediocre work just because the illuminator had laid a hand on a subprior. And that subprior should have known better than to make a spectacle of himself in the face of an abbot who had just received the archbishop's word that he was master of his own house.

The second reason was that Edmund had reinstated Winston's agreement on the spot. No sooner had the words left Simon's mouth than his superior stepped forward and proclaimed that of course the agreement was still in force. Winston had reached his agreement with the prior, not his underlings, so only the prior had the power to annul the agreement.

Simon pouted at me, and it was all I could do to conceal my condescending laughter. But having been put in his place by his prior, a man who would not stand for a subordinate assuming any of the powers that were rightly his, Simon didn't say anything.

In addition to that, Simon was then forced to put up with Edmund asking me to command their spearmen until we reached Peterborough. Because, well, as he put it, "It's only a day's ride, but the men need someone in charge."

I said yes, mostly to annoy Simon, but I was also glad to hand over command of the men as soon as we were safely inside Peterborough. I would still like to be a thane someday, but if I'm going to command men, let them be my own, not the ragtag flock of soldiers scraped together by a couple of monastic farts.

Winston was given space to work in Peterborough's library, and we were housed outside the monastery in the town that had grown up around it, in a house owned by the monks. It was a good, solid post-and-plank structure, weatherproofed with moss and clay, and it had a freshly thatched roof. In addition to the common room with the kitchen at one end, there were three bedrooms, including a large one that Winston and Alfilda claimed. I took the somewhat smaller one at the other end of the house to be as far away from Winston's snoring, and other nighttime noises, as possible. We kept our things in the room between us.

I was not really sure how Alfilda spent her days, apart from ensuring a proper meal for us. For my part, I explored the little town and found myself a couple of drinking buddies among the spearmen but quickly grew tired of our very limited conversations about weapons, battles we'd heard about or participated in, and women they'd bedded or would like to bed.

So one day I wandered out of town and strolled along the River Nene, which flows calmly in these parts. When I spotted a flock of geese grazing in the meadowlands along the riverbank, I sat down with my back against an oak in the late-afternoon sun to watch the birds waddling around—not because I'd taken a sudden interest in how grass is converted into plump, succulent roast goose, but because I'd noticed the leggy wench who tended the geese.

She was somewhat cool toward me in the beginning, but after a few days of attention—I even offered her wheat bread and mead—she warmed up, and on the fifth day after we met, she allowed me into her bed.

We had a few good weeks together, and then her betrothed, who was a spearman for the monastery, came home from a ride to Worcester on which he'd accompanied a delegation of monks. I had to make my exit then, which I did in a peaceful, orderly manner, without the fellow suspecting that his intended hadn't been missing him all that much.

So now I sat outside our temporary home, yawning. The sound of someone clearing his throat made me open my eyes. I found myself looking up at Godskalk's calm face.

Winston did not like to be disturbed while he was working, and he turned his back to me in irritation three times before he finally heard my quiet message that the king's thane wanted to talk to us. Not that that made him stop working on the illumination he was putting the finishing touches on, but he did at least acknowledge that he'd received the message by snapping that I could certainly look after a housecarl until he came home.

Godskalk and I found a fairly respectable tavern, and by the time I figured Alfilda would have dinner waiting for us, I had heard all the news Godskalk thought might interest me. Although none of it was important enough that I remember the details today. For my part, I had only one question for him: Would his road be taking him toward Brixworth when he left here?

His response was yes.

Winston was waiting for us at the house, and he got up from his seat and greeted Godskalk politely before inviting the thane to join us at the table. Alfilda brought in a simmering pan smelling of thyme-rubbed lamb chops and butter-fried root vegetables. She set it on the table in front of us and took her own seat on the bench next to Winston.

We ate with a good appetite. Then Winston sat up and pushed himself back a little from the table, and Alfilda followed suit. Godskalk and I shared the last contents in the pan, and then we, too, were full. Once all our tankards were refilled, Godskalk cleared his throat and said, "The king is satisfied with your report."

I cocked my head and gave Winston a questioning look. He explained that he had prepared a report and convinced one of the monastery's messengers, who was heading south, to deliver it to the king. "While you were off bedding another man's woman," he added unnecessarily, thus provoking me to snap in retort that if my having a good time bothered him so much, he could simply have sent me as the messenger instead of entrusting our confidential messages to a monastery soldier.

"Whatever," he said, making light of my ruffled feathers. "All the same, I am glad Cnut is satisfied."

"For the moment," Godskalk said with a wink.

That's how it is with kings. Something always comes up that worries them and ruins their satisfaction.

"Part of his satisfaction is because Leofwine's son Eadwin renewed his oath of allegiance to the king," Godskalk said with an impish smile. "I don't suppose any of you have any idea what might have prompted the jarl's son to do that?"

Ah yes. We had guessed as much. Ælfgar had told Leofwine that Cnut had sent us to Mercia, and it wasn't hard for Leofwine to work out why. A renewed oath of allegiance was the best guarantee that not just he, but also his youngest son, would keep the peace.

"Plus you cleared up the murder case nicely," Godskalk said with a satisfied nod and took a swig.

We looked at him with suspicion.

"Cnut is satisfied that the two men went free? Two men who murdered someone who was doing Cnut's bidding?" I asked skeptically.

Godskalk nodded. We all exchanged looks.

"Well, I suppose Thurbrand, who also killed on the king's orders, shouldn't feel too safe then," Alfilda said with a smile.

Godskalk smiled back, and we all nodded at each other. No one needed to put into words what we all knew: as long as Thurbrand had to fear revenge from Uhtred's family and friends, he would remain loyal to Cnut, who was the only one who might be able to guarantee his safety.

Godskalk bade us good night but left a tied leather pouch behind on the table. As soon as the door closed behind him, Winston opened the pouch, and out rolled coins worth a pound of silver.

When Winston went to the monastery the next morning, I left the house as well. I visited a fabric merchant's stall that I'd had my eye on for several days now.

Once my purchase was neatly packaged, I sought out Godskalk, who was just on his way to the stable for his horse.

"Are you going through Brixworth on your way to Hampton?" I asked and added, "It wouldn't add much distance to your journey, and you could do me a favor."

Once he'd agreed, I described Elvina and her father's farm to him and asked him to give her the package I handed to him.

I was confident she would appreciate a blue kerchief.

Epilogue

t was raining when Ealdred and Ulf rode into Bamburgh Castle. The ride from the south had been uneventful. No soldiers had bayed at their heels. No attackers had jumped them from thickets or shrubbery. They'd spent nights in ditches and outbuildings, in haylofts and stable lofts, never with both of them asleep at the same time, always looking over their shoulders, their ears alert to every sound.

And now they'd reached Bamburgh. They'd ridden across stubble fields and fallow fields, crossed the tops of dunes and finally the bridge into the castle itself, which had proven impregnable until forced to succumb to a Viking army forty years earlier. After that it had risen again as a fist, one the defeated clenched at their victors.

Ealdred swung himself out of his saddle with difficulty. They'd been riding since early morning, and he was beat. The guards who came over to them had their arms outstretched, a clear sign that they were recognized. The leader of the guard greeted them and then let them continue, without demanding that they hand over their weapons.

They walked toward the hall side by side. Ulf carried his sword in front of him in both hands. He hadn't drawn it since Brixworth, and he could no longer wear it as his own weapon.

Ealdred, son of Uhtred and jarl of Northumbria, greeted them from his high seat, but when he saw who it was, he got up and came over to meet them. Ealdred and Ulf stopped two paces in front of him.

"Thane Ealdred, my namesake and friend," the jarl said, and then turned to Ulf. "And you, Ulf, my father's trusted man. We thought you dead."

"It was best that way," Ealdred explained.

The jarl's eyes were drawn to the sword; Ulf knelt and held it out to him.

"This was my father's?" the jarl asked.

"Yes," Ealdred said with a nod. "Now it can rest with him."

Standing in the hall before the kneeling Ulf, the jarl listened to Ealdred's recounting. His men sat and stood around him. Those who had cried at not having been able to fall beside his father, Uhtred, sat shoulder to shoulder with younger men, whose fathers, uncles, and brothers had been killed at Wiheal. They had all sworn their oaths to the current jarl, and they all listened to the account in rapt silence.

When Ealdred finished, there was a profound silence in the hall. Then a murmur spread, a sound like waves on the beach, rising into a mighty roar when the jarl drew the sword and swung it over the heads of the two men. The jarl's thunderous voice yelled that the footpath of revenge begun by these two men would grow into a broad street that he would lead the men of Northumbria down.

"And this sword," the jarl declared when the silence had once again settled over the hall, "will not rest with my father. It will be the tool in my hand, which will strike down the murderer and his scions."

Again the murmur grew into a churning sea of sound, rumbling between the hall's walls, penetrating them, and billowing upward toward the sword-gray autumn sky. Then it faded, again becoming a promising silence, a peace that settled over them all and bound them together like the oaths they'd sworn to their master and jarl.

"And you, who before were the most welcome among us, will now be the most honored of us all." The jarl extended his hands to Ulf and Ealdred, guided them to his high seat, positioned them on either side of him, and let them yet again receive their companions' roaring adulation.

Once it was quiet again, Ealdred rose.

"Have I kept my word to your father?" he asked the jarl.

"In truth, yes," the jarl replied, looking at him in puzzlement.

Thane Ealdred bowed his head and sighed. When he raised it again, he looked the jarl in the eye.

"So am I released from my oath?" he inquired.

"If you wish to be," the jarl said with a nod, astonished.

"Wish it, I do not," Ealdred said, and sighed again. "But my honor requires me now to give my oath to another."

Only then did he explain how he and Ulf had made it out of Brixworth with their lives intact.

When he concluded, the jarl rose and extended him his hand. And this time the men in the hall honored both him and Thane Ælfgar, a man who was unknown to them, by hammering their swords against their shields.

Author's Note

hen I traveled around eastern England along with my editor, Svend Åge Petersen, in the spring of 2010 (I would like to thank the Literature Committee of the Danish Agency for Culture for the travel grant), I visited a bookshop in Ely where I happened upon a fascinating work by Richard Fletcher titled *Bloodfeud: Murder and Revenge in Anglo-Saxon England* (Oxford University Press, 2003) that discusses the murders of Uhtred and his followers in AD 1016. This story, as recounted in the prologue to *Oathbreaker*, is thus true in the sense that Uhtred of Northumbria was a historical figure who was killed by Thurbrand the Hold in the village of Wiheal (wherever it may have been located) on King Cnut's direct orders—or at least with his approval.

In his learned and thoroughly researched book, Professor Fletcher also discusses the repercussions of that incident on three generations of Uhtred's and Thurbrand's families, who ravaged each other with bloodthirsty acts of revenge until the final killing (probably) took place, between 1073–1074.

The story of the event in Wiheal is an example of how actual history exceeds even an author's imagination, since I must simply admit that it would never have occurred to me—not even in a murder mystery—to kill off forty-one men who rode to their deaths confident in the knowledge that they had been guaranteed safe passage by those who had sworn their allegiance to the king.

My trip to England in 2010 actually began with a three-day stay in Brixworth, home to All Saints' Church, a structure that to this day displays prominent Saxon features and is what many consider the finest remaining example of a seventh-century building north of the Alps.

After spending three days exploring the church and wandering about the surrounding countryside, I was convinced that this was where the second story about Halfdan, Winston, and Alfilda would play out. Once I finished Professor Fletcher's book a few weeks later, I started picturing the contours of a plot—a chain of events that gradually took shape and ended up as the present novel.

A few—and by no means anywhere near exhaustive—words about the construction of Anglo-Saxon society are probably appropriate here.

Excluding slaves, the basis of Anglo-Saxon society was freemen, called *ceorls* in Anglo-Saxon (cf. Modern English *churl*). Their freedom was defined by three things: service in the *fyrd* (England's national militia), the right to attend and speak at the *gemot* (cf. Modern English *moot*), and their value in *wergeld* (blood money) of 200 shillings.

Above the freemen was the aristocracy. A member of this class was called a *thane* and was tied to the king or to another lord, at whose pleasure he served. The lord could terminate this service abruptly—including by deprivation of land and in some cases deprivation of life—if the lord felt the thane was not meeting his obligations. A thane's wergeld was set at 1,200 shillings.

A step up from a thane was an *ealdorman*, who pledged his oath directly to the king and acted as the king's representative in one or more shires. (The local judge of a shire was called a *reeve*, or *shire reeve*, whence the word *sheriff*.) An ealdorman was responsible for making sure court was held in the shire, for assembling and leading the fyrd in battle, and for being the king's hand and eye in every way within his shire. The title of ealdorman, like the office, was hereditary, but from the eleventh century on, ealdormen were selected from a limited number of families.

Shortly after Cnut's conquest of England, and in the setting of the stories about Winston, Halfdan, and Alfilda, the Anglo-Saxon title of ealdorman started to be replaced by the Old Norse title *jarl* (which is cognate with the English word *earl*). I use *jarl* or *ealdorman* in the books to communicate whether the nobleman feels himself to be English or Danish (Old Norse being the precursor to Danish, as Anglo-Saxon is the precursor to English).

At the top of the social hierarchy was the royal family. The king and his closest relatives led the nation and the people in war and peace, controlled the army, and guaranteed law and order. The title of *cyning* (Modern English *king*) was not originally hereditary, unlike the title of *wita* (plural *witan*)—designating the noblemen, prelates, and influential officials who met periodically in the *Witenagemot*, a sort of senate. The witan had the right and power to choose the member of the royal family they considered best suited to rule, but from the middle of the ninth century on, the royal family of Wessex became the only recognized family from which the witan could elect England's rulers. This was a tradition that Cnut broke when his father and he conquered the country.

The supremacy of Wessex meant that previously independent kingdoms—including Essex, Mercia, Bernicia, and Deira, for example—became jarldoms (or earldoms). Over time even the names of these jarldoms faded as their boundaries changed—whether due to kings seeing advantages to moving boundaries at their discretion or jarls moving the boundaries themselves in their incessant struggles against each other.

One particular region of England was called the Danelaw: After the Viking chieftain Guthrum's defeat to Alfred the Great at Eathandun in the late ninth century, England was divided, and Guthrum received, roughly, what lay to the north of the old Watling Street. Some of Guthrum's army displaced or intermarried with the Saxon and Angle farm families in the area. They settled down and lived among the English but in accordance with Danish law—and over the subsequent centuries they managed to make the area so wealthy that the Danelaw itself became a target for new Viking attacks.

In the novels, therefore, I distinguish between Danes, the descendants of Guthrum's men who had settled in England and had been living there for well over a century by the time this story is set, and Vikings. The Vikings were of the same ethnic group as the Danes—but I use the term to describe the raiders who arrived much later, with Sweyn I Forkbeard and Cnut the Great.

About the Author

© Ilona Dreve

Best-selling Danish novelist Martin Jensen was born in 1946 and worked as a teacher and a headmaster in Sweden and Denmark before becoming a full-time writer in 1996. The author of twenty-one novels, he has been honored by the Danish Crime Academy twice and was awarded the Royal Library's Prize for his medieval novel *Soldiers' Whore*. He and his wife are botany enthusiasts who also enjoy bird-watching and gathering mushrooms.

About the Translator

© Libby Lewis, 2006

Tara F. Chace has translated over twenty novels from Norwegian, Swedish, and Danish. Her most recent translations include Martin Jensen's *The King's Hounds* and *Oathbreaker* (AmazonCrossing, 2013 and 2014), Camilla Grebe and Åsa Träff's *More Bitter Than Death* (Simon & Schuster, 2013), Lene Kaaberbøl and Agnete Friis's *Invisible Murder* (Soho Crime, 2012), Jo Nesbø's *Doctor Proctor's Fart Powder* series (Aladdin, 2010–2013), and Johan Harstad's *172 Hours on the Moon* (Little, Brown Books for Young Readers, 2012).

An avid reader and language learner, Chace earned her PhD in Scandinavian Languages and Literature from the University of Washington in 2003. She enjoys translating books for adults and children. She lives in Seattle with her family and their black lab, Zephyr.